The Book of Hours

T. Davis Bunn

A
JANET
THOMA
BOOK

THOMAS NELSON PUBLISHERS
Nashville

Published in Nashville, Tennessee, by Thomas Nelson, Inc.

Scripture taken from the HOLY BIBLE, NEW INTERNATIONAL
VERSION®. Copyright © 1973, 1978, 1984 by International Bible Society.
Used by permission of Zondervan Publishing House. All rights reserved.

Library of Congress Cataloging-in-Publication Data

Bunn, T. Davis, 1952–
    The book of hours / T. Davis Bunn.
      p. cm.
    ISBN 0-7852-7088-4 (pbk.)
    I. Title.
PS3552.U4718 B6 2000
813'.54—dc21

99-089593
CIP

Printed in the United States of America

1 2 3 4 5 6 QPV 05 04 03 02 01 00

1

*B*rian Blackstone gripped the banister and eased himself down the left-hand set of stairs. The creaking bounced back and forth through the vast formal hall. This one room, the entrance hall to what had once been a splendid English manor, was half the size of his former house. The railing shook and rattled beneath his hands like ill-fitting dentures. But his weakened state forced him to lean heavily on the banister, and each step groaned as if it was ready to break and pitch him headlong. When he reached the stone landing, he heaved a sigh of relief. He heard sounds emanating from the downstairs apartment and hurried for the front door. He needed to meet whoever shared this house, but not now. One thing at a time. It was a creed that had served him well for the past two years.

Outside the solid-oak door, Brian almost stumbled over his two valises. The leather suitcases were battered and grimy from two hard years of third-class travel. He had left them there the previous night because he had not felt able to carry them up the winding stairs. And the taxi driver who had brought him in from London's Heathrow Airport had certainly not been willing to take them anywhere, not after he had seen the paltry tip Brian had offered. Brian really was in no shape financially to take a taxi at all. But so late at night there had been no other way to journey from the airport to the village of Knightsbridge.

He walked down the graveled drive, sheltered beneath the tallest elms and chestnut trees he had ever seen. To his right stood a converted stable, red-brick and crumbling. The gatehouse and the manor's main entrance rose just beyond. The entry's tall stone pillars supported a pair of rampant lions clasping some long-forgotten family shield. The iron gates were a full fifty feet wide and thirty high, now rusted permanently open and sagging with age. The gatehouse was probably as derelict as the stables, but it was hard to tell since the entire facade was covered in roses. Brian found it the most charming scene since his arrival. Some of the vines, where they emerged from the earth, were as thick as his thighs. The roses framed the big lead-paned windows and the doorway, draping around the metal plate set above the mail slot announcing that the house was called Rose Cottage. Brian walked on, feeling that no name had ever been better deserved.

As he passed through the main gates, he could not help but glance back. His first genuine view of the manor rising above the chestnuts was astonishing. No photograph could possibly do the estate justice, and upon his arrival the house had been reduced by the night and his fatigue to a hulking shadow. Now not even the trees could hide its massive girth. The house only had three stories, but the ground and second floors were both more than twenty feet high. The front of the Cotswold-stone manor was nine windows broad, and each window measured five feet across.

As he walked the narrow village lane, Brian found himself thinking back to what the taxi driver had said about Knightsbridge. Strange that the man's words seemed clearer now than they had the night before, when the world had drifted vaguely through the mists of Brian's exhaustion. Now, as he walked past brick-and-flint walls bowed with the pressure of uncounted centuries, he heard the man's voice anew. The taxi driver had related how the village was older than London itself, a thousand years and more. Knightsbridge had been the first capital of William the Conqueror; the ruins of his castle still stood within the village green. The present bridge was erected upon stones set in place by the Romans themselves. The village was filled with centuries of rumors about knights and clandestine monasteries and hidden secrets and mysteriously vanished treasures. On and on the taxi driver had prattled, while Brian had huddled in the dark backseat and struggled not to groan.

He felt better after a night's sleep, but slightly feverish and still very weak. The smell of freshly baked bread was the first sign he had of approaching the village's heart. The lane opened into a central market square, filled with stalls and chatter and people, flanked by buildings as old as the manor. Brian followed his nose to a stall with a rainbow-bright awning and a portable stove displaying trays of hot-cross buns. He pointed and asked, "How much for one of those?"

"Fifty pence, love, and a better bargain you won't be finding here today."

Fifty pence was eighty American cents, too much for a raisin bun as far as he was concerned. But his sense of prices had been seriously distorted by all the places he had recently left behind, and his stomach now clenched with hollow hunger. It had been quite a while since he had felt much appetite for anything. "I'll take one, please."

He stepped to the corner of the stall and stood tearing off

tiny fragments of the hot bun. Experience had taught him it was far safer to take solid food in small segments. He finished the bun, wiped his sugar-coated hands on his pants, and waited to see how his stomach responded. When all appeared calm, he returned to the stall's front. "I'll have another, please."

"Knew you would." The woman was as broad as her stall, and the morning's heat caused her to glisten like the buns she sold. "Grand fellow like you couldn't get by on just one."

Brian handed over his money, trying not to wince at the cost, and asked, "Could you tell me where I'd find the Whitehorse Realty Company?"

"Just behind you, love. No, over there, by the solicitor's."

Brian thanked the woman and moved back out of the way. The day was surprisingly hot for England, or at least for what he had heard of English summers. He had never been in England before. In fact, he had spent two full years avoiding this very arrival.

He felt eyes on him, and knew it was not just his imagination. He tried to remind himself that eyes had followed him through many of his travels, for he had been in a number of places where white men were an oddity. But he could not fool himself into thinking that it did not matter. Here was different. Here he was supposed to feel at home.

A strident shouting match across the square caught his attention. He could not make out the words, but the banners above the two opposing camps were clear enough. Two elderly ladies staffed a narrow stall whose banner read, "Buy a raffle ticket and save the heritage of our village bells." Two hefty women shouted at them and gestured angrily, waving placards as though wishing they were holding battle-axes. Brian squinted and made out the placard's words: "Ban the noise; ban the bells. Sign our petition today." Just as the argument threatened to come to blows, a lean middle-aged gentleman wearing a vicar's collar rushed up and swiftly stilled both sides. Brian found himself admiring the man and his ability to calm waters with a few quiet words.

Then he heard two women behind him talking loudly and assuming the noise from across the market masked their voices. Brian realized they were speaking about him.

The first woman said, "He doesn't strike me as a posh gent."

"What, you were expecting the Yank to show up wearing a pair of shiny gray shoes, them with buttons up the side?"

"All I'm saying is, a deep-pockets like him ought to pay a little mind to how he goes about town. Look at him, will you? Skin and bones, he is. Not to mention brown as a native. Clothes flapping on his frame like they was hanging on a line out my back garden."

"Don't be daft. A bloke that rich can ruddy well dress how he likes."

"Say what you like, I'm thinking the new master of Castle Keep is as batty as the old maid herself was."

Brian finished his second hot-cross bun, brushed his hands on his trousers, and moved off. There was nothing to be gained from correcting them. Nor from asking how they knew who he was. The busybody attitude of small village life was one of the reasons he had avoided coming to Knightsbridge for so long. One of many.

Nor were the market women the only ones who knew of him. For as he crossed the cobblestone square, the realtor's door opened and a man bounced out. Everything about him was tightly compressed. The man did not rise above five feet six inches nor weigh more than a hundred and fifty pounds. He sported a double-breasted blue blazer, a flamboyant yellow polka-dot tie and matching pocket handkerchief, and a trim beard. As he offered Brian a small neat hand, even his smile was condensed, slipping in and out of view in seconds. His voice popped out words like a softly cracking whip. "You must be Mr. Blackstone. Hardy Seade. Such a pleasure, sir. A pleasure. Please, come in. Come in."

The office was compact as well, the ceiling so low-beamed Brian had to stoop to cross before the receptionist's desk. Hardy Seade asked, "Will you have a coffee, tea?"

"Nothing, thanks."

"Sorry about the ceiling heights. They weren't built with Americans in mind." A quick laugh as he led Brian into the back office. "Naturally not, since this building was erected before America was discovered. Most of the Knightsbridge market predates your aunt's estate. Have a seat there, Mr. Blackstone."

Brian slid into the chair, eased the crick in his neck, and corrected, "My wife's aunt."

Hardy Seade hesitated in the act of seating himself. "I beg your pardon?"

"Heather Harding was my wife's aunt."

Seade lowered himself and proceeded tensely. "But all the documents list you as the new proprietor."

"That is correct." Brian realized more was going to have to be said, so he braced himself and added, "My wife is deceased."

"Oh. How, well, tragic." Seade's tone of voice indicated his dislike for surprise news from his clients. "My condolences."

Brian deflected the discussion with, "I thought I heard noises downstairs this morning."

"Well, of course you did. Any house with spaces that large is bound to reflect a bit of sound. But I assure you, the tenants in your ground-floor flat are of the highest possible caliber—"

"I'm sorry, the what?"

"The flat, sir. The apartment. At the back of the house overlooking the grounds and the river."

"No. You said I have tenants?"

"Well, of course you do. The ground-floor tenants, the Wainwrights, have been there for years. Your aunt had the flat converted specifically for them. Then there is a local doctor in Rose Cottage, and I rent the stable grounds myself. These funds are the only way we have managed to meet the estate's basic expenses. As it is, I am forced to pay the gardener out of my own pocket. He's a fine young man, by the way. No doubt you'll be seeing him around from time to time. Joe Eaves is the name." Hardy Seade suppressed his irritation by thinning his lips until they almost disappeared. "Really, Mr. Blackstone, I do feel it would have been best if you had examined all the documents I've been sending before your arrival."

"I haven't been home in two years," Brian replied.

This news pressed the real-estate agent back into his seat. "Then you don't know about the sale?"

"Sale of what?"

"Your aunt's estate, sir. That is, her former estate. Yours now, I suppose, at least for another week. Eight days, to be precise. Castle Keep is to be auctioned off to pay the outstanding death duties."

Brian felt the first tendrils of fatigue lace their way out of his gut. It was such a familiar sensation that he scarcely paid it any mind. It was more like an internal alarm clock, chiming the first note of the call to rest. Which meant he had to wrap up the meeting and make it to his next stop as quickly as possible. "Pay what?"

"Death duties." Seade noted Brian's lack of comprehension and added with disdain, "I believe you call them inheritance taxes."

"I am not interested in selling the place."

"If you'll forgive me for saying so, the matter is out of your hands. The death duties are two years overdue, notices have been filed, and a date for the foreclosure auction has been set."

Brian pushed himself from the seat. "The house is not yours to sell."

Hardy Seade came fully erect. "I regret to inform you that come the end of next week, unless you muster up the six hundred and thirty thousand pounds still outstanding in death duties and interest, the estate is not yours to keep."

"Hand me that wrench, Arthur."

"The what, dear?"

"The wrench. Right there by your feet." Dr. Cecilia Lyons emerged from her dark corner behind the pantry cupboard. "No, not . . . Look there, that metal dingus."

"Ah. We Brits prefer to call it a spanner." Arthur Wainwright, retired brigadier general of the Royal Air Force, former chief of the largest military air base in Great Britain, rummaged through the toolbox. "It keeps us from confusing it with all the world's other dinguses."

"Spanner, wrench, whatever." Cecilia accepted the tool and

slipped back behind the pantry cupboard. The antique oak shelves were seven feet tall and weighed a ton. As far as she could tell, the pantry had not been moved since the house wiring had been installed. She and Arthur had spent a very dusty half hour easing them off the side wall. She sneezed into the cramped space and asked, "Can you shine that light over here, please?"

Arthur did as he was told. With the cupboard drawn out, the pantry was too small for them both to fit inside. Arthur was forced to hold the heavy flashlight out at full reach, and the light tended to waver. Shadows danced about the ancient water-stained walls, highlighting the age and neglect. Rose Cottage was one of the things Cecilia Lyons loved most about the English village of Knightsbridge, and her home's dilapidated state was enough to make her weep.

Rose Cottage was the former gatehouse of the manor known as Castle Keep, and it had long been Cecilia's dream to buy and restore the place. But the five-hundred-year-old gatehouse was not for sale.

Two years earlier, the former proprietor had passed on, leaving the manor to a mystery man no one had met. Or heard from. Until now. For that period Castle Keep had been left in the hands of a local real-estate agent who was known far and wide as being so tight he could make a penny squeal. Hardy Seade remained utterly unfazed by the state of disrepair.

Arthur Wainwright, her neighbor and friend, watched her struggle with the bolt and asked, "Are you sure we shouldn't wait until the electrician arrives?"

"Not a chance." Cecilia struggled with a bolt caked in rust. "Can you find the big screwdriver?"

"Just a minute."

Instantly she was left in darkness. Cecilia said to the gloom, "I've lost all power in my kitchen. You haven't had electricity in your bedroom for what, a week?"

"Longer, I'm afraid. Not to mention the bath." The light returned, and the old man handed over a long-handled screwdriver. "Gladys had a frightful tumble last night. Gave us both a start, I don't mind telling you."

"I've been by the realtor's office four times this week. We've got a list long as your arm of urgent repairs. All we get from Hardy Seade is the royal runaround." She set the screwdriver onto the bolt and banged the handle with the wrench. The bolt's covering of rust did not budge. Cecilia reared back, aiming not at the bolt but rather at the snooty realtor's nose.

She hammered down, and the bolt broke off clean. "Uh-oh."

"I told you we should wait, dear."

"What should I do in the meantime, cook over a fire in the garden?" It took both hands to pry open the fuse box lid. "I wonder how long it's been since somebody's had a look in here."

"You can hardly blame Mr. Seade for being forced to deal with an absentee landlord."

"It doesn't stop him from collecting the rent." She squinted over the row of cardboard-capped tubes. They looked like a row of shotgun shells. "I think I remember seeing a box of these fuses under the kitchen sink."

"Let me check." Arthur tottered over and groaned as he lowered himself to floor level. His knees were severely arthritic, as were his hands and right shoulder. He had what appeared to be the onset of a cataract in his left eye. His liver was damaged from six tours of duty in the tropics and all the related illnesses, and there was every indication that he was beginning to suffer from osteoporosis. Cecilia knew because she had been his doctor since her arrival in Knightsbridge eighteen months earlier. Arthur might be old and increasingly frail, but his mind was sharp, and he was proving to be a genuine friend.

"Here they are. And there's a fire extinguisher as well." He returned with both box and extinguisher. "How many do you need?"

"Shine the light over here again, please. Right. There's one with a burn mark in the middle."

Arthur set the extinguisher at his feet, fished out a fuse, inspected it doubtfully. "I don't see a sell-by date."

"That's because they probably didn't know what shelf-life was when this was made." She pried out the charred fuse, then held up the replacement to the light. "I wonder if it makes any difference which way I stick this in."

"Cecilia, dear, I really think—"

"Never mind." She gripped the fuse by its cardboard middle and rammed it home.

Instantly there was a huge *BAM* followed by a shower of sparks. Cecilia shrieked and covered her head. Hazarding a single glance, she cried, "The wall's on fire!"

"Not for long, it's not." Arthur took aim with the extinguisher and hit the trigger. "Stand back!"

A torrent of white foam exploded from the ancient device, drenching the fuse box, the wall, and Cecilia. She hardly noticed. "The wall is still burning!"

A change had come over the old man. Gone was the doddering gentility. The voice was crisp, stern, and twenty years younger. "Take the wrench and break through. No, not there.

11

Higher up. Above the fire line. That's it. Strike harder."

The smoke was acrid and burned her eyes and lungs. A bright peak, almost like the burning end of tinder, hissed and smoldered its way slowly up the wall above the fuse box. Cecilia gripped the wrench with both hands, the metal handle made slippery by the foam. She hammered at the wall plaster. A spidery crack appeared about six inches above the burn line. She pounded again.

"That's it. Once more, now."

The plaster broke and fell at her feet. Arthur squeezed in beside her, stuck the nozzle directly into the opening, and pulled the trigger. Foam splattered around them both. Arthur pulled back and inspected the smoldering wall. "One more for good measure."

Cecilia squinted through the white torrent, and when the nozzle was pulled back a second time she asked, "Is it out?"

"Give me the screwdriver." Arthur set down the extinguisher and pried off another section of plaster. He reached into the wall and levered out a segment of what appeared to be newspaper. "Here's your problem."

Cecilia leaned over his hands. "What is it?"

"The *London Illustrated News*, by the looks of things. They used to wrap copper wiring with newsprint for insulation."

She felt her anger coming to a boil. "How long ago are we talking here?"

"Oh, I doubt it's been used much since the thirties. By then they'd figured out how to wrap the wire in rubber."

She used the wall for balance as she stepped across the foam-slippery floor. "So the wiring in my house hasn't been touched in seventy years."

"Longer, I warrant. Probably hasn't been altered since they went off gas." Arthur followed her into the kitchen. "My dear, you look a frightful sight."

Cecilia looked down at herself. Gone were the trousers and sweater she had donned for work. In their place was a dripping cascade of white bubbles. "Is it in my hair?"

"Is it . . ." Arthur was encased in the same foam. A long streamer grew from his chin like an immense white beard. He could not keep the chuckle from his voice as he replied, "Well, perhaps just a little."

She pushed shut the pantry door. On its back was an old-style mercury mirror, now smoky and cracked with age. Everything about Rose Cottage was ancient. That was one of the things she loved about the place.

Cecilia did not recognize herself, save for the eye opening in her white mask that mirrored the shock she felt. "I look like a walking snow cone."

Arthur was laughing outright now. "Gladys will be terribly sorry to have missed this little show."

She raised her wrist but could not see her watch for the foam. "I have to get to the clinic."

"I'll clean this up." Arthur raised one foam-encased arm before she could protest. "It's all right, dear. I've actually rather enjoyed our little experiment in home improvement. When I'm done here, I'll go put a flea in the ear of our friend Hardy Seade. Mark my word, we'll have an electrician in this very afternoon."

"You can have him move this cupboard back when he's done and save us both the risk of a hernia." Cecilia started from the kitchen, only to be halted by the view through her front window. Across the weed-infested lawn rose the hulking presence

13

of Castle Keep. Beneath the curved front portico, beside the mammoth front door, stood two leather suitcases. She asked, "Have you seen him yet?"

She knew Arthur had moved up beside her because she could hear the foam dripping softly on her flagstone floor. "Not yet. He must have arrived very late."

"Late is right." If her anger had generated heat, the foam would have evaporated in a flash. "I can't wait to meet that guy."

Arthur warned, "Perhaps a frontal assault is not the best way to endear yourself to your new landlord."

But Cecilia paid the caution no mind. "Look at him. Couldn't even bother to take in his own luggage. Was probably expecting one of us to drag it upstairs for him."

A note of the former commandant returned to Arthur's voice. "In that case, I would say the gentleman doesn't have the sense to run a bath, much less an estate of this size."

Cecilia turned from the window. "I hope he doesn't ever plan to get sick. Not on my watch."

2

***

$\mathcal{D}$espite her hasty shower, Cecilia Lyons arrived at the Knightsbridge clinic still feeling foam in her ears. And her hair. Her left foot squished soggily in her only other good pair of shoes. The back of her right knee tickled, and her fingers still wanted to stick together. But all she could think about was the arrogance of a landlord who waited two years to show up, then left his valises on the front portico expecting others to step and fetch at his command.

The level of bile was almost enough to carry her straight through the reception area and back into her office. Except for the fact that a large woman in tweeds planted herself in Cecilia's path and declared, "You're the new doctor."

Cecilia disliked tweedy suits primarily because she detested the kind of woman who tended to wear them. "That's right."

"I am Lavinia Winniskill, chairwoman of the Keep Knightsbridge Peaceful Committee."

"This must be about the bells," Cecilia guessed.

"Exactly." She waved an impatient hand toward Maureen, the clinic's receptionist and secretary. "I have tried to explain to this person here just how vital it is I speak with the head of your clinic. This matter is not only urgent, it is *imperative*."

Cecilia took aim at the woman's third button and struggled

to hold her voice level. Because she was small and fine-boned, certain people tended to think Cecilia could be pushed around. But if a certain woman wasn't careful, she was going to find out just how wrong such an observation could be. "This is a medical clinic," she replied. "Our sole purpose is to serve the ill of Knightsbridge."

"Which is precisely why I must speak to your director! You of all people must know how vital it is to have peace and quiet here in the heart of our village. *Not* to have the bells of *seven* different churches ring every hour of the night and day!"

Cecilia's glance was enough for Maureen to offer, "Dr. Riles has minor surgery this morning."

"*Well!*" Lavinia huffed. "Whatever else the matter of our bells might be, it is not *minor*."

"Minor surgery means anything that can be taken care of in the clinic," Cecilia explained. *Like sewing a certain pair of lips shut*, she thought.

The explanation was waved impatiently aside. Lavinia Winniskill took a step closer, so as to tower over Cecilia. "Now you look here. I realize from your accent that you are an American interloper. But if you are to make yourself an acceptable member of our society, you must understand that certain issues and certain people require special consideration. Which means—"

"Please leave the clinic."

"—that I have every intention of being shown into . . ." The mouth continued working, although the mind had finally been snagged by Cecilia's quiet words. "I beg your pardon?"

"We don't have time for the bells around here; we're too busy trying to help the ill and suffering." Cecilia kept her voice calm, her gaze unflinching. "So the next time you come in here, I will expect your moaning to be medically related."

"Now see here!" But something in Cecilia's gaze caused Lavinia Winniskill to turn and move for the door. From a safer distance she turned and declared, "You have most certainly not heard the last of *this*!"

As soon as the door closed behind her tweedy back, one of the elderly patients declared to his neighbor, "Now that was better than a poultice on a boil, it was."

Cecilia turned from the door and the patients, only to see Maureen raise her hands and applaud silently. All Cecilia said was, "Give me a minute."

But scarcely had she entered her office when Maureen appeared in the doorway. "I'm sorry, dear, but Angeline Townsend is on the phone," Maureen said.

"Not today," Cecilia groaned. "Not now."

Maureen handed over an envelope from the lab they commonly used for clinical testing. "This just came in. Should I have her call back?"

"No. No. I need to take it." Cecilia shrugged off her jacket and let it slip to the floor. When the line clicked, she said, "Don't tell me. There's still no change."

"Tommy's no better, I'm afraid. The medicine hasn't helped a bit."

Tommy Townsend was a four-year-old patient whose symptoms had baffled Cecilia for almost two months. And despite her best efforts and twice-weekly consultations, the child was not getting any better. Cecilia gave her head a vigorous scratch, and felt her finger come away sticky from the traces of foam that remained in her hair. "You'd better bring him in again, then."

"I've already asked. All your appointments are taken today."

"I'll make time. And I want Dr. Riles to have a look at him. Come in just before lunch. He's doing minor ops until then."

"All right." Angeline's voice held all the quiet desperation of a worried mother. "Did you get the lab results back?"

"Just this morning." Cecilia slit open the envelope, read the results, and sighed, "Inconclusive again, I'm afraid." She hesitated, then added, "It might be a good idea to move Tommy into Reading."

Reading was the closest major city. And the nearest major hospital. Clearly the mother had been thinking the same thing, for all she said was, "I'll see you in a couple of hours."

Cecilia dropped into her seat, wishing she could dash back home for another shower and a nap. There was a knock on her door, and Maureen poked her head in. Cecilia told her, "It's not even nine o'clock, and I'm already exhausted."

But the clinic's chief assistant was beaming. "I've got just the remedy for what ails you."

"What are you talking about?"

The smile grew grander still. "You won't believe who just sauntered in."

Cecilia started to snap that she was in no mood for guessing games, when it hit her. "You have got to be kidding me."

"Suffering from a tummy ache, he is. And wanting to see a doctor."

Cecilia leaned back in her seat, just as the day's first ray of sunshine rose above the neighboring roofline and lanced through her window. "Well, for goodness' sake, don't keep the fellow waiting."

Maureen's eyes glittered with the effort of holding in her laughter. "Somehow I thought you'd be saying that."

The village clinic was housed two streets off the central market, in a stone cottage as old as the rest of Knightsbridge. Thankfully, the renovators had thought to lower the original floor, which meant Brian was able to stand upright and not strike his head on the ceiling beams. He stood by the central counter, filling out a sheaf of forms. At the point where he was asked to give his last address, he hesitated, then wrote out, "Central Hospital, Colombo, Sri Lanka." A five-week stay seemed enough to qualify it as an abode. From the sound of things, it was several weeks longer than he would have here.

The receptionist took the completed forms and gave him another queer look before directing him to take a seat. Brian crossed the broad plank flooring and sighed gratefully onto the wall bench. He took in the scene about him. The morning's early gloom was gradually burning off, and sunlight fell through the lead-paned windows to cast people and chamber alike in tones of ruddy gold. Everyone seemed to know one another and their complaints. The talk was easy and low, the comforting sound of folks who had lived in one another's pockets for so long they knew what would be said long before mouths opened. Glances were tossed his way, which only seemed to echo the refrain running through his brain. He did not belong here and never would. That was scarcely tragic, seeing as how the matter had already been taken from his hands.

Six hundred and thirty thousand pounds, the realtor had

said. One million, one hundred thousand dollars. Brian leaned back in his seat. The bench was high-backed and extremely uncomfortable, but he had sat on far worse. Nothing could compare to the third-class wagon of a Malaysian train for discomfort. His backside still bore lumps from a two-day run to Kuala Lumpur. Brian made himself as comfortable as possible and gave into the sense of defeat. Six hundred thousand pounds. He would be hard pressed to come up with even six hundred dollars. No matter what promise he might have made to his wife, Castle Keep was lost almost before it was found.

"Mr. Blackstone?" The receptionist stood in the middle of the chamber and beamed at him. "Dr. Lyons will see you now."

Every eye in the room seemed to track his progress. In the sudden silence his voice seemed to echo. "Most of these people were here before me. I don't mind waiting my turn."

"You just go right on down the hall there." The woman seemed hard put not to laugh out loud. "Dr. Lyons's office is the second door on your left."

Brian had the distinct impression that several others in the waiting room shared the receptionist's humor. As he started down the hallway, he heard an old man wheeze, "I'd give me good arm to be a fly on that wall."

The doctor's office was surprisingly large, the doctor herself surprisingly small. It was hard to tell her height, as she did not rise from her seat. But the oversized desk and antique swivel chair left her looking like a dark-haired child playing in an adult's seat. "Yes?"

"Dr. Lyons?"

"That's right. Come sit down."

Brian did as he was told. "Are you American?"

"Father. Mother's British." The accent was as clipped as the words, the tone utterly flat. The dark eyes were bright, the features slightly off-kilter. The nose tilted upward, the lips much too full for such a fine-boned face. Her head was cocked at a funny angle, and the short raven hair was pushed impatiently back behind her ears. "What seems to be the matter?"

Her abrupt attitude brought back memories of all the bad doctors he had suffered through to get here. Which was why he fished in his pocket and said merely, "I need to get a refill for a prescription."

She accepted the vial, read the label, demanded, "Where did you get this?"

"Sri Lanka."

"I'm afraid, Mr. . . . ."

"Blackstone."

"We do not automatically accept diagnoses and prescriptions from other countries." She set down the vial and cocked her head once more in his direction. "This is for a very strong antibiotic."

"That's because I was very ill. I had either food poisoning or dysentery, I'm not sure which, and neither were the doctors."

"I see." She seemed neither impressed nor all that concerned. "What are your symptoms now?"

"About what you'd expect." He had met a couple of American doctors who had lost their license to practice in the United States and fled to places that were only too glad to have medical care, no matter how questionable their abilities. He had just never expected to find one in Britain. "Weak, shaky, still a little fever."

"Any nausea or abdominal pain?"

21

"Not for the past couple of days."

She was out of her chair almost before he had spoken. "Take off your shirt and come sit over here."

Reluctantly he followed her to the corner bench. She examined his eyes, pricked his finger for blood, and inserted a thermometer before returning to her desk and filling out several forms. She returned to check his temperature and might have sniffed at the result, he wasn't sure. She inspected his tongue, listened to his chest, prodded his abdomen, and finally announced, "Other than signs of dehydration and weight loss, I'd say you were in fairly good shape."

"Would you." Another wave of fatigue swept over him. Brian fumbled with the buttons to his shirt and willed himself to remain upright. "Well, given your fantastic three-minute examination, I can't tell you how reassured that leaves me."

She crossed her arms. "We do not like to overprescribe medication in this country, Mr. Blackstone. Particularly antibiotics. And especially not antibiotics as strong as the one you've been on."

He started to explain how he had bribed the hospital pharmacy clerk in Colombo twenty dollars to give him a prescription for the antibiotic most recently arrived from overseas. How this was an old trick for seasoned travelers, since many Third World pharmacies did not bother to store antibiotics in cool, dry places, which meant they rapidly lost their potency. But he decided it was not worth the bother. He had met doctors like this before, people who assumed they had nothing to learn from anyone, especially not the patient. "I need another round of treatment."

"I'm sure you *think* you do."

"Look, is there another doctor I can see around here?"

She bridled. "You're welcome to check up front. I'm sure Dr. Riles can fit you in. Perhaps sometime next month will be convenient."

"Great. Just great." He rammed his shirttail into his trousers and hoped she did not notice his swaying. "Thanks for nothing."

But she did not move back to her desk; she merely stood in the center of the room with her arms crossed. "I happen to be renting Rose Cottage."

Bitterness rose like gall in his throat. "I guess that means you've heard about the sale of the property."

The change came as fast as a lightning strike. Eyes flashed wide, arms cocked on hips, face flushed crimson, voice rose to high-pitched clamor. "So *that's* it! You let this place fall into utter ruin, and then show up only to *sell* it!"

"I don't—"

"I should have known it the instant you walked in here! You . . . you moneygrubbing weasel!" She cocked back an arm, and for an instant Brian thought she was going to strike him. But she merely flung it toward the door. "Get out of my office!"

Brian stalked down the hall, feeling wind batter his back as the doctor slammed her door at his departure. The receptionist greeted him with a cheery smile, one shared by several of the others in the waiting room, and asked, "Feeling all better now, are we?"

3

$\mathcal{T}$he morning continued pretty much as it had begun. A steady stream of patients' sniffles and aches kept Cecilia's thoughts partly at bay, but the sense of dread rose steadily. When Maureen finally called back to say Grant Riles was ready to see her, she found it hard to rise from her chair.

There had been quiet but fierce opposition to the idea of an American doctor being given a place in Knightsbridge. At first Cecilia had thought it was because she was viewed as too foreign, and at every opportunity she had repeated the fact that she had been born here and her mother was English. It was only several weeks into her position as locum, or temporary GP, that she learned the truth. The people did not doubt her ability as a doctor and had no objection to her American heritage. They simply did not think she was going to stay.

The only reason she had been granted a chance at all was because the white-haired senior doctor had vouched for her. Dr. Grant Riles was a man of remarkable energy. At sixty-three years of age he remained pestered by his inability to speed up the world to a more acceptable pace. He tended to bark where others spoke, and flipped through medical journals with such impatient force that Cecilia normally received them with the pages torn halfway out. But he was a walking dictionary of medical treatments and a fierce advocate of preventive medicine. He had watched her closely through the six-month trial period, then asked Cecilia only one question: Would she give him five years? Cecilia had answered with an unequivocal yes.

As she passed through the waiting room, Cecilia gave Angeline Townsend and her son a vague smile. She then entered the clinic's other front room, larger than her own office with frosted panes turning the street traffic into shadows. Dr. Riles was scribbling impatiently, bearing down so hard he seemed intent on drilling the pen through both page and desk. Without looking up he said, "I understand you proposed inflicting grievous bodily harm upon one of our local citizenry."

"It was completely out of line," Cecilia said, panicky over what was to come.

"I agree." He looked up. "Do you have the Townsend boy's file there?"

"Yes."

"Let's have it then."

Only when he was deeply absorbed in the notes did Cecilia realize that that was to be the extent of her dressing-down. Weak with relief, she sank into the chair across from him.

"What is your assessment of Tommy's condition?"

"That's just it. I don't have one." The day had robbed her of any ability to hide her confusion. "He complains of vague pains that track all over his body. He's seriously underweight, less than two-thirds of the norm for his age."

"Which is?"

"He'll be five in two months."

"Fever?"

"Off and on. Two bad spikes, the last eight days ago, all the way to a hundred and four. Lasted ten hours and then disappeared without a trace. His mother is beside herself with worry."

"Quite understandable, given the circumstances." He flicked through the sheaf of lab reports. "I see you've given him all the normal tests."

"Most of the blood work I had done twice, just to be sure." She could not help but clench her hands in her lap. "Leukemia, hepatitis, encephalitis, meningitis, E. coli, everything I could think of. They all came back negative. Every time I do another test, the mother lives through nights of terror until the results come back."

"Then I suppose it's time to have a look at the boy." But when she started to rise he halted her with, "May I ask you a question?"

Cecilia braced for further condemnation. "Of course."

Grant Riles had the most unruly eyebrows she had ever seen. They arched across his forehead like silver-gray brushes. His eyes seemed to hunt for her through the undergrowth. "Have you ever lost a young patient?"

The question struck like a blow to her midsection. "No."

"I have. Three times. And each one was a harrowing experience." He turned his attention back to the open file and muttered quietly, "Most trying."

She licked dry lips and found sufficient breath to ask, "Do you think that's what we're facing here?"

"The issue is not what I think at this point. I haven't been watching the patient's decline all these weeks. You have." He slapped the file shut. "The question you need to be asking yourself is, Are you ready? Have you prepared yourself the best you can? Because sooner or later it is going to happen. You will come up against the unsolvable. We are only human, and death will one day win out." His eyes were a light green in color, as mild as his tone, yet they pierced her very soul. "The hardest task most doctors ever face is accepting defeat with a young patient. Especially one they have become attached to. You care for this Tommy, I take it."

"Very much." The words were barely more than a whisper.

"Well, I can't tell you not to care. But I can urge you to fortify yourself. Not that it will necessarily happen." He leaned across the desk. "*This time.*"

Cecilia did not want to hear any more, and she could think of no other way to halt the discussion than to rise to her feet. "I'll go—"

"Just one moment more, please." He waited until she had turned back around. "I would advise you to have a word with the vicar. Trevor Parkes is a good sort, as you no doubt know. It may help you to establish a line in the sand, don't you see. Between where your provenance ends, and God's begins."

Brian sat in what before had probably been Castle Keep's formal parlor. It was at the back of the second floor, with four tall windows overlooking the sweep of grounds. At the garden's far end ran the sparkling liquid ribbon of the River Thames. He had chosen this room to occupy because it was next to the kitchen. He had set one of the high-backed dining chairs directly beneath the window and pulled the smallest of the side tables up in front of him. His bedroll and sleeping bag were spread upon a threadbare Persian carpet. He knew all the bedrooms were upstairs. Although he had not ventured farther than the four rooms in this corner of the house, Brian had a vivid picture of the entire manor. He had no intention whatso-ever of going upstairs. The one positive outcome of selling the house would be not having to enter the room his wife had once called her own.

He ate slowly, pausing between every second or third bite to ensure that his stomach was not rebelling. He had only been back on solid foods for about a week. He ate a poor man's meal of beans and brown rice and dark bread, no seasoning except for a little salt, no butter, no grease of any kind. It tasted positively divine.

His attention was caught by a lone figure crossing the weed-infested garden, heading down to the river. Brian ate and watched the dark-headed doctor move easily along the rocky path. Clearly this was a walk she knew well. She wore an almost shapeless man's gray cardigan, the sleeves rolled up until they bunched like woolen balloons around her wrists, the bottom edge almost trailing in the dirt. It made her look even smaller than she already was.

His stomach knotted and then released, the spasm so familiar he paid it no conscious attention at all, merely set down his fork and continued to stare out the window. He knew tomorrow he would be angry with her, but toward evening his energy flagged, and all he could feel right now was a mild annoyance. She had seemed so passionate about the place, so *angry* over losing it. A trace of breeze lifted the sweater's trailing edge, and she wrapped her arms more tightly about her slender frame. She stood at the riverside, staring down at the flowing emerald water, as darkness began to gather. Brian finished his meal and sat there still, watching her and wondering why she was so involved in a place that was not even hers. Only when she turned and wended her way back around the side of the manor did he himself rise and go into the kitchen.

Over and over a dual refrain played through his mind—first the promise he had made to his wife, and then the impossible sum. Six hundred and thirty thousand pounds. He had never had anything close to that much money in his entire life. They might as well be asking for the moon.

Brian was more awake tonight, and the house's many flaws seemed etched upon the gathering dark. Many of the switches did not work, and those lights that did come on flickered and cast fitful glows over the high, shadowy ceilings. His wife had often spoken of her aunt as a mad and fanciful woman, and here in her old estate Brian saw evidence of this everywhere. Only a true eccentric would feel comfortable in this half gloom, with neither television nor radio by the looks of things. The windows did not close properly, and damp drafts filled the long chamber even on this summer evening. The floors creaked and sagged. The pipes in the bathroom rattled, and there was no hot water to speak of. When he finally lay down on his bedroll, the sounds became even clearer. The entire house groaned with age and lack of proper care.

It seemed as though Brian had only been asleep for an instant when the pains began.

The agony was so savage, he could scarcely believe it was happening. In his foggy condition it felt like a nightmare had crept into his waking state. The more awake he became, the stronger grew his torment.

The pain was so feral he felt as though some invisible beast were gnawing bites from his side. He opened his mouth, gasping for air as he rolled about on the floor. Moonlight streamed through the chamber's high windows, illuminating the ancient phone on the table by the door. Brian found he could not even rise to his feet. He crawled on three limbs, his left arm curled protectively about his side.

When he heard the dial tone, he sobbed with relief. He dialed for the operator, and as soon as the woman's voice came on he croaked, "I think I'm dying."

The phone's ring crashed about the house like a battery of cymbals. Cecilia had once tried to muffle the telephone bell, but it did no good. No matter how soft the sound, being awakened in the middle of the night was hard on the nerves, and her shattered sleep amplified the sound. She fumbled for the receiver, pulled it to her head, and said, "Yes?"

"Dr. Lyons?"

"Yes."

"This is the central exchange. Are you the doctor on call?"

"That is correct." It was a telephone operator, one she did not recognize. Which meant either a traffic accident or an emergency at the police station. Or perhaps a guest in the town's only hotel. The locals knew to call the clinic, where the nurse on duty would try to make sure it was a case genuinely requiring that the doctor be awakened. If so, they were patched through, with the nurse giving the doctor on duty a moment to come awake. Cecilia swung her feet to the floor and rubbed her face. Hard. "What is it?"

"We have an emergency heart case."

The worst possible scenario. She was already up and fumbling for her clothes. "What's the address?"

"Castle Keep, Knightsbridge. Sorry, I don't have a street—"

"Arthur!" She dropped the phone, slammed her feet into bedroom slippers, leapt down the stairs, grabbed the emergency bag she always left on the hall table, and raced out into the night.

The trees rustled and shivered overhead, as though sharing her fear. Arthur Wainwright was an anomaly, healthy as a horse and yet frail as anyone his age. She had never suspected him to have a weak heart, but anything could have set off an attack. Such as moving a heavy wall cupboard and hefting a bulky fire extinguisher and chasing a fire up a pantry wall. Cecilia bounded up the stairs and slammed open the front door with such force that it struck the side wall with a sonic boom. The front hall light was a flickering glow somewhere far overhead, turning her shadow into a leaping fool. She pounded on the apartment door with one hand, pressed the buzzer with the other, and shrilled out, "*Gladys!*"

But it was a sleep-tousled Arthur who opened the door, his wife of fifty years cowering behind him. He gripped an industrial-strength flashlight like a mallet, stared down at her, and demanded sternly, "What on earth?"

She had to take a moment to catch her breath. "They said you had a heart attack."

"Merciful heavens," Gladys Wainwright said, gripping her chest. "He hasn't yet, but give us time. We just might make the journey worth your while."

But Cecilia was already turning away. "The operator distinctly said Castle Keep. It's got to be him."

The elderly couple demanded in unison, "Who?"

"Him. Our landlord. Mr. High Muckety-Muck himself."

Arthur Wainwright stepped out into the drafty hallway. "The man's had an attack?"

"For his sake," Cecilia said, taking the stairs two at a time, "I certainly hope so."

The three of them burst through the unlocked door to find the new arrival scrabbling down the hall on hands and knees. He halted midway and came up into a crouch. Leaning against the side wall and gripping the base of his rib cage with both arms, he bared his teeth in a tight grimace and wheezed, "It's getting worse."

"Is that so," Cecilia snapped, surprising even herself. She was not known for her bedside manner, but she did not go out of her way to offend her patients. Yet this man was different. She had despised him long before they ever met.

Brian Blackstone seemed to find nothing untoward in her response. He merely gripped himself harder and panted, "It feels like a red-hot poker is being drilled through my side."

She walked over and knelt in front of him. He was clad in a pair of ragged boxer shorts and a tan so dark it looked painted on. Even in the hall's feeble light she could see the sheen of perspiration covering his body. "Unlock your arms and show me where it hurts."

"I'm not sure." His breath came in quick little gasps, as though breathing too deeply might cause something to unspring. "I think under my ribs, but it moves around."

"Is it more to one side?"

"I think . . . Yes. My right." Another spasm hit him and he groaned.

"Well, unless your heart has shifted under its load of guilt, I think we can rule out cardiac arrest." She gripped the upper arm and tugged. "Let's try to see if we can make it back to your bed."

Gladys stepped forward, her voluminous nightdress billowing like a starched sail. She looked reprovingly at Cecilia, for clearly her tone did not sit well with the older woman. But all Gladys said was, "Shall I make us a pot of tea?"

"We won't be here that long." Cecilia could not help but glance around as she entered the front parlor. It was her first time on the manor's upper floors. The room was not nearly as tall as the entry hall, but grand in its own faded way. Not even the feeble lighting could mask the fact that this had once been a truly stupendous salon. Gilded cherubs reached across the domed ceiling to hold the crystal chandelier in place. Only two of perhaps thirty bulbs worked, however, and these gave off fitful illumination. What they revealed spoke of seedy opulence. The rumpled sleeping bag sprawled across the shabby Persian carpet only added to her ire. She eased her patient back down, knelt beside him, and declared flatly, "You're not having a heart attack."

"I never—"

"And you're not going to die."

The reassurance, no matter how it was delivered, helped to calm him and clear his vision. Instead of expressing relief or gratitude, however, Brian Blackstone said simply, "Another of your thirty-second diagnoses."

The words struck hard, particularly because it was at least

partly true. Cecilia snapped open the catches to her bag and pulled out her stethoscope. "The pain is centered below your rib cage and on your right side, is that correct?"

"Yes."

"Hold still." She placed the stethoscope to his chest. The pulse was frantic from pain, but strong. Chest clear, though the breathing was somewhat irregular, as was to be expected. She freed her ears and set the instrument to one side. "Place your arms to your sides."

She palpitated his upper abdomen but found only the tightness of clenched muscle. "Do you feel nauseous?"

"I told you this afternoon—"

"Not from your previous illness. Now. Do you feel anything different at this present time?"

"I don't know. Maybe."

Gently she prodded his sweat-dampened skin. "Is this where it hurts most?" She was rewarded with a wince and a nod. "Does it radiate downward along this line?" Another nod. "All right. From your dehydrated state, the perspiration, and the specific location of your pain, I can say with great certainty that you have experienced an attack of kidney stones."

"Poor fellow," Arthur murmured from somewhere by the doorway.

The expression of sympathy only heightened her ire. Cecilia searched in her bag and came up with a pair of vials and two syringes. She ripped open the containers and said, "Let me share a little something with you, since this will hopefully be the last time you and I ever meet. I did my undergraduate studies at Duke before studying medicine here in England at Oxford University. I was offered the chance to specialize at Guy's

Hospital in London. I turned it down because all my life I've dreamed of practicing family medicine in a small English village. Something that I am absolutely certain will make no sense to you whatsoever."

She ripped open the package of sterilizing gauze, swabbed his arm, prepared the tourniquet, and used her middle finger to thump up the vein. All the while she continued speaking. "I came here because this is the home village of my mother's family. I was one of fourteen candidates for the job. Despite what you might think, this is a highly sought-after location."

"My dear," Arthur protested quietly, "I hardly think this is the time or place—"

"When I had my final interview with the town's chief doctor, he said I was far and above the most qualified candidate," Cecilia went on, ignoring Arthur entirely. She filled the first syringe, squeezed out the air bubbles, and inserted the needle into the vein. "Then he told me he was going to have to offer the post to someone else. The reason was simple. He did not think an American doctor, no matter how strong the connections to this place, would ever be able to overcome the inclination to chase the almighty dollar. Those were his exact words."

She observed the patient's gradual relaxation as the strong painkiller took hold and released him from the agony. She pushed the plunger fully down, then placed a cotton swab on the point of entry and removed the needle. "I answered the only way I could, which was to say I would work at half-pay through the six-month trial period. I went into debt to live and work here. This is a lovely village. It's bursting at the seams with history and charm. The longer I stay here, the more . . ." She halted because she had no choice. It felt as though a fist had closed about her throat. She swallowed down the constriction and the sorrow and finished, "Rose Cottage is also my *home*."

She inserted the second needle a few millimeters up the arm from the first, and went silent for the time it took to inject the muscle relaxant and observe his response. His body continued to slacken in stages. His eyes held her attention most of all. They were gray and surprisingly clear, but their calm was unearthly. As though he were detached from everything about him, including his own distress. Now that the pain was gone, he seemed scarcely connected to this place, this world, even his own body.

Cecilia rose to her feet, and in turning met Gladys's and Arthur's reproving stares. She knew then that she would have to be the one to break the news. "Castle Keep is going to be sold."

"What?" Arthur's words were punctuated by a gasp from his wife. "When?"

It was the patient who responded, his voice utterly blank and uncaring. "Next week."

"That's why he came to Knightsbridge, to collect his money and run." Cecilia looked into the man's clear gray eyes, empty of even a hint of shame or remorse, and wondered what made him so utterly cold. "You might have the power to kick us out into the street and take off with all the riches you can carry. But the truth is, you've missed the opportunity of a lifetime. You've lost the prize." She picked up her bag and started from the room, shepherding the elderly couple before her. "That is, if you ever had it at all."

4

*W*ednesday's dawn was long in coming, as slow as the pulse of returning pain. Brian lay on his pallet, drifting in and out of slumber. He knew the pain was not vanquished but merely set aside for the moment. Thankfully, his mind cleared before the agony resumed. He had much he needed to think over. But instead of dwelling upon the surprises the night had revealed, Brian found his thoughts returning again and again to the doctor and her opinionated prattle.

Two years away from the United States, two years of traveling back roads and places with no roads at all, had left him with an ability to view all of life from a tourist's safety. Just passing through, involving himself in nothing. And yet one addle-headed woman packing more degrees than was healthy had wormed deep under his skin. Now that he was alone and the house was quiet and the pain stilled, Brian found a hundred different ways to put her in her place. Not all the world could be boxed up neat and tidy with a ten-second assumption. Dr. Lyons jumped to conclusions because it kept her from needing to think deeply about anything or anybody. She had built her entire life around the stopwatch a doctor used to ratchet up the number of patients. She might not be hunting for money, but she still carried all the bad habits, all the shortsightedness. Oh yes, he could tell her a thing or two. If only he had a chance.

But this was not the night's surprise. No. Brian had met a lot of doctors and liked very few of them. He had no time at all for the way some lorded over people in their moments of weakness. Or for the way others barricaded themselves away emotionally, discussing the most sensitive and tragic issues in the coldest of terms. They pretended it was to protect themselves from becoming overinvolved. But after years of observing doctors, Brian had decided that in truth many had never learned to care. Medical schools taught would-be doctors everything there was to know about the human body, except how to locate their own hearts. No, there was no surprise whatsoever in Dr. Cecilia Lyons's response to the vagaries of life.

What had astonished him in the night was his own reaction. Not to the doctor, but rather to the pain. Brian lay on his pallet and watched the first streaks of crimson appear in the sky outside the grand windows. The glass panes were centuries old, and their warped surfaces turned the simple scene of first light into a living impressionistic painting. He thought back to other illnesses and earlier dawns. Mornings he had greeted in the hospital in Colombo, and those before the tummy bug had laid him low. Dawns he had watched from the shelter of palms on the coast of Thailand. And before that had been some remarkable sunrises where desert met the sea in northern Australia. Earlier still had come the soft gray light of a rainy New Zealand morn, and before that the semitropical heat of Tahiti daybreaks. On and on the list of names and places went, most of them scarcely remembered. Brian stared at the strengthening light and felt his pulse press upon the muted pain in his side, and he knew that he was seeing this dawn with a clarity he had thought lost and gone forever.

What had surprised him most about the night was that in the moment of worst pain, he had wanted to live. So many days gone by he had greeted as one already dead, one whose heart had been torn from his body, and whose corpse could not realize it was time already to cease the useless task of living. A year ago, the news that he was going to perish would have been greeted with a single word—*Finally*.

But as he lay and waited for the pulse of pain to return, he realized he no longer wanted to depart. Why, he could not say. He had no good reason to want to hang around. But he could not argue with what had resounded through the pain and the night.

Brian winced as the first discomfort sliced cleanly through his side. He knew an instant's fear, for he was certain the doctor had meant exactly what she said. Dr. Lyons was not going to return.

The pain subsided momentarily, long enough for him to knead his side and take an easy breath. But it was just a fleeting lapse; he could almost see the clean ice-blade of coming agony poised over his belly. He wanted to shout, to call and plead for someone to come and help. But the manor's interior walls were so thick he doubted anyone could hear. And certainly no one who would be able to help stop the pain.

Fear of what he was about to endure pushed a sheen of sweat to his face. But it was not just the fear. Brian curled up on his side, pressing hard to shield himself from the torment, and heard the silent cry resound through his panic-stricken mind. *He wanted to live.*

Cecilia was out the main gates and a hundred yards down the road before she finally accepted that she had to go back.

No matter how hard she argued with herself, she could not leave her landlord unattended until the duty nurse made morning rounds. It might be another two hours before the nurse arrived, and Cecilia had seen enough patients with kidney stones to know those minutes could last a lifetime. She turned back, resigned to the fact that she could not even become angry with the man. She was too busy worrying over little Tommy Townsend.

As she passed back through the front gates and crunched down the weed-infested drive, her mind continued to circle over the latest developments in the child's case. The previous day's examination had yielded nothing new. Cecilia took no comfort in the youngster's proving an enigma to her boss as well. Tommy was nearly five years old and was not growing. He suffered from undefined aches and pains. One day it was his chest, the next his knees. He slept too much. He was listless. His fever varied by as much as four degrees in a twenty-four-hour period.

As Cecilia pushed through the front door, crossed the gloomy front hall and started up the stairs, she reflected that Tommy's mother was almost as great a worry as the child himself. Angeline followed every diagnostic test with an overwrought horror.

She was halfway up the stairs when it hit her—the test she had failed to carry out, principally because she had never heard of it being used. It harked back to earlier times, when tiny babies refused to grow, and underweight children were a tragic norm. Cecilia hurried on, determined now to finish here and get to the office so she could call Angeline Townsend and prepare her for yet another night of worry and dread.

The world and the morning did not truly come into focus until she pressed the doorbell and heard the scraping sound inside. She felt a rising tide of guilt, which crested when Brian Blackstone opened the door and stood there clenching his side and breathing in tight little gasps.

"Here, let me help you back to bed." She slipped under his arm and felt the perspiration that sheened the skin of his chest. These panic-sweats were a classic symptom of kidney stones, and along with the off-side pain offered one of the speediest diagnoses in medicine. Together they made the journey back down the hallway and into the formal parlor. The air of faded grandeur was even stronger in the morning light. As was the desperately grateful look that Brian gave her as he returned to his pallet.

The man's grateful gaze left Cecilia feeling even worse. No matter that he was stealing away her beloved Rose Cottage. He was a patient, and he was in great pain. It went against the foundations of her profession to realize that she had caused him to suffer unduly. "How long since the pain returned?"

"About an hour." His face twisted into a parody of a smile. "But it seemed like closer to a year from this end."

She tried to return the smile but could not. She wanted to apologize for her behavior but found that impossible as well. So she glanced at her watch, counted back, and came up at five hours since the earlier injection. "I'll make sure to return and dose you again before this batch wears off."

"Thank you," he whispered, the abject relief so strong in his voice and eyes that it pierced her heart.

"I assume from your reaction last night that you've not had a previous attack."

"Never."

"The muscle relaxant should help you pass the stone, especially if it is just dust. If it is a larger stone, we'll know by tonight." She did not bother to explain that the total blockage caused by a large stone would result in a pain not even her strongest drugs could dull. No need to worry him with what hopefully would not happen.

"I'm sorry for scaring everybody last night."

The fact that he was doing what she could not halted her in the act of opening the syringe package. "That's all right."

"I never knew a pain could be as bad as that and not kill me."

Cecilia went back to preparing the first injection. "My third year of medical school, when we were first starting our hospital rounds, a doctor listed all the nightmare agonies we could expect to face in our patients. It was her way of preparing us for the shocks to come. Kidney stones were right up there with terminal cancer, childbirth, and cardiac arrest."

Brian watched as she tightened the tourniquet, thumped his vein higher, and inserted the needle. "How long will this go on?"

"If you haven't passed it by tonight, I'll need to move you to the local clinic and put you on a drip." And possibly a catheter, but again there was no need to frighten him with that just yet. "Any nausea?"

"This morning."

"That can be a side effect of the muscle relaxant." She completed the first injection and began preparing the second. "Try to drink as much as you can. I'll leave you my direct number. If the pain starts again, or if you begin to spasm, you must call me immediately."

His eyes never left the syringe she was preparing. "Thank you."

Her mind went back to the meeting in her office the previous morning, and shame almost engulfed her. She cleared her throat and asked, "How long were you sick . . . where did you say you'd come from?"

"Sri Lanka." As she inserted the second needle and pressed the plunger, his breathing eased. "I was in the hospital for almost five weeks."

That bit of news halted her once more. "What?"

"It was my own fault. I was living rough and eating rougher."

"How long have you been traveling?"

"Two years." A film began to settle over his eyes, and the words became more labored. "Ever since my wife died."

She completed the injection with the motions of a well-programmed robot. "You lost your wife?"

His nod was drugged and slow. "Hairy cell leukemia."

The news pushed her off her knees and sat her on the floor. "How long was she ill?"

"Four years. In and out of remission three times." He turned his face toward the window. The English sunlight seemed overweak falling upon his leathery skin. His voice grew ever more slurred as the second drug took hold. "I think we were both ready by the time it finally happened. But it didn't make it any easier."

"No, I suppose not." With numb fingers she began gathering her bits and pieces. "I have to get to the clinic."

"I promised her I'd hold on to the place. But I can't." The words gathered and pushed against one another, the act of forming them distinctly lost to him now. "Least, that's what the realtor told me."

The realization that he was talking about Castle Keep caught Cecilia in the act of rising. She sank back to her hands and knees and drew in closer to his face. "What did you say?"

"Six hundred and thirty thousand pounds," he mumbled. "Never had that much money in my entire life."

"What are . . . death duties, is that what you're talking about?"

"Six hundred and thirty thousand," he said, and the eyelids slid slowly down. "Got to go with the auction. Don't have a choice."

"Mr. Blackstone, wait. Hold on a moment longer, please." She raised her voice and almost shouted, "When did you hear about the auction?"

He mumbled something that might have been, "Yesterday."

"Mr. Blackstone?"

Brian raised his right hand slightly from the pallet and mumbled, "Sorry, Sarah. So sorry." Then his breathing deepened, and he was gone.

5

─────────

*B*rian drifted in and out of the clouds and the sunlight and the day. Perhaps the drugs had a cumulative effect, perhaps it was simply the result of a stronger dose; whatever the reason, Brian felt as though he were swimming not through hours, but rather mysteries of time and place. He was only partially aware when he passed the stone around midday, a gift he did not genuinely appreciate until later that afternoon, when the drugs finally began to wear off.

Which was why, when afternoon shadows stretched long musty arms across the parlor and a man's voice called from his front hall, Brian was able to rise and walk out to greet him.

"Oh, hello." He was tall and a few years older than Brian, lean and hard. "I'm Trevor Parkes, the vicar." He hefted the pot he was holding. "Gladys, your tenant downstairs, has made you some soup. She wasn't certain whether you'd be presentable, so she asked me to bring it up."

"Come in." Brian leaned heavily against the wall. "The kitchen is back this way."

"Yes, I know." The vicar moved in close enough for the soup to waft tantalizingly. "You seem remarkably mobile for someone suffering from kidney stones."

"Not anymore." Brian was surprised at how weak he felt. Rising from the pallet and walking the hallway proved enough to exhaust him. He entered the kitchen and collapsed into a high-backed chair by the central table. "Passed it a couple of hours ago."

"Oh, well done." The vicar hefted the pot. "Shall I do the honors?"

"Please. I imagine there are some bowls around here somewhere."

"Yes, just over the sink here." The vicar moved into the light of the western window, revealing the strong features and corded arms and neck of a serious athlete. Which made his voice sound even milder than it actually was. "I wager the drugs have left you rather washed out."

"Limp as a wet rag," Brian agreed. "You've been in this house before, I take it."

"Any number of times. I had the honor of calling Heather Harding a friend." He set the pot on the stove, found the matches, lit the flame under one eye, and moved the pot into position. "I arrived in Knightsbridge just as she started her decline. Enjoyed many a pleasant cup of tea here at this table. Do you have any bread?"

"Sorry. The cupboard is totally bare."

"Well, I'm sure Gladys can spare you a slice or two. Hang on a tic." Before Brian could tell him not to bother, the vicar was out the door and gone.

Brian sat at the table and felt the lowering sun warm him to his bones. The ruddy glow was kind to the old chamber, painting the dilapidated appliances and peeling walls and worn plank floor with glowing strokes. He heard pleasant voices echo from downstairs, and someone laughing. The faint sound convicted him of his own loneliness.

The vicar returned swiftly, carrying a half-loaf with him. "No good soup should go undipped."

"I'm surprised they were willing even to give me crumbs from the table," Brian said, trying to respond with humor of his own. "Seeing as how they're about to lose their home."

"Yes, Arthur showed a marked unwillingness to join me in my mission of mercy." He fished in the drawer for a ladle, washed it and the bowl and the spoon thoroughly, then ladled out a generous portion. "All of which I find quite strange, I must say."

"I don't see why." Brian watched the vicar set the bowl down in front of him. The fragrant steam caused his entire body to clench with sudden hunger. "It must be hard to look around for a new home, especially at their age."

"No, what I meant was, I find it remarkable that Heather did not make any mention to me of the house being auctioned off." Trevor slid into the seat across from Brian, observed the way the spoon trembled as it rose. "When did you last eat?"

"Last night. Beans and rice. Only been back on solids a week." The split-pea soup was as thick as goulash. "This is great stuff."

"Yes, Gladys is quite accomplished in the kitchen. You've been ill?"

"Food poisoning. Sri Lanka." The short responses were fit in between bites. Brian felt the first faint twinge and forced himself to slow down. But it was hard. His body seemed desperate, beyond famished, no matter what state his stomach might be in. "Spent over a month in a Colombo hospital."

The vicar grimaced in sympathy. "That must have been dreadful."

"Beyond belief." He pushed the scenes away by returning to

matters closer at hand. "You say Heather never mentioned anything about planning to sell the house?"

"Not a word."

"Maybe she didn't bother to think about death duties."

"She was frail; she was old. And she was very ill, particularly toward the last. She was also a genuine English eccentric." The memory brought a smile to the vicar's face. "But one thing Heather was not, to the very last, was forgetful."

"I wouldn't know. I only met Heather once. She despised me."

"Oh, I very much doubt that."

"Loathed the ground I walked on." Even after all these years, the memory still rankled. "She came to Philadelphia the month after I asked Sarah to marry me. At least, she said it was to visit. What she really wanted was to convince Sarah to break off the engagement."

To his surprise, Trevor's smile resurfaced. "Yes, I'm afraid that does sound like Heather."

"For the first week she was over, Heather and I fought constantly. I finally told Sarah I was leaving and would be back when Heather returned to England. That is, if Sarah still wanted me."

"Which she did, I take it."

"Heather wouldn't even come to the wedding, not even when Sarah traveled over and begged Heather to be her bridesmaid." He scooped up the last spoonful. "I've never been to England. Sarah came over a few times more before she became ill, but she always made the trip alone."

"I never met your Sarah, of course. I believe her illness started around the same time as Heather's own decline."

The sunset dimmed, the colors gradually washed of their glow. "That's right."

"Heather talked of her constantly. Your wife must have been a remarkably beautiful woman."

Brian turned to the window, only to find his late wife's face etched into the sky, the evening, the life that still remained to him. "Inside and out."

With a pastor's understanding, Trevor rose to his feet and turned his back to Brian and his moment of remembered pain. "Should I put on some tea?"

"I doubt there's anything to make it with."

"Oh, Gladys thought to give me a few bags. Couldn't see you go without a cuppa." He turned around long enough to offer a quick flash of a smile. "Not even the man planning to rob them of their beloved home."

"It's not my idea."

"So I gather." Trevor opened the cupboard by the stove and exclaimed, "What on earth do we have here!"

"What is it?"

"A letter from Heather!" The vicar turned back around, holding a slender pink envelope yellowed with age. "It's addressed to you."

Brian stood and felt the world swim. "Uh-oh."

Trevor was instantly by his side. "Let me help you."

Brian had no choice but to lean heavily on the other man. "Maybe I'd better go lie down."

"Of course. Slowly now, that's it."

Weakness rose like a relentless flood tide. "I didn't come here to sell the place. I promised Sarah I'd keep it."

"I must say, I find it baffling that Heather had not seen to the death duties." Trevor waited until he had settled Brian on his pallet to ask, "Why are you down here and not upstairs?"

"Two choices up there," he mumbled, the fatigue tugging relentlessly at his eyes. "Heather's bed or Sarah's."

"Oh. Of course. I understand perfectly." He rattled the letter he still held. "Shall I read this to you?"

Brian was about to agree, when sleep rose up and covered him with the mantle of night.

Brian knocked on the downstairs apartment door, then stood in the gloom and listened to the vague sounds within. The door finally opened to reveal the stern-looking older man. "Oh, it's you."

"Goodness, Arthur, that's no way to greet the fellow." His wife was shorter but about one-and-a-half times as wide. She pushed by her husband and beamed at Brian. "How are you, dear?"

"Much better. I can't thank you enough for the soup." He handed back the empty pot. "I just had a second helping, and it was better than the first."

She preened with pleasure. "Trevor says the nasty little stone things finally decided to leave you in peace."

"This afternoon."

The old gentleman was stiff in the manner of a man born to command. "Had four bouts of stones myself over the years. Terrible, they were. Dreadful."

Gladys added, "Arthur and I spent eighteen years in warmer climes. Africa, mostly. Stones develop more swiftly in hot climates. Dehydration."

"Plus three years in Delhi," the old man said. "RAF. You know Delhi?"

"I had planned to go there," Brian replied, surprised at his own gratitude for the old man's willingness to unbend this much. "But I ate something that didn't agree with me in Colombo."

"Arthur has been to Colombo, haven't you, dear. With the queen."

That pushed Brian back a step. "As in the queen of England?"

"Arthur flew her plane," his wife proudly announced. "Twice."

But Arthur was fastened upon an earlier thread. "Gut-rot is a risky business. Laid you up for long?"

"Almost five weeks."

"A month and more in a Colombo hospital." A faint hint of a smile appeared beneath the neatly trimmed mustache. "That must have been a lark."

"It was," Brian replied, "a living nightmare."

It might have been a cough or perhaps a laugh. Then Arthur Wainwright said, "You'll have to come down sometime; we'll trade a few tales of war wounds and warmer climes."

"I'd like that. Very much."

"What must you think of us," Gladys scolded. "Making you stand here in the drafty hall. Come in and have a glass."

"Actually, I was wondering if you could loan me a flashlight. I need to go upstairs, and I can't seem to get the lights to work."

"Oh, they haven't worked for years. Arthur, go bring the man the big torch. It's on the bathroom sill." To Brian, she added, "The electrics in this house are atrocious. Heather was always going on about them, promising to have the walls torn open and all the wiring replaced. But she never did."

"Never did get around to much of anything," the old man grumbled, disappearing into the gloom of the apartment's dusky interior. "More's the pity."

Brian asked, "So my wife's aunt never mentioned anything to you about planning to sell off the house?"

"Not a word. Which is more than passing strange, seeing as how we were Heather's closest friends."

A voice from the dark muttered, "Or we thought we were."

"Hush up, you." Gladys leaned forward. "Did Trevor really find a letter from Heather amid the teacups?"

"Yes."

"How utterly thrilling. Imagine, sitting there for two years, just waiting for you to show up."

The old man's silhouette reappeared from the murk. "Just goes to show the sort of job the cleaner was doing."

"She didn't have any reason to go fishing in among the china, now, did she?" Turning to Brian, Gladys explained, "The real-estate agent sent his cleaning lady over once a month to do a spot of dusting."

"Spot is right," Arthur grumbled. "And a ruddy lot of good it did us, having the hall floor swept when it's so dark we can't see a hand in front of our faces."

Brian caught the drift. "So the realtor hasn't been keeping up on the repairs?"

"Now don't you start us on that." She blocked Arthur with her girth. "You just go get some rest, and we'll save all that for when you have time to come down for a spot of dinner. So nice to finally meet you proper, dear."

"Glad to see you up and about," her husband added before the door closed.

Brian stood and felt the air impacted by the shutting door and the voices within, Arthur grumbling and Gladys chiding, two people so used to living together they could not consider a life alone. He started up the stairs, lit now by the flashlight's gleam, and wondered if he would ever grow used to the void within.

When the house had been refashioned to include a down-stairs apartment, a wall and a set of grand double doors had been inserted on the upstairs landing. The sweeping twin staircase joined on what was now a broad balcony, as large as a parlor and embellished with a chandelier that did not work. The doors opened into a wide hallway running the length of the house, leading to what had once been three grand salons and a library, with the eat-in kitchen at the house's south end. Refrains of for-mer grandeur were everywhere, crowded by shadows and age. Brian walked down the hall away from the kitchen, opened another door, took a deep breath, and started up the stairs.

The envelope in his shirt pocket seemed to reopen and whis-per to him. The voice of a woman he had met only once reached across the impenetrable distance and spoke in time to the squeaking stairs, repeating all the letter's surprises.

"My dear Brian," Heather wrote. "I wish to apologize. My hands no longer follow my mind's command, so my letter must be brief. In the space of too few words, I offer you years of repen-tance. I was horrid to you. Not because of who you were. No. Because I was a selfish old woman. I tried to force dear Sarah to choose between the two people she loved most, you and me. What a dreadful mistake that was. I deserve all the loneliness that life has punished me with.

"You, however, do not. I understand the agony you are going through. Oh yes. Far more than you would ever imagine. For I, too, have lost a love. You probably never knew that. How could you? I never gave you a chance to know me at all. Until now."

The manor's third floor was a narrow copy of the second, with lower ceilings and somewhat smaller rooms. The chambers and windows were modest only in comparison with those downstairs. The dust was thick enough to clog the still air, the scents stuffy and very old. No cleaning person had ventured up here in a very long while.

Brian entered the room closest to the stairwell, and though all the furniture was draped in yellowed white dustcloths, he knew instantly he stood in Sarah's room. To his vast relief, there was no sense of tragic longing. The room was just a room, despite matching her descriptions exactly. He tried the wall switch and was rewarded with a yellow glow from the dusty, fly-specked chandelier. It, too, matched his wife's account, hand-blown in the shape of an hourglass. Brian turned slowly, reliving the nights they had spent sharing her happiest memories, almost all of which began here in this room. And all the while, Heather's murmurings and the letter in his pocket kept him company.

"Once I knew the love of a soul mate," Heather wrote. "Forgive my brevity. It hurts to write of that time. Even saying these few words leaves my heart as pained as my hands. His name was Alexander. We were married three short years, and then God took him away from me. I fear the loss drove me a bit mad.

"A year and five months later, a little princess arrived at my doorstep. She was eight years old and as beautiful as an English summer dawn. Her name was Sarah. She was sad, lonely, and terrified of me. And with every reason. It was her presence that drew me back from the depths of my own living death. And returned me to God. For I knew that alone I would not be able to find either the love or the answers that this little child required."

Each wall held a mural, painted at Heather's request by a local artist. They depicted passages from Sarah's favorite books. It had become part of Sarah's excitement over returning to Castle Keep each summer, waiting to discover what Heather had ordered up. The entire right-hand wall showed a covered bridge from whose heights Christopher Robin and Pooh and Tigger raced twigs upon a smooth-running stream.

The room was dominated by a four-poster bed, which beneath its dustcovers looked like an ancient vessel ready to sail upon the seas of night. Brian stared at the bed and felt the first heart twinges as he imagined his little Sarah nestled there, sent by parents who had never really been parents at all. Lost and frightened and alone, she had hidden deep within the covers of a bed so big it seemed to go on forever. She had felt trapped here inside a house so huge it took even her tiny footsteps and echoed them over and over like ghostly drums. And watched by an aunt whose eyes did not seem able to track together, especially at night. That first summer, Aunt Heather had cast a terrifying figure, with a rat's nest of graying hair and hands that danced to music Sarah could never hear. Yet somehow this strange old biddy had become Sarah's grandest friend, introducing her to the wonders of a house filled with mysterious places and ancient secrets, acquainting her with other mysteries as well—those of faith and hope, those of laughter and belief in a tomorrow worth living.

Heather's quiet chant was still with Brian as he turned from the room and its treasured yesterdays, and it sent him down the hall on a quest he still did not understand. "Sarah arrived wounded by her own past," Heather wrote. "Don't ever think children are incapable of harboring tragedy. Their spirits can also be stained crimson by the injustices of life. I wanted to help her, but could not do so alone. So I turned to God for help, and found that He had brought Sarah just for that purpose. Such wondrous subterfuge within the divine mind."

Heather's own chambers were also as Sarah had described, a series of four adjoining rooms that flowed one into the other. Brian's footsteps made a dusty trail across the ancient carpets as he walked and searched. Here in these rooms, with the covered paintings upon the walls staring at him like sightless eyes, Heather's voice seemed clearer still.

"To my delight, I discovered that Sarah loved puzzles. I turned this grand old house into one large maze and used its mysteries to teach her both to discover herself and to trust me. I found a healing in this. For me, and thankfully for Sarah as well. And in the making of my clues and watching her uncover the rewards, I found a bond growing between us. And a miracle. For it was not only Sarah who was learning to trust and love and laugh and live. I was as well."

The bedroom opened into a small salon, with its high-backed padded chair and fainting couch both made lumpish and vague by yellowing covers. All the lights worked, revealing a blanket of dust upon the hardwood floors and making the tattered velvet wallpaper appear faded as sun-bleached parchment. From there he entered a dressing salon, with a marble-tiled bath beyond. Brian halted in the dressing room, took the letter from his pocket, and listened as Heather's scratchy voice finished reciting the final passage.

"This, then, is my gift to you. Rather, it is *our* gift. For Sarah has worked with me every step of the way. All those conversations through the good and bad times of our respective illnesses, this is much of what we spoke of. We recalled the past. Did you ever hear her laughing on the telephone with me, even when the pain and the weakness crippled her? What a miracle our memories can be. We spoke and remembered better times. And we planned, Sarah and I. We gave ourselves hope of a future, which illness had robbed us of, through hoping for you, dear Brian. I pray you will permit me to say those words, for through Sarah's love and her sorrow of leaving you, I have learned to care for you as well. Dear, dear Brian, mainstay of my darling Sarah's life. I pray that you shall heal. I pray that you will come to know hope in a future. Not the future you might have wished for yourself. No. But a future just the same.

"Our gift is to be a series of puzzles. In reading our clues and seeking our answers, we hope and pray you will find a future as well. A morrow filled with reasons to live, and a purpose grand enough to bestow upon you the gift of hope. For you deserve it all, my dear Brian. All the hope a tomorrow worth living can bring.

"Here, then, is the first clue: From the hope tossed skyward on your beloved's happiest day, in a grand palace made to make a child feel grander still, search for the heart, search for the heart, search for the heart of your beloved. Yours ever, Heather."

With a single, ragged breath Brian drew himself back from the realm of memories and silent voices. He stared into the dressing room's mercury-backed mirror, but felt as though he had been observing a vision, one where angels with wings of gossamer dreams whispered songs from realms where lovers never mourned.

He wiped his eyes to clear them, when suddenly he found himself caught by a living apparition. It took a long moment to realize what it was he was seeing. Then he turned slowly, almost afraid to reach out and touch it.

It was the ribbon that convinced him. Faded and tattered as it was, there could be no mistaking Sarah's handwriting.

The bouquet was of miniature water lilies and teacup roses, dried and faded to the color of time-washed silk. Upon the ribbon that bound the flowers was written a passage taken from the book of Ruth, which Sarah had woven into her marriage vows: "Where you go I will go, and where you stay I will stay. Your people will be my people and your God my God."

Brian forced himself to pick up the marriage bouquet, marveling at how it had come to be here. Heather could not have caught it, for she had refused to attend their wedding. In fact, Heather had neither written nor answered any of Sarah's entreaties for more than a year. Brian held the bouquet in his hands and wondered at a young woman's love, one so strong it would retrieve the tossed bouquet, then hold it until it could be taken to a cross and lonely old woman. One who Sarah had always wished would remarry and start life anew.

Brian stared at the whitewashed wall, from which hung a collection of hats and slippers and gloves. Then he realized that there was something remarkable about this particular hook which had held the bouquet. In fact, upon closer inspection it looked almost like a lever. Hesitantly, Brian reached forward a second time and pulled the lever down.

The entire wall clicked back slightly. Brian set the bouquet down on the dressing table, lifted his flashlight, and pressed. When the wall gave only a fraction, he put his shoulder against the door and pressed harder still. With a squeal of hoary protest, the wall gave way.

Brian pointed his light inside the windowless room, smaller still than the dressing chamber. For a moment he saw nothing, until he aimed his light lower. Then the sight of the past coming vividly alive caused him to cry out loud.

6

$\mathcal{C}$ecilia Lyons stood by her parlor window on Thursday and tried to enjoy the slow July dawn. The day was overcast and cool, a temperature more suited to October. The sun had not yet crested the horizon, and all the day was pewter and still. The air was so windless she could hear the faint thunder of wings as birds flittered to and from her feeder. The day's soft beauty seemed only to deepen her gloom. She had not slept well, worried as she was over Tommy Townsend. The previous afternoon she had done what was inelegantly called a sweat test, scraping the child's skin with a sterilized ruler, gathering perspiration and then sealing it into a small glass vial. She had not bothered to hide from Tommy's mother that she was checking the child for yet another early killer. Cystic fibrosis was to become Angeline's latest nightmare.

Cecilia sighed hard, trying to push away worries over what the lab might report back. She decided to take her second cup of coffee and the morning's work out to the riverbank.

Once every two weeks Cecilia had a half-day free for study. There were several such time-slots built into her schedule—classes every quarter, conferences, opportunities to train further. She took advantage of them all. A plastic box intended to cart drugs from the suppliers to the pharmacies sat beneath her tall pantry cupboard, which had been moved back into place by the same electrician who had returned power to her kitchen. On these free mornings the plastic box was jammed with medical journals, both English and American, and dozens of drug circulars left by the pharmaceutical company salespeople. She slipped into her favorite tattered cardigan, balanced the cup on top of the pile, and carried the box down the drive.

As she rounded the corner of the manor, the sun edged its way over the horizon. The narrow ribbon of blue between the meadow and the cloud-covered sky was instantly transformed into an eternal doorway, and all the world sang a golden chorus to greet the new day. Cecilia continued on as much by memory as by sight, for she walked straight eastward into the sun, and little was visible beyond the world of golden silhouettes. She knew the manor gardens so intimately she thought of them as her own, and yet she entered a thrilling new realm. Even the grass she crossed was made fragile and jewel-like. The sky was no longer gray, but rather draped in streamers the length of heaven, a symphony of color. A pair of magpies flew to each side of her, seraphims sent to welcome her into this new day. She felt convicted by her inability to be happy with the gift, her heart made sadder still by this new failure. Tommy Townsend was not here, but he might as well have been. Her inability to help the little child left her veiled in a sorrow not even the morning's glory could pierce.

She was almost on top of Brian Blackstone before she saw him.

Brian had a curious expression on his face as he watched her approach. Almost as though he was struggling with himself. And yet he offered her the quiet greeting, "You look so sad."

All the resentment she had been carrying came rising up,

filling the morning so tightly she could scarcely manage, "I don't want to talk about it."

"I understand." He was silent a long moment, then added, "Would you like to sit down?"

She hated the fact that it was his right to invite her. This was *her* table and *her* garden, no matter whose name might be on the papers. But there was no alternative except to go back to the house, and the morning beckoned too strongly to retrace her steps. Cecilia set her box down on the wrought-iron table, retrieved her mug, took time for a sip and a long look at the horizon. The sun was a rounded crest upon the eastern hills, framed by trees and clouds of fire.

Brian's hands were busy with something shielded from her by the table's edge. The garden table was long and broad, intended to host as many as two dozen people. At each end, low iron side tables had been planted to support serving dishes and drinks. Cecilia liked to sit here and imagine how grand it all must once have been. But now the wild wisteria clambered up the table legs and anchored the rusting chairs in place. Summer flowers fought for space amid the weeds, while jasmine and thyme added their scent to the dawn.

"You were right."

The words were so quietly spoken that Cecilia had difficulty believing they were directed at her. "I beg your pardon?"

"About the antibiotic. I didn't need it after all." Brian raised what appeared to be a tiny high-backed chair to his mouth and blew gently. But before she could see for certain, his hands disappeared back below the vine-covered table. "I've eaten three full meals since the stone passed and haven't had any problems."

He looked at her then, the strengthening light turning his gaze as clear as a child's. "I can't thank you enough for your help in the night. If you hadn't come, I don't know what I would have done."

She dropped her gaze, unable to meet either his eyes or her own flush of shame. Even the cup's faint tendrils of steam were laced with color from the sunrise.

Brian sensed her muddled confusion and clearly misunderstood the reason. "I know, I know, doctors are like anybody else, they hate talking about their work outside the office. But I need to thank you." He bent over his work, whatever it was, and continued, "In Colombo, the ward they stuck me on had twenty-seven beds and sixty-one patients. I had a bed all to myself only because I was so big. Most beds had patients at each end, and the beds with children held three, lined up like dark sardines." Again he lifted and dusted and blew, this time holding what looked like a miniature chest of drawers. "I spent over a month staring through my mosquito net, watching the fans whirl overhead, listening to the other people around me, watching the families move back and forth in front of my bed and staring down at me like I was caged in a zoo, and wishing I was anywhere but there. It left me terrified of not ever getting better."

Cecilia's own sense of remorse and confusion only deepened. She reached inside her box, pulled out the top item, and stared blankly at the page. She could not apologize. Yet no matter what her mind might be saying, her heart would not still its remorseful beat.

As though in response to her own silence, the sun rose and slipped into the gray glove of day. Instantly the wonder was gone, the colors muted, the day chilled. The river turned to sullen slate. She forced herself to focus on the pages she held, only to exclaim, "How on earth did this get in here?"

"What?"

"Oh, it's the latest village battleground." She rattled the pages in the distance between them, glad for something safe to talk about. "The vicar is trying to raise funds to repair the church bells. Last month he took them down from all seven village churches at once to save money. The bells are hundreds of years old, and they're in pretty sad shape."

Cecilia looked up from the pamphlet and noticed for the first time just how handsome Brian Blackstone was. He was lean to the point of emaciation, but in the veiled daylight his skin looked as fresh and clear as his eyes, and the angles of his face looked as strong as an Indian's. "A group of locals want to keep the bells from ever going back in. They call it noise pollution."

She realized just how lame the whole thing must sound and hurriedly pressed on, "You'd have to live here to understand how hot people get over the silliest things. I try not to have anything to do with either side. But Trevor Parkes, the local vicar, has become a dear friend. These bells mean a lot to him, and he's become so worried over this battle . . ."

She halted because Brian had frozen in his bent-over position. "What's the matter?"

"It's another letter." Slowly he leaned back, drawing into view a folded envelope, brittle with age. "From Heather."

"Heather was writing you?" Curiosity got the better of her, and she rose up in her seat to see what he had been working on. She gaped at the sight of a dollhouse, one so beautifully designed she could identify it as a copy of the manor even with its roof propped against the vine-covered table leg. As soon as the object came into view, she could not help but cry, "I want it!"

7

$\mathscr{B}$rian sat in a high-backed horsehair chair, one that gave off
a vague musty odor every time he shifted his weight. Beyond his
parlor window, an ancient river craft chugged along the
Thames. The Victorian slipper launch was all inlaid wood and
brass fittings, with a softly puffing steam engine set amidships.
The passengers had dressed for the occasion, the men wearing
high-collared suits and flat straw hats called boaters. The
women were in crinoline and carried parasols. A silver tureen
full of freshly cut roses rested upon a table beside a wicker pic-
nic basket. The woman's laughter tinkled as fresh as birdsong
upon the still July air. Brian sipped the remnants of his tea and
discovered that the sound called to him. This surprised him. For
two years he had done his best to avoid places filled with light-
hearted people. Such contacts exposed his own wounds, as
though he had been banned from a realm where laughter was
welcome and cares could be set aside for an afternoon of sunlight and smooth-running water. But this day was different, and
in a subtle way that suggested that he was healing. Not just in
mind. But in heart as well.

He glanced down to his pallet and the letter lying alongside.
He had been rereading the second message when he had fallen
asleep. It had been such a deep rest that there had been no

dreams, only fragments of whispers as though the short sentences had followed him into slumber. His mind echoed with them still.

"Dear Brian," Heather wrote. "Today's weather has turned cold and damp, which means my joints are even more of a bother than usual. My hands are battling me, turning this letter into a struggle with pen and paper both. Age is such a dilemma; it traps the memory of youth within the dread reality of departure. I had hoped your darling Sarah would be writing these missives. But she has put her foot down, and we both know there is no shifting that woman when her mind is made up. She says her time in your life is over, and to write now would only cloud the waters of your transition. Hers is the voice of the past, and mine is to be that of your future. So it has fallen upon these fragile shoulders to say that somehow I am certain she is with you still.

"My day is not a good one, so that is all I have to say for now, except to share the next puzzle with you. The riddle is as follows: A little girl came to England and thought that her sorrows had not just followed, but multiplied with her arrival. Yet it was in this place of supposed darkness that she found not only a turning, but a healing. Seek where the darkness gathers, and find wings for your own renewal. Yours ever, Heather."

Brian took his empty cup back into the kitchen, pleased that his stomach rumbled with hunger. All he had in the pantry was a last slice of Gladys Wainwright's bread, which he ate as he inspected the prize discovered from Heather's first letter. The dollhouse stood on the kitchen table, burnished by the brilliant afternoon light. It was an astonishingly exact replica of the manor itself, down to the columned portico and the portraits on the parlor walls.

As he inspected the chambers through the tiny windows, he felt Heather's words striking with a resonance that shook him still.

He had come to England only because he had almost no money, resigned to entering a realm of memories that were not even his, and confronting sorrows that had pursued him all the way around the world. Instead, he was indeed greeted by a healing. The perception was so peculiar he did not know what to think of it or how to respond.

The voices rose to greet him as he came down the stairs. He spotted Arthur standing in the front doorway silhouetted by the sun. Arthur turned at the sound of his footsteps, revealing a face creased with worry, and said, "I am astonished the grass does not wither beneath her feet."

Brian stepped to the doorway and observed a tall woman dressed in Burberry serge. She wore no-nonsense lace-up shoes and a peaked hat with a feather that shivered under her torrent. "I have been a loyal citizen of this village for decades. Not to mention a regular attendee at church! I have every right to request, nay, to *demand* that you halt your fiendish plot!"

Her prey was the vicar, and there was no sign of yielding within the man's sinewy form. "Mrs. Winniskill, I regret to inform you that no amount of church attendance excuses either ill conduct or a desire for conflict."

From his position beside Brian, Arthur murmured, "Lavinia Winniskill. Resident mover and shaker. Married into the town's wealthiest clan. Her husband is director of several large companies. The woman loves nothing more than a reason to stir the pot."

To Brian's mind, Lavinia Winniskill brayed like a donkey

learning to yodel. "What an offensive and uncouth thing to say. I desire nothing but an end to that infernal racket!"

"Some people happen to find our village bells very appealing."

"Then they are not in their right minds!" She flung her arm about, missing the vicar's nose by mere inches. "They live in some archaic past filled with romantic claptrap!"

"I happen to love those bells," the vicar replied. "And I class myself as neither archaic nor particularly romantic."

"Then you have most certainly taken leave of your senses!" She took a threatening step forward. "I warn you, this has gone quite far enough."

"Indeed it has," the vicar agreed. "I must therefore request that you cease in this senseless and argumentative stance you are taking."

"You . . . I . . ." Clearly the woman was unused to having someone oppose her so directly. "I'll have you know Bishop Henries is a personal friend!"

"Then he has my abject sympathies." Trevor Parkes showed all the resilience of good English oak. "Now I, for one, have more important matters to attend to and must bid you good day."

But when he started up the stairs, she spotted Brian there on the stoop and cried, "Oh no, you don't! Mr. Blackstone, I implore you, don't listen to this man's ramblings!"

"Actually, I am here to see my old friend." Up close, the strain was etched much clearer upon the vicar's features. "Good afternoon, Arthur. Hello, Brian. How are you feeling?"

Lavinia started up the stairs herself. "Mr. Blackstone, you are *surrounded* by the *enemy*! Arthur Wainwright is a *traitor*! He is aiding their plan to repair and replace those wretched bells! He has sold out his heritage and left this village to die on its feet!"

"Oh really, Lavinia, do be sensible." Arthur affected a condescending drone. "We're talking about a few church bells, not the invasion of Hitler's army."

Lavinia pushed herself up close. "Mr. Blackstone, I beseech you. There are seven churches at various locations around the center of our village. Seven, Mr. Blackstone. These deranged folk insist upon ringing them every hour of every day. When those bells are replaced and all start banging away at once, the racket is enough to drive a person *mad*. As a local landowner, you of all people must see how utterly vital—"

A voice down the lane called out, "Don't bother with Mr. Blackstone, Lavinia dear."

The big-boned woman heeled about and cried, "Hardy, thank goodness. You of all people must talk some sense—"

"I said don't bother." The real-estate agent climbed the stairs and nodded a languid greeting to the gathering. "Afternoon, all."

Brian noticed the chill that entered Arthur Wainwright's voice. "Finally come to see to our electrical problems, Mr. Seade?"

Hardy Seade cast an indifferent glance toward the old man, but directed his words to the woman. "Our dear Mr. Blackstone will only possess this property for another few days. Isn't that so, sir?" When Brian did not respond, the realtor continued, "The estate is to be auctioned next Wednesday. And a buyer has already come forward with a most impressive bid. So I regret Mr. Blackstone will not be around long enough to weigh in on the issue of the church bells."

Brian's disappointment over the coming loss and dislike of the man smirking at him fought for position. Then an idea struck, one powerful enough to make Brian smile. He stepped inside and said, "I'll be right back."

He raced up the stairs as swiftly as his weakened legs would permit, and returned to find the same tableau. Clearly a few more words had been exchanged, for all the faces smoldered. Brian held Heather's prize with both arms and said to the vicar, "I don't have any money for your cause, but you can have this if you think it would help."

The sun chose that moment to emerge from behind a lonely cloud, and splashed golden and generous upon the front terrace. The miniature manor Brian held was suddenly no longer just a dollhouse. The tiny windows and perfectly proportioned rooms shone with a brilliant luster, as though all the diminutive chandeliers had suddenly come alight.

"How absolutely marvelous!" Arthur bent over for a closer inspection. "I say, it appears to be an exact replica of Castle Keep."

The vicar's eyes had gone all round with astonishment. "Mr. Blackstone, really, this is too generous."

"Call me Brian. And no, it's not."

The woman spluttered, "You can't *possibly* be serious!"

Arthur offered, "We could raffle it off. A pound a ticket."

The vicar nodded vigorous agreement. "We'll clear out the church charity's shop-window and put this inside with a great sign. 'Win a piece of village heritage and save the church bells.' Marvelous, I can't thank you enough."

The real-estate agent shouldered his way closer. Hardy Seade was no longer smiling. "I'll give you a thousand pounds for it."

Arthur chortled, "Really, what on earth would you want with a dollhouse at your age?"

"It's for my niece." The words came out clipped with anger.

"I happen to know for a fact," Arthur countered, "that you are an only child."

Rage rose from his reddened cheeks to fill Seade's gaze. "A thousand pounds, Mr. Blackstone. You and I both know it's not worth half that."

Brian handed the dollhouse to the vicar. "It's not mine to sell."

The agent shot Brian a venomous look. "The offer stands, Vicar. A thousand pounds for the model."

"Hardy!" Lavinia shrilled. "You can't possibly mean to give money to that man and his demented cause!"

"Oh, do be quiet," Hardy snapped. "A thousand pounds cash, Vicar. Here and now."

"That's most generous of you, Mr. Seade, I'm sure." Trevor carried his dollhouse and his smile down the broad front stairs. "And I'll be delighted to accept any donation you care to give us, just as soon as our raffle tickets are printed up."

Hardy Seade almost steamed with rage as he turned back to Brian and snarled, "I'll have a court injunction placed against you this very afternoon. You'll not carry a single stick of firewood from this place."

"Oh, I very much doubt it will be as simple as all that." Arthur held to the same cheery tone as the vicar's. "I went by the council offices this morning, and I happen to know that the auction refers to the house and grounds. No mention was made of the furnishings."

"We'll see about that." Hardy Seade thumped down the stairs. "Come along, Lavinia."

Arthur waited until they had carried their mutterings down

the line of elms to turn and pat Brian on the shoulder and say, "That was a most generous act."

"They sure make a pair," Brian observed.

"Yes, Lavinia Winniskill and Hardy Seade are certainly flies in the marmalade. And I must say, seeing their faces when you offered the vicar your little prize, why, it was better than a day at the races." The old man turned his back on the angry couple. "You really must come down for a spot of dinner tonight."

"Thanks, but I don't want—"

"Now, now, none of that. You'll find Gladys is a marvelous cook."

8

The day cleared with such a gradual transition that Cecilia really did not notice it until the sky had bloomed to full and open blue. She began her Thursday afternoon at the village wards. That was a fancy name for a converted fifteenth-century cottage. There were several of these ancient structures about Knightsbridge, given to the town at some earlier point because the landowner couldn't bear to tear down a house that had stood since the days of good Queen Bess. Now they were worth a fortune, and the heirs were constantly trying to wrest them back.

The cottage stood down a narrow walk connecting the market square to the village green. The front door opened straight into the nurse's station, essentially a beamed front parlor where the duty nurse sat and knitted through the night. Each of the wards held six beds, but rarely were more than three or four of them in use. Today the women's ward held a recent stroke victim and a mother in her late thirties being tested for a new medication. The male ward held one patient, a highly educated man and binge drinker. Once every three or four months Robert would be found in Cork Talk, the local wine bar, either propping up one corner or slumped on the floor.

Cecilia found the patient awake and relatively clear-eyed,

and began the lecture that had become standard fare between them. "You have what we call multisystem failure. Because of this drinking, your liver isn't functioning properly. As a result your skin is breaking down. This is the worst case of eczema I've ever seen."

"You know why it is I insist on your treating me," he drawled. "Your lithe tongue and your winsome walk. I've always found the white doctor's robe to be most evocative."

"Speaking of walking, let me see you cross to the door and back."

He remained where he was. "I'd rather not."

"Feet bothering you again?"

"Of course they are. It's part of the burden one bears for being old."

"False. It comes from a lifetime of bad habits, as you well know." She studied the man and let some of her concern show. "Why do you do this to yourself? You have so much to offer."

Robert sensed the change, and his own tone grew hollow. "Offer to whom, my dear? There is no one who finds the least bit of good in this dried-up sack of flesh."

Cecilia lowered herself to the edge of the bed. "Have you ever spoken with the vicar?"

"The vicar is but a man. A good man, but a man nonetheless." His wit sliced through her question like a knife through butter. "What you intend to ask is, Have I ever spoken with God. And the answer is, What would God want with a poor fool like myself?"

"You don't know that."

"No, perhaps you're right. Perhaps what I fear is the responsibility of discovering that someone might care for me after all."

His expression turned sadder still. "The resulting guilt would surely kill me stone dead."

She completed her examination and departed, carrying with her all the words she wished she had known how to say.

Thursday afternoons had two hours set aside for her home visits, and there were seven names on her list. Nothing in the National Health Service charter required doctors to make house calls except in an emergency. But many village doctors did, and this was one of the reasons she had decided to practice in England. She wanted to see her patients as *people*. She wanted to know where and how they lived. She wanted to find the root causes of illness and treat those as well as the symptoms. It was an unreasonable hope, for there was never time to visit anyone save the long-term ill. But the goal remained with her still.

Between patients she found her mind returning to her conversation with Robert and the challenge their words had contained. Not for Robert, but rather for herself. While in medical school a fellow student, a person of far stronger faith, had once described Cecilia as a part-time believer. He had said that people like Cecilia were the hardest to reach, for they were content with acknowledging God and holding Him ever at arm's length. At the time Cecilia had laughed it off, but this walk through the warm July afternoon left her feeling both exposed and convicted. The unanswered questions about little Tommy Townsend—and the need to offer something to his mother—sharpened her sense of failure.

When she returned to the practice, Maureen was up and moving before Cecilia made it through the door. "You'll be coming with me right this instant."

Cecilia caught sight of a waiting room filled with smiles before the other woman wheeled her about and dragged her back onto the street. "What's the matter?"

"Nothing and everything. I thought I would positively burst before you got back." She hustled Cecilia down the cobblestone way leading to the market square. "I can scarcely believe it, even after a dozen people have stopped in to tell me."

"Tell you what?"

"We're almost there. You'll see it for yourself." As they entered the market square, Maureen took a sharp left-hand turn and halted at the outskirts of a large chattering crowd. "Make way for the doctor, please."

A tiny space opened. Cecilia readied herself for the victim of an accident or a heart attack, though the surrounding smiles and the chatter left her utterly confused. The final grouping by the charity window was all made up of young girls with their noses pressed hard against the pane. Maureen touched the shoulders of two youngsters and chided, "Let the doctor have a look, that's a dear."

Reluctantly the girls made a space for them. As soon as Cecilia saw the center of their attention, she repeated what she had said that morning. "I want it!"

"Get in line, dearie," said a voice from behind them. "So does half the town."

A little girl to her left said, "It has little sofas and beds and curtains and everything."

Her neighbor added, "The front parlors have five paintings on the walls. Five. I counted them myself."

The normally cluttered charity window had been cleared of everything save the manor dollhouse. A large banner had been hung overhead that read, "Donated to the Church Bell Campaign by Mr. Brian Blackstone, Esquire. Raffle tickets, one pound."

"I suppose the man must have a heart after all," Maureen said. "Whoever would have thought. Perhaps he keeps it in his back pocket, just so it doesn't get overused."

One of the children said, "I wonder how they got all those things in there so neat and all."

"The roof comes off," Cecilia answered, pressing her face up close to dispel the glare. Inside the shop, the front display was ringed by yet another crowd of mothers and daughters.

Cecilia felt more than saw Maureen's slow turning in her direction. "And just exactly how would we be knowing such a thing as that?"

"I saw him cleaning it up this morning."

"Oh you did, did you. And where was this taking place?"

"Out by the river." To her surprise, Cecilia felt her cheeks reddening and added, "I met him there by chance."

"Oh. By chance, was it."

"That's right. I went out there to watch the sunrise, and he was sitting there cleaning it." She realized she was the center of attention but could not help going on. "The top floor lifts off as well."

This news was greeted by oohs from the little girls and a crossing of arms by Maureen. Cecilia added, "He found another letter from Heather Harding inside the front parlor."

This brought a stir from the ladies as well. One of the women behind her said, "So it's true then, the vicar finding a letter the old lady herself wrote and left for him?"

Another voice pressed, "What did it say, dear?"

"I don't know. He didn't read it until after I left."

A child asked, "Did you help him carry it back inside?"

Another child elbowed the first and chided, "Letters don't weigh anything, silly."

"*You're* the silly one. I meant the dollhouse, you git."

Cecilia answered, "Brian said the house is light as a feather."

"Oh," Maureen purred. "*Brian* was saying that, was he."

Cecilia turned from the window to find her assistant smiling at her. "What's that supposed to mean?"

"Nothing. Nothing at all." The eyes twinkled mischievously. "It's a shame the bad ones get all the good packaging, isn't it?"

It was Cecilia's turn to cross her arms. "What are you talking about now?"

One of the ladies to her right offered, "I hear he's ever so handsome."

"Lean and mean," Maureen said, her eyes still on Cecilia. "And dark as a little brown nutkin. Which is no surprise, seeing as how he's been living in those far-flung places for ever so long."

"Tall, dark, handsome, and rich to boot," one of the other ladies said. "I suppose I could put up with a little meanness now and then."

Cecilia glanced around, found smiles directed at her from young and old alike. "This is the silliest conversation I've ever heard."

"Is it, now," Maureen said.

"I don't know about you, but I've got a waiting room full of patients." As she started back down the way, there was nothing silly about the blush she carried with her, nor the chuckles and quiet comments she left in her wake.

Cecilia saw anywhere from fifteen to thirty patients in any full morning or afternoon at the practice. Some were old favorites, particularly the elderly and the lonely. She would ask them to come back every three months and there they were, as regular as clockwork. She would take their blood pressure, run down a quick checklist of questions, then sit back and let them talk a bit. Most were suffering from little more than the desperate solitude of old age. After almost two years in the village, she was coming to see this as one more illness she could treat, but never cure.

That afternoon there were four in a row, their complaints very similar, their attitudes utterly different. Two were bitter and morose and sullen with ancient rage—at their children, the day, their aches and pains, the hand life had dealt them. The third was a former bank director, too stodgy to ever admit to the feelings that hollowed his gaze and slackened his features. The fourth was sadly quiet and resigned. All seemed to expect answers from Cecilia, ones she did not have to offer. After the fourth had left, she sat for a long moment, her hand on the buzzer that would signal Maureen to send in the next patient. She stared at the sunlight splashed upon her window and wondered at how the entire world conspired that day to ask such questions of her.

To her relief, her next patient was an attractive woman in her mid-thirties, dressed in a success suit of dark blue with no-nonsense pumps and immaculate makeup. Cecilia breathed easier at the thought of finally having someone come in with a complaint she could treat.

The woman came immediately to the point. "I've recently moved to the area and started a new job. But I'm encountering difficulties in the workplace."

Cecilia took out a new-patient form. "Where were you living before?"

"North London." The woman hesitated. "You're American."

"That's right."

The woman struggled for a moment with something internal, then said, "I'm sorry, I was expecting someone . . ."

"Older?" She smiled, and when the woman attempted to smile back Cecilia continued, "You were saying that you're having a health problem related to your new work."

"No. Not exactly. That is . . ." The polished veneer was becoming frayed. "I have a problem entering the building."

Cecilia set down her pen. "What sort of problem?"

"I can't seem to find breath." One hand rose to fiddle nervously with a strand of hair. "My heart rate goes right through the roof. My legs are as weak as water."

"I see." She settled back in her chair. Another patient with a nonmedical crisis.

But the woman was not through. "I get so dizzy I have to lean on the wall. I break into a cold sweat."

"I get the message," Cecilia muttered to herself.

"I beg your pardon?"

"Nothing. What I meant was, this is not exactly a health issue."

"But you can prescribe some pills, can't you?" The tone turned desperate. "I have to have help."

"There are pills, yes, but they only treat the symptoms."

The woman's voice rose a notch. "But it is precisely the symptoms that are driving me around the bend!"

"Yes, of course." Cecilia forced her own voice to remain steady. "What I meant was, there might be some underlying cause that needs your attention."

"Oh, piffle. I've been through a very hard time, which I am already fully aware of. I accepted a new job, which meant I had to leave London." The woman had regained control of her voice, but not her hands. They danced from her lap to the arm of her chair to the ends of her hair. "Because of that I've had to break up with my boyfriend. I'm having trouble with my family over my decision, not that it's any of your business. They want me to settle down, but I've spent my entire life dreaming of a chance like this. It's just a spell, that's all. A hard transition."

"I'll give you a prescription for something to help your nerves," Cecilia decided. "But I'd like to see you again at the beginning of next week."

"All right. Fine." The woman's gaze remained intent upon Cecilia's hands as she wrote on the pad and tore off the sheet. "Thank you."

"Please make an appointment with the receptionist as you leave." Cecilia found herself wondering what answers she would have then that she did not have now.

But as the door closed and she reached for the phone, Maureen called through to announce, "The lab just sent over the results of Tommy Townsend's sweat test."

Cecilia felt wrenched by the news, so much so that she could not keep a tremor from her voice. "We weren't supposed to get them until tomorrow."

"I suppose they're as worried about the kid as we are. They see his name often enough." When Cecilia said nothing, Maureen asked, "Shall I open it, then?"

"No, no, I'll be right out. And do me a favor, would you? Call Trevor and ask if I can stop by the vicarage after work."

9

When Cecilia arrived at the vicarage, the sky had darkened to the final rose-tinted hues of a long and stressful day. The lab results on Tommy Townsend's sweat test had come back negative, which meant she was no closer to knowing what ailed the little child.

A light breeze cast itself down the ancient lane, perfumed by wildflowers along the riverbank. The vicarage stood behind the village's central church, a structure whose stone skirting had been laid more than twelve hundred years before. The church's Norman tower was one of the first built in England, set in place by William the Conqueror himself soon after his invasion from France in 1066. Knightsbridge had been the staging point for William's conquest of London, and his first capital in England. The castle ruins still rose like stunted teeth along the village's north border. This evening the ancient church rose to capture the day's final colors, glowing with a quiet pride of place and heritage.

The vicarage had been erected using stones taken from the ancient castle and looked like a medieval keep—there was even a tiny square turret to match the church's bell tower. The lead-paned windows glowed warm and welcoming as Cecilia let herself in through the gate and walked to the front door.

But the day continued to mock her, for when Molly, the vicar's wife, opened the door, her first words were, "Thank goodness you rang, I was about to call and ask you to stop by."

"What's wrong?"

Molly glanced behind her as her two teenage children began quarreling somewhere down the back passage. "Oh, Trevor's healthy as a horse. As always. But he's not sleeping well, and he's just wearing down to a nub."

Cecilia did not need to ask. "The bells."

"He blames himself, you know. He thought it would save the church money to have all the bells down at once. But of course that was just the opportunity the 'Keep Knightsbridge Peaceful' brigade were looking for."

"Lavinia Winniskill is a menace."

"Oh, it's not just her. She likes to be the lightning rod, and the town malcontents are only too glad to let her stand in the limelight." Molly Parkes pushed open the door. "Anyway, I'm glad you've come. The bell keepers were around this afternoon, and they're ready to put them all back in next week. We were planning to have the official rededication a week from Sunday. But today Trevor's learned the Keep Knightsbridge Peaceful Committee has managed to place a motion before the town council. They intend to block the bells' return to the towers."

"Poor Trevor."

"The man is beside himself, I don't mind telling you." She led Cecilia down the house's flagstone hallway, past the high-ceilinged parlor where Molly's youngest daughter was studying at the dining table. She stopped before a closed door, knocked, and when a muffled voice responded from within, Molly mouthed the words "Thank you."

Cecilia had no choice but to push open the door. "Trevor?"

"Oh, it's you." Trevor Parkes was a former all-county crick-eter and had once been slated as an alternate to the England squad. Normally he held the quietly focused intensity Cecilia had found in many such athletes, especially in a game that could last as long as four full days. This evening, however, he looked to have aged twenty years.

He waited until she had shut the door to declare, "Our little village is about to become a victim of its own complacency."

Cecilia hesitated long enough to realize this was the only invitation Trevor was able to offer. She crossed the room and seated herself on the other side of his desk. Trevor watched her and yet did not seem to truly see her at all. Certainly not enough to be dragged from his thoughts. "I imagine the vast majority of villagers would claim to believe in God. But so long as their lives meander along in comfort and ease, they are more than happy to keep God at arm's length."

Trevor's features seemed slackened by defeat. "They are a smug lot, my parishioners. They are surrounded by all the beauty this world has to offer, all the ease of modern life, all the warmth of friends and people whose job it is to smooth out all the bumps. Why should they allow God any closer than is comfortable? He's just someone to greet on the Sunday street." His tone burned with bitter mimicry. "A good chap, really. But a bit too pushy if you let Him be. Demands all sorts of things. Lost in the past. Thinks in terms of black and white, when any-body with sense knows the world is shades of gray, particularly in this day and age. No, no. Getting too involved in this reli-gion business simply wouldn't do."

Cecilia found herself unable to observe him any longer.

Though she knew he did not mean it as such, his features held too strong a conviction of her own casual faith. She glanced at the side wall, with its floor-to-ceiling bookcases, before her gaze rested upon the fireplace. The house had been built centuries before the notion of central heating, and each of the rooms still contained a working fireplace. They were small affairs, the log-holders not much bigger than salad bowls, with cast-iron frames intended to heat up and radiate warmth.

"But faith is not a matter of convenience. God is not a divine waiter, standing about until we decide we require His help. He calls us to *commit*." His words were stretched and racked by the pain of seeking to reach those who did not wish to hear. "We are not invited to a dinner party where we can pick and choose among the courses. God calls us to be His children, loyal and selfless, eager to strive forward until we are ready to join Him at the eternal wedding feast." He was glumly silent for a long moment, then added, "Perhaps it's my fault."

"No, it's not," Cecilia responded quietly, still unable to raise her eyes from the cold and blackened fireplace.

"If I could only find a way to reach them. To make them see it's not just about a group of bells. Bit by bit we are relinquishing the standard of God and the heritage that helped to build this community and this nation."

She only partly heard him. Cecilia found herself recalling another night, one from her first winter in the village. She had been frightened by so much—the alienness of the place and the people, the way everyone seemed to stand back and measure her, the inability to make friends, the loneliness and the questions and the doubts that she had indeed done the right thing by moving to Knightsbridge. Night after night she had come to this very room and sat with Trevor and his wife. They had been comfortable with the silence of intimate companions, content to let her play chess with their son or watch television or read or simply reflect upon the day's challenges. Cecilia had spent hours staring at the tiny fireplace, where a pile of coals always glowed as strong as sunset jewels, hissing and whispering in the tongues of night and winter. Now she stared at the cold, empty place and felt convicted by how the fire was going out—not from the room, but rather from this fine man. And she was partly to blame. She had come when she needed something, then allowed pressures and work and her own selfish direction to stand between her and all this good man stood for.

"These bells were set in place by people who wanted the very hills to ring with God's call," Trevor went on. "They have rung the time to pray for more than seven hundred years. It would be a desecration to their memory and all they stood for to let them go silent."

Cecilia lifted her gaze and said, "Tell me how I can help."

"We can't simply . . ." It took a moment to realize what Cecilia had said. "I beg your pardon?"

"I want to help," she repeated, more firmly this time. "What do you want me to do?"

"My dear . . ." His gaze remained clouded. "These are powerful people within the community. I'm only coming to realize just how potent. I very much doubt you would want to make them your enemies."

She swallowed. "You just said we need to commit. All right. I'm committed."

Trevor stared across the desk at her for a long while, long enough for her to realize that the man's wavy blondish hair was not graying so much as turning transparent, as though the winds of time were blowing out the color. For some reason she found this strengthening her resolve, such that she seemed almost to expect it when he said, "Saturday evening there's to be a special open meeting of the town council. They are going to put forth a motion to halt the bells' reinstallment. I was going to speak, but—" he paused.

"I'll do it," Cecilia offered.

"It would certainly carry more weight if someone who is not directly connected to the church were to speak on our behalf," Trevor mused.

"Fine," she answered, though it turned her stomach to jellied ice to think of standing before the village assembly. She was indeed committed. "Tell me what you want me to say."

10

$\mathcal{H}$ardy Seade is himself the third tenant on your estate," Arthur explained to Brian over dinner Thursday evening. "He uses the old stable block to house his collection of antique cars. He also heads the group wanting to buy the estate at auction."

"Oh Arthur, don't bother the young man so," his wife complained.

"It's all right." Brian went on to Arthur, "Any idea what they plan on doing here?"

"Oh, they make no bones over their desire to tear down all the outbuildings and build a high-tech office and laboratory complex."

Brian froze with his fork in midair. "You're kidding."

Arthur Wainwright possessed the chiseled features and wayward white hair of an aging movie icon. He shook his head sadly. "I wish I were."

"Now the both of you just stop it. All this misery and mayhem can wait until coffee." Gladys Wainwright hefted a platter heaped with slabs of mutton. "Do have some more lamb, dear."

"I wish I could, but I just don't have room left for anything."

"Oh, but you must. I've been baking all afternoon, making one of my famous brambleberry pies." She stood and picked up a tray, then when Brian started to rise she stopped him with, "Stay right where you are, dear. We don't allow guests to help until their second visit."

Brian turned back to Arthur and said, "You're right, she's a great cook."

"Yes, the only thing my Gladys likes better than gossip is baking." Arthur rose and began gathering plates. "I won't be a moment."

Brian settled deeper into his chair and stared around him. The ceilings in these back downstairs rooms were lower, the rooms more cramped. Gladys had explained that this rear section had once been the servants' quarters and contained the oldest portions of the house. The kitchen certainly looked it, with a flagstone floor sculpted by feet until it rippled with the tides of centuries. The entire apartment sighed with weary overuse and a lack of care. The whitewashed room where he sat was stained by water and time, the floor so scored the last flecks of varnish peeled from the scarred wood. Brian tried to tell himself that it didn't matter, it wasn't really his.

Even so, when Arthur reappeared, Brian's voice grated with frustration and helplessness. "I just don't see how Heather could have let Castle Keep get so run down."

"Yes, well, there you are." Arthur set down the cheese board and eased into his chair. "Heather was a dear woman. Her husband, Alex, was one of my closest friends. When I retired, Gladys and I experienced a number of financial setbacks, most especially a brother-in-law who needed psychiatric care."

"Call a spade a ruddy spade, dear." Gladys walked in and set down the plates and turned back to the kitchen, saying over her shoulder, "My brother was an alcoholic and a spendthrift. The only reason he didn't perish in prison was because of my Arthur's generosity."

"When I came out of the force, we were skinned. Dead broke," Arthur continued. "Don't know what we would have done if Heather had not offered us this flat."

"Starved on the street," Gladys called from the kitchen. "Begged pennies from passersby."

Arthur waved it all aside. "You asked how Heather could have allowed the place to fall into such disrepair. The answer is simple. When Alex died, she went a bit mad."

Gladys returned bearing a steaming pie so large it seemed ready to lift itself from the pan. "Alex was a dashing figure of a man. And such a charmer. He could draw a chuckle from a cadaver."

"Heather just fell to pieces," Arthur continued. "We were stationed in Kenya when it happened, but her letters were eulogies that would break your heart to read. When we came back on leave, well, we found a shattered spirit."

"A hollow gourd." Gladys placed a slice dripping sugar and berries onto a plate and set it in front of Brian. "I simply don't know what would have happened if your Sarah had not appeared on the scene."

"Heather would not have survived," Arthur responded. "It is quite that simple."

"Do go ahead and start, dear. It's not as good when it grows cold."

Brian took a bite, and exclaimed, "This is incredible."

Gladys beamed as she placed a plate in front of her husband. "Yes, well, I do make a rather good pudding, if I say so myself."

"After Sarah arrived, Heather's letters went through a dramatic shift," Arthur said between bites. "Day and night, really. In the space of one year she went from a shroud seeking the tomb to a woman with a reason to live."

"Still, she never did see to the estate after Alex passed," Gladys said. "The only work she had done was to paint the walls of Sarah's room. Alex was the one who loved this place. He was passionate about it. Heather lived here because her family had been here for generations; I don't suppose she really cared one way or the other very much. But not Alex. He adored Castle Keep."

"An estate like this requires work all the time. Manors are funnels into which one is always pouring money. A year without work, and they begin to wear. Twenty years, and . . ." Arthur waved his fork about the room. "You see the result."

Gladys peered tightly across the table. "Perhaps you'd rather we not speak of your departed wife."

"No, it's all right," Brian said, immensely glad it was the truth. "Sarah talked so much about Castle Keep, I feel like I know its every nook and cranny."

"Oh, I very much doubt that," Gladys replied. "This is a house that dearly loves its secrets and its mysteries. The foundations are over a thousand years old, laid by monks who established a monastery at the ford of the river Thames."

"Rumors and unfounded suppositions," Arthur scoffed.

"It's not and you know it." Turning back to Brian, Gladys continued, "That's why William the Conqueror chose this ford to cross the river and build his castle, because the monks had located a market village here in the Dark Ages. He needed supplies for his armies, and a spiritual anchor for his life."

"There's never been any documented proof of that," Arthur countered. "And the theories are hotly disputed."

"Well, be that as it may, this house is full of spaces and secrets it shares with no one," Gladys replied. "I know that for a fact, and so do you. The old place has been built on and added to so often no one has any idea what it contains. Why, Alex himself hired an architect to come in and draw up plans, and the poor man almost had a seizure trying to fit the interior within the exterior. The measurements simply would not add up."

But Brian remained caught by memories all his own and the ease with which they arose in this ancient chamber. He tasted the words before he spoke them and found a sense of rightness there. As though here in this place he was protected. Safe and welcome to share a part of what he had carried all the way around the world. And sought to run from as well.

"The last couple of months before Sarah died, we talked about how it would be when she was gone." Brian stopped there, only mildly aware that the room had gone utterly still, as though his words had sucked out not only discussion but even space within which the couple could move. He was too focused on his own internal state, too satisfied to find a rightness in speaking of these secrets he had never shared with anyone. "I didn't really want to, but Sarah said it would help her face what was coming if she knew she could have a little hand in planning my future."

A ripple in the window's drapes caught his attention, as though a gentle spirit had passed and drawn one invisible hand along the printed fabric. He continued, "I knew what Sarah was doing. She wanted to force me to look beyond the moment and what we both knew by then was coming. I had always wanted to travel but never really had the time. So we spent hours plotting a course. The plan was for me to come here to

Knightsbridge and use the manor as a base, then travel on, going to all the cities she had read about and dreamed of going with me—Venice, Zurich, Cairo, Paris, dozens of places." He took a deep breath, pressing his heart back into a semblance of proper shape. "After the funeral I took off all right. But I couldn't bear the thought of going here or anyplace else that held memories of Sarah. I traveled in the exact opposite direction. Flew across America, hopped a plane to Hawaii, and from there on across the Pacific."

Gladys asked from across the table, "Did you have children, dear?"

"No." Another pain there, which was not why he smiled. No, his mouth was lifted by the fact that the irony did not hurt him as it once had, but rather allowed him to feel just how sheltered he was here by the night and the manor. Why this was the case did not matter so much, not now. For the moment it was enough to be able to lift the borders of time and peer into things that once had hurt like blades scouring the surface of his heart. "We wanted to, but we couldn't. It was actually when we went for a diagnosis that the doctors learned my Sarah had leukemia."

It was not the old couple who murmured, but the room and the manor itself. As though the centuries had granted the walls an ability to share in human sorrow. Brian continued, finding a vague pleasure in the fact that he could speak in a voice calm and steady. "Sarah talked to Heather on the phone all the time, every day if she could. It was her way of dealing with her favorite relative being deathly ill and her not being there."

"Heather missed Sarah terribly," Gladys murmured. "It hurt her so not to be with Sarah in her own hour of need."

Brian nodded acceptance, not willing to move further than the simple motion from his own recollections. "Sarah's parents did not have a happy marriage. They divorced when she was nine, and her mother remarried a man who didn't have time for Sarah or any other child. Sarah's Aunt Heather and the summers she spent here were what really gave her a reason to live and a love for life."

Arthur offered softly, "Heather always referred to Sarah as the child she had long dreamed of but never deserved."

Suddenly Brian had to rise. Not from sorrow, but rather because his wife was too close just then to share with anyone else. He stood by the table and mouthed words he could scarcely hear. "I can't thank you enough for a lovely evening."

The older couple's eyes were filled with the act of silently sharing. "You really must feel free to return any time, dear," Gladys said.

Brian said his good-byes and left the apartment and climbed the stairs. To his relief, the upper chambers did not rattle with loneliness or pain or the dust of all that was lost and gone forever. For the moment at least, he was able to look back without bitterness, anger, or lamentation. As he prepared for bed and felt the house creak and sigh companionably, Brian knew it was safe to remember . . . and to move on.

11

$\mathcal{T}$hat Friday morning, Brian awoke to a vague sense of fear. He lay in the gray light of an unfinished dawn, pinned there by the hollow dread that he was returning to the bad old days. Other mornings crowded about him, reminding him of the hard times, back when he would awake to the empty knowledge that his life was over and gone. That he would walk through another day alone and without purpose or direction or even a sense of life.

And yet, this morning's fear seemed fashioned from something else. Brian lay upon his pallet and tried to put a name to what was so new it would have been easier just to assume it had come from the previous night's dinner conversation. He almost *wanted* to think that he was trapped once more in the painfully familiar. But it was not so. He knew this without understanding why or what he faced.

Two years of habits took over, and he rolled from his little bed, dressed, and took his coffee out to meet the day at riverside. All the while, he felt a tremendous pressure within, as though he were being blown up tighter and tighter. His mind returned to the previous night and the dinner and his confession. He expected to feel remorse, or at least unease, over having been so open with strangers. But that was not the case. Nor was his fear based upon having exposed his wounds to the raw light of inspection. Brian felt the same pressure in his chest as the night before, but pressure from what he could not tell.

Then he heard the footsteps swishing through the grass behind him, and even before he turned, he understood. Not what was behind his fear or his internal pressures; no, that would have been asking far too much of a newborn day. But at least he knew what he needed to do now.

Cecilia had always been an early-morning person. While still very young she had learned to push the chair over to the kitchen counter, climb up and pull out the bowl and the cereal, and make her own breakfast. Throughout school she had loved to rise before the world was reshaped and revel in hours that were hers and hers alone. So it was that she stood by her kitchen window rinsing out her breakfast dishes when Brian came out the manor's front door. Her hands froze in the process of drying a plate as she watched him walk around the manor's corner and disappear in the direction of the river.

Before she could think things through and come up with reasons to remain where she was, Cecilia was moving. She poured another half-cup of coffee, picked up the book she had been reading when she had fallen asleep, and headed out.

Twice she almost halted and turned back. The farther she walked down the elm-lined lane, the louder became her internal objections. The loss of her beloved Rose Cottage, the man's two-year absence, the apology she knew she owed him; this and a new vague unease left her regretting her impulsive action.

Even so, it was somehow easier to continue than to go back.

When she was halfway across the back garden, Brian turned around. And there in the gladness of his smile, and the way he raised his cup to her in easy greeting, Cecilia found a rightness in her coming after all.

Once more she found herself startled by the clearness of his gray gaze, as though life had washed away all but the very essence from his eyes. His features were even, granted a stark edge by his leanness and his tan. He was both young and old, his years overtaken by experience, his age no longer measured by time alone. He turned back to the river and the eastern horizon without saying a word.

Cecilia smiled in reply, recognizing another spirit shaped by too many days in solitude to ever feel the need for vacant speech. She walked over and seated herself, then looked up toward the dawn.

The day arrived as gentle as birdsong, as soft as the river's whispered journey. A predawn veil remained cast over the sky, softening and spreading the light. The colors rose in gradual crescendo, from rose to palest yellow to the gold of heaven's crown.

Only when the sun finally appeared, and the veil was cast aside to reveal the new day, did Brian finally speak. "For the first six months or so after Sarah left me, I couldn't even name the places I visited while I was still there. It really didn't matter, because most of the time I couldn't see beyond the burdens I was carrying."

Cecilia was shocked to realize Brian spoke of the days following his wife's funeral. She turned slowly toward him, astonished by the way he had gone from utter silence to deepest confession. Yet what surprised her most was her own internal reaction. For by speaking in this way, it felt as though he were not exposing his innermost self, but rather her own.

Brian kept his gaze fastened upon the river, which was transformed into a billion mirrors by the day and the morning breeze. "I had to have something to aim toward, though. Something to give me a sense of direction. So I always aimed for a place near water. I wanted the expanse, the chance to look out and see nothing but an empty horizon. Every morning and evening I would go out to the water's edge, marking the slow beat of empty time. And I'd try to see beyond the walls I had inside of me."

Cecilia felt ashamed by her lack of anything to say. His words felt like a gift, one that would be incomplete without something in reply. But what could she tell him of worth? That she had been alone so long that she could not imagine a different life? That she had grown used to the fear that she would never find anyone to ever care for her as he had for his dead wife?

A shiver went through her, as though a trace of winter's breath had drifted across her heart. In truth, what she wanted to say was that she had prayed the previous evening and again that morning. The first two such prayers she had said outside of church walls for years. But how could she share such a thing with a stranger? The shiver strengthened, and with it an unreasonable desire to speak nonetheless. It was silly. She was overreacting to a strange journeyman's disclosure of nothing to live for. Cecilia found herself trying to respond with an anger, but the man's calm matched the day, and together they left her without the ability to escape.

The silence weighed upon her now, and she dropped her head, defeated by the absence of something to confess. Her eyes then settled upon the book, and it was almost with relief that she said, "I went by the vicar's yesterday evening."

Brian seemed to have been waiting for a reason to turn her way. "Trevor?"

She nodded. "He's been living through a terrible strain."

"The bells?"

She met Brian's gaze for the first time. "How did you . . . Oh, of course, the dollhouse. That was a lovely gesture, by the way."

The clearness was still in his eyes, the extraordinary directness to his words. "Some of Sarah's finest childhood memories were centered around that dollhouse. I couldn't sell it."

"Even so, it was such a nice thing to do."

He turned back to the day and the river. "Sarah had a terrible childhood. She was terrified when she first came here. Heather designed a series of mysteries, puzzles. Each one led Sarah to know the house better, and each one had a reward at the end. The first riddle's reward was the dollhouse." His tan seemed almost golden in the morning light, as though it was for moments just like this that he had been darkened. "What's the matter with Trevor?"

"The fight is wearing him down. The bells . . ." She dropped her gaze to the book in her lap and only then realized that she had been staring at him. "He gave me a book about the town's early history. I had no idea the bells were so important to Knightsbridge's heritage. But that's not the problem. He wants me to speak on the church's behalf at tomorrow's town meeting. I hate speaking in front of a crowd. The thought alone is appalling. And I've never had to address a hostile audience." She swallowed, her throat so tight the noise drowned out the birds. "I can't believe I agreed to do it."

Cecilia waited with head bowed for him to offer some platitude, something to the effect that it would all turn out fine. Instead he spoke so softly the words were almost lost to the morning symphony. "You're talking to the wrong guy."

She raised her head and had to squint against the sun's glare. "Why do you say that?"

"Because I've spent the last two years running away from every commitment I ever made." He seemed not to speak to her, but rather to unburden himself to the sun. "Since I've arrived here, I feel like there has been a swirl of thoughts blowing around my mind. Once in a while I pull out a single shred and then spend hours trying to make sense of it."

The lines of his face seemed to grow sharper and the edges clearer with each minute of strengthening day. There were tiny flecks of silver in his dark hair, or perhaps it was just the sun's bleaching. Cecilia found herself resisting a sudden urge to reach out and draw a wayward lock of hair off his temple. To cover herself, she added swiftly, "What about commitment?"

"One of the things I learned during the hard times with Sarah was that when you commit to something, it's not just to the good times. I think too many people go through life assuming everything is going to work out just like they want, and then when it doesn't, they feel like this gives them the right to pull up stakes and move on. But life isn't like that. Some of the most beautiful times I had with Sarah were also some of the most tragic."

Brian started to raise his cup, realized it was empty, and set it down on the table. "I don't miss the burdens of commitment, but I sure do miss belonging somewhere."

Almost before she realized what she was going to say, Cecilia asked, "Would you come to the town meeting tomorrow?"

That brought him fully around. "Are you sure about that?"

"Yes." Confusion leaped into her mind, a clutter of reasons and desires for having asked him at all. "I have to be going. You could perhaps walk over with Arthur and Gladys; I know they plan to attend."

"All right." Brian rose with her. "This is going to sound a little crazy, but I have a favor to ask."

Nothing, she told herself, would sound as bizarre as having just invited this man to a village gathering. "What is it?"

"Heather has left me some riddles of my own. That's what was in the letter Trevor found in the kitchen, and there was another in the dollhouse letter." He dug in his pocket and came out with a much-folded sheet of yellowed paper. "I'm terrible with puzzles."

Cecilia backed away from his hand and the risk of further entanglements. "I really have to be going. But you might ask Arthur. I'm sure he'd be happy to help."

12

---

*B*rian walked down the line of elms to the sound of a lawn mower. Through the trees he glimpsed a handsome man with a shock of red hair and the build of a wrestler almost jogging behind an ancient machine.

The man looked up and flashed Brian an easy smile. He cut the motor back to idle and walked over, grassy hand outstretched. "I'm Joe Eaves, your lordship. Welcome to Castle Keep."

"Thanks." The gardener was about his own age, with a grip like sweaty iron. "The name is Brian, and I'm not lord of anything."

The news only broadened Eaves's grin. "Mr. Seade's paying for the work I do 'round these parts, so you don't have to worry about a thing. Any questions you have, just take them up with Mr. Seade." He gave an easy nod and started back toward the idling mower. "Grand weather we're having."

Brian watched as Joe Eaves wheeled about and pushed the mower in the direction of the outside wall. Brian found the gardener's presence disturbing. He continued down the lane, watching Joe mow a neat pair of green ribbons in the scraggly lawn. Despite the man's friendly efficiency, Brian could not get over the fact that Hardy Seade was paying for the work.

The thoughts stayed with him as he wound his way toward

the central market square. In ways he could neither explain nor deny, he was also certain his sense of transition was connected to this place. Somehow a ramshackle manor in an English market town was charged with a potential for change. And the realization left him sorely distressed that the manor would soon belong to others.

Sunlight adorned the ancient village with an enticing sparkle. Centuries and secrets reached out from both sides of the lane to catch his eye and slow his walk. A beamed lodge with the date 1614 branded over the doorway stood next to a trio of town houses whose dressed Cotswold stone was turned honey-blond by the morning. Beside them ran a bowed wall of brick and flint, the hard stones as translucent as uncut diamonds. Lead-paned windows watched his passage within a pair of newish homes designed to blend comfortably with the ancient street. Brian walked and took in lace curtains and cobblestones and medieval peaked doors and blooming wisteria and a sleepy kitten watching from a recessed portico. The way narrowed just as the central church spire came into view, and as he walked he decided that in his two years of travel he had never come across a place as gentle or as appealing as Knightsbridge.

Two friendly passersby directed him across the square and down a short cul-de-sac to the modern building at the back. He climbed the stairs to the second floor, read the sign, and knocked on the door. When the voice inside answered, Brian opened and asked, "Are you the county finance manager?"

"That's right." Then the woman's head lifted, and her features turned to stone. "Oh, it's you, is it. Well, come in. I've been wondering when you'd show up."

Brian had no choice but to enter and shut the door. "You know who I am."

"Let's say your reputation has preceded you, shall we?" Her head dropped back to her papers. "By approximately twenty-four months."

Brian settled into the chair opposite her desk and listened to the pen scratch angrily. She was in her late thirties and would have been very attractive were it not for her frosty air. She wore a silk blouse of bright yellow, the one touch of color in the austere office. Her forehead creased as the pen traced its way down a long line of figures, then she scribbled at the bottom. Brian realized she was giving him the treatment, placing the new manor owner in his place. He was tempted to leave, but there were answers he needed, and there was nowhere else to turn.

"All right." She slapped the file shut. "You are aware of the upcoming foreclosure auction for Castle Keep, I take it."

"I was actually wondering if you might be willing to postpone it."

She looked genuinely aghast. "Postpone?"

"Yes. I've just heard about the unpaid inheritance taxes. A postponement would give me a chance to put together the money and pay—"

"Now look here, Mr. Blackstone. That is your name, correct?" She eyed him as she would a bit of refuse. "I fail to see how you can waltz in and talk about slamming this great huge change right smack-dab in the middle of our town's scheduling. *Our* town, mind you. Not yours."

He struggled to keep his tone mild. "All I'm asking—"

"I have nothing against the casual honest visitor from

111

America." The words were as flinty as her gaze. "What I do object to is the wild gadabout who blows in and expects the town to offer him the bended knee."

Brian decided he had no choice but to sit and simmer and wait her out.

She rose from her desk, crossed the room, flung open a filing drawer, and said as she riffled through the files, "We will not thrash about merely because you finally elect to show your face." She pulled out a file, opened it, and set it on the drawer. "Your property is in arrears, Mr. Blackstone. To the tune of six hundred and thirty-four thousand, five hundred and twelve pounds."

"So I've heard."

"Well of course you have, since I have personally written you nineteen letters to that effect. Nineteen, Mr. Blackstone." The accountant eyed him from the heights of power. "I'm rather confused. Precisely why has it taken you two *years* to finally respond?"

"I've been away."

"Away."

"That's right."

"For two years?"

"Yes."

"Rather a bizarre manner to see to your duties as heir, wouldn't you agree? Or were you not informed the place was bequeathed to you?"

"I thought it was being handled by a local property agent."

"Ah." The news took her back around to her padded executive chair. "You did not feel it was worth your while to check matters out for yourself?"

Brian rose to his feet with a swiftness that drove the accountant back in her seat. He took no pleasure from the flicker of unease in her eyes. At that moment, all he could think of was that to remain meant telling her about Sarah, and that was not going to happen. Not with this woman. Not ever. "Thank you for your time."

"Enjoy your brief visit to our town, Mr. Blackstone." Her icy tone pushed him back and through the door. "Castle Keep is to be auctioned off five days from today. And I for one will not be the least bit sorry to see the back of you."

The first thing Cecilia heard when entering the clinic on Friday was Maureen declaring, "If I didn't know better, I'd say I was greeting a woman in love."

She was vastly relieved to see that no one else was there to observe her turn crimson. "What on earth are you talking about?"

"Well, let's see." Maureen had a way of cocking her head that made whatever she said sound comic. "Your face is shining like a little lighthouse."

"I've never heard—"

"And you're carrying the funniest smile, like the world's told you a joke and you can't quite decide whether to laugh out loud."

Cecilia slammed the outer door hard enough to make the panes rattle. "Maureen Dowd, you are positively the most irritating woman it has ever been my misfortune to work with."

"Let's see." Maureen pretended to pat her curls into place.

"Could it be that your landlord is no longer a beast with scales rising from the swamps?"

Cecilia's denial was halted by Maureen's knowing smirk. "If you must know, I had a chat with Brian this morning in the garden."

"I know," Maureen declared smugly.

"You know . . .?"

"Gladys Wainwright stopped me in the marketplace this morning. Seems she observed your two heads together for quite a while."

"That does it, then." Cecilia walked over and slumped onto the corner of the counter. "If Gladys knows, then so does the whole town."

"Have a fling with the man if you want, dear, but have a care who you trust your heart to."

Cecilia toyed with her keys. "I've pretty much given up hope of ever finding someone to fling with at all."

"Oh, come now. A lovely thing like you?"

"A woman with a very clear idea of what she wants out of life," Cecilia corrected. "I've been in love. Three tries, three strikeouts. Twice with young men who were certain that if I learned to love them enough, I'd give up on my dreams of becoming a village doctor. The third try was the worst mistake of my life. I guess I got tired of being hurt by men who accused me of putting my dreams before love."

"I didn't know. Not about them all. Of course I've heard . . ." Maureen's smile was no longer in sight. "I'm so sorry, dear."

Cecilia found her thoughts circling back to the morning's talk. "I told the vicar I'd speak at the town meeting."

Maureen showed genuine surprise. "I didn't know you felt so strongly about the bells."

Cecilia's thoughts on that were so confusing it was easier to reply, "I'm terrified of standing up in front of people."

"Then why on earth did you say you'd do it?"

She thought of Brian's words and answered with a conviction that surprised even her. "Because I belong here."

"Well, of course you do, dear." Maureen rose to her feet. "Now you just settle yourself back in your office, and I'll bring you a nice cup of tea."

But before Cecilia could move from her perch, however, the front door clicked open. As soon as she heard the sound, she knew who it was. Before turning and seeing the overly small child and his desperately frightened mother, she knew and felt a rightness that defied all logic and her own quaking heart. So she was able to rise and greet Tommy Townsend with a heartfelt smile and say, "I'm so glad you came."

"Mr. Blackstone? Nigel Gelding, assistant manager of Barclay's Bank. I understand you're interested in applying for a loan?"

"Well, a mortgage is more like it." Brian watched the young man take in his pressed khakis and the faded denim shirt and knew he was wasting his time. "I'm not sure what you call it here."

Chubby cheeks pressed back in a banker's smile. "Let's just step into my office, shall we?"

When the door was closed and Brian was seated across the polished desk, the banker drew out a series of forms, lined them up carefully, selected one of his trio of silver pens from the holder, then gave Brian yet another bland smile. "Just how much were you wishing to borrow?"

"I'm not sure."

The banker lacked a single sharp edge. He possessed the round face of someone who had grown from a chubby childhood into overweight maturity. His cheeks pushed forward, drawing his mouth into a little cherub's bow, which opened now into an "O" of surprise. "You don't know?"

"Not for certain."

"Mr., ah . . ."

"Blackstone."

"It is, well, customary in this country for someone who wants to borrow money to have some idea of the amount required."

"I know it's going to be more than six hundred thousand pounds."

"Six . . ." The brow managed to wrinkle somewhat. "That's rather a lot."

"It will probably be more. I want to bid on my house when it goes up for auction."

Clearly the man did not like surprises. "You what?"

"I've just inherited Castle Keep, and—"

"Oh, yes. Now I understand." He slipped the pen back into the holder. "You're that fellow, are you."

"Yes. The house is to be auctioned next week, and I want to bid for it."

Another glance at Brian's rumpled form, then, "And could you tell me what exactly it is that you do?"

"Until two years ago, I managed a wholesale supply company."

The banker made no move to write this down. "And since then?"

"I've been traveling."

"Ah." Two chubby, manicured hands gathered the forms and stacked them neatly. "Is there a great deal of money in traveling?"

"None at all."

"No. I thought not." This time the smile held all the warmth of a locked vault. "Mr. Blackstone, it is also customary in this country for someone who wishes to borrow money to be able to show how it will be repaid."

"But I thought I could use the house as collateral and—"

"I'm afraid not." The banker stood and offered his hand. "Thank you so much for stopping by."

Little Tommy Townsend had been through the routine so many times he climbed straight onto the examination table and began unbuttoning his shirt. As always, Angeline Townsend parked herself in the corner, crossed her arms, and clenched her upper body so tight the flesh puffed up around her collar, like a balloon being squeezed out of shape. Cecilia fitted the stethoscope to her ears, listened to a heartbeat she had come to know so well she heard it in her sleep. The chest was far too small for a four-year-old boy, the weight well below the norm, the skin so translucent she could trace the little blue veins with her fingers. The lungs sounded slightly congested—nothing new there, either. "Do your joints still ache?"

"My knees." The boy was all skin and bones and eyes. His voice was just barely above a whisper, his features sad. And scared. "And my neck."

"It was your ankles last time, wasn't it." She did not need to check her patient's notes. The vague swelling of his joints, and the way this symptom moved randomly about his body, was one of the many enigmas about Tommy Townsend. Gently she probed the offending knees. "Does that hurt?"

"Yes."

She hated the way he sounded resigned to his pain. Hated even more her inability to do anything about it. "Have you had any fever?"

Angeline answered for him. "Not last night. But the night before he was bathed in sweat. I had to change his nightshirt."

Cecilia's gaze fastened upon the child's upper arm, and she felt her gut clench tight. The limb was as light as a bird's and scarred by countless needles. The little veins were discolored and bruised, and the three latest marks had stained the fresh Band-Aids with blood. Cecilia ran one finger down the inside of the boy's arm, and Tommy shivered in response. He knew what was coming and could do nothing about it.

From her post against the opposite wall, Angeline asked tightly, "Have the lab results come in?"

"They were negative as well," Cecilia replied.

"Then Tommy doesn't have cystic fibrosis?"

"Definitely not." She lifted the boy's shirt and helped him slide in one arm, then the other. She brushed his little hands aside and began doing up the buttons herself. "The results were absolutely conclusive."

"Well, that's good, I suppose." But she did not sound the least bit happy. And Cecilia could well understand. They had run the gamut of diseases, and with each series of tests, Angeline Townsend suffered. "So what do we do now?"

Cecilia sat down beside Tommy on the padded couch, steeled herself, and met Angeline's tormented gaze. "That depends on you."

The pale features blanched. "Me?"

"That's right. If you insist, we can put Tommy into the hospital and have him run through more tests."

As the mother studied her for some signal, Cecilia heard Tommy give a tiny whimper. It was the most natural thing in the world to reach over and draw the little boy into her lap. As Tommy turned so that he could rest his head on her chest, Cecilia realized that it was the first time she had touched the child for anything more than an examination. She had tried hard to hold herself removed from the boy, and for all the right reasons. But now, as she stroked the feather-soft brown hair and felt his skinny arms reach around her, she found herself missing what she had denied herself.

"But that's what we should do, isn't it?" Angeline's face screwed up with all that had happened and now all that was to come. "It's the way forward, wouldn't you say?"

Cecilia hugged the child tighter, met the mother's gaze, and said firmly, "No. I wouldn't."

"But . . ." She gestured at the child in Cecilia's lap. "We don't know what's the matter!"

"That's right. And in trying to put a name on it, we've subjected this child to far too much already." She continued to stroke the hair, feeling her confusion diminish in the process. "I think we should gamble that Tommy has something called postviral syndrome. It's a sort of catchall term for any number of symptoms. The records show that Tommy had a bad chest infection several months before this started."

119

"That's right. He was in bed for almost two weeks."

"And he hasn't felt right since then?"

"He's lost weight, he's had fevers, he seems to catch everything that goes around."

"Well, we've eliminated all the real threats—meningitis, hepatitis, leukemia." Cecilia halted her list. There was no need to repeat the worry. "If Tommy goes into the hospital, they will start by repeating all the tests we've already run."

The little arms tightened around Cecilia's waist, and the child whimpered, "Don't let them hurt me any more, Mommy."

The mother's lip trembled, and the words came out choked. "But I have to know!"

"I need to know also. But at what price? And if it is postviral syndrome, there is no cure except time and rest. Admittedly Tommy is younger than most, but it isn't unknown for a child of his age to come down with it."

Angeline Townsend wrenched herself off the wall and collapsed into one of the chairs by Cecilia's desk. "I can't take much more of this."

The child whimpered in agreement. Cecilia said, "I understand."

"You can't. You don't . . ." She forced herself to take a steadying breath. "I had three miscarriages before Tommy."

Cecilia nodded. She had seen the woman's records. Her heart burned with what the woman had not actually said. No, it was true. She didn't know what it was like. She couldn't.

"Every time you start on another of those tests, I spend the nights in agony. Every test is another disease, and in my heart Tommy has suffered them all."

Cecilia felt the child stirring. She released him and watched as he slid from her lap and walked over to his mother and climbed into her lap and whispered, "Don't cry anymore, Mommy."

"That's why I feel that we should stop altogether," Cecilia replied and felt an uncommon ache where the child had been. Perhaps that was what the professionals had always warned her about. But in all of the moment's honesty, she could not call the sensation unwanted. "The tests have worn us all out and given us nothing but conclusive evidence of what Tommy does *not* have."

She pulled a tissue from the box by the table and handed it to Angeline. "I simply cannot recommend that we put Tommy through anything more. Or you."

Angeline held her child with one hand and wiped her eyes with the other. "How long before we know?"

"It could be weeks, it could be months. Postviral syndrome affects different people differently. What we need to do now is put Tommy on a high-protein diet and see if we can help him gain some weight."

Angeline stroked her child's head. "Steak and ice cream for you tonight. You'd like that, wouldn't you, sweetheart."

"I'll want to see you every ten days or so, just to chart his progress and make sure there aren't any new symptoms." Cecilia walked to her desk and began writing on her pad. "We'll try to help things along with a few vitamin supplements you should mix with his milk, morning and night."

The young mother rose to her feet, accepted the pages, and said to the child, "What do you tell the doctor, sweetheart?"

Tommy turned toward her and sang shyly, "Bye-bye, Cecee."

"Take care, Tommy. And grow strong." Cecilia walked them out, shut the door behind the little boy, and smiled a greeting to the crowded waiting room. On her way back to her office, she stopped by the counter and leaned over to quietly tell Maureen, "I've just been renamed."

"Yes, children will steal your heart if you let them." But Maureen's gaze remained on the now-closed door. "Do you know, I believe that's the first time I've ever seen Angeline Townsend smile."

Cecilia took that bit of news back into her office, buzzed for the next patient, and cast a glance at the sunlit window. What a grand day it was turning out to be.

13

It took Brian the better part of Friday afternoon to admit defeat over the latest clue and accept that he needed help. Even so, he was reluctant to take Cecilia's suggestion of asking Arthur. He could not imagine how the stern old gentleman would view a foreigner popping up on his doorstep and asking for advice about a riddle from his dead aunt-in-law. Even so, his visits to the village finance office and bank had left him resigned to the fact that he was going to lose the house. The tall grandfather clock in Heather's upstairs corridor had been stopped for years, yet as he descended the right-hand staircase, it seemed to Brian that he could hear a ticking echo in time to his tread. He had no choice but to ask the old man. He needed help, and he needed it now.

Arthur's response to his request could not have been more astonishing. The old gentleman lit up with an incandescent flash. "My dear boy! You don't mean to tell me Heather has left you puzzles!"

"Well, yes. I'm sorry to bother you, but—"

"Bother? Why, nothing could be further from the case!"

Brian found himself able to hand over the note and explain, "Apparently my wife and Heather planned these clues together. On her good days, I'd come into Sarah's room and find her giggling with Heather on the phone. When I asked her what they were doing, all she'd tell me was, 'Planning.' It was so good to see her laugh, I never had the heart to push for more."

His words halted Arthur in the process of opening the letter. "My dear fellow, how tragically touching."

"I just thought you should know," Brian finished. "Some of the letter is pretty personal."

Brian studied Arthur as he read. Age had softened his features and planted a few spots on his neck and left cheek, but Arthur Wainwright remained both virile and handsome. The timeless polish was intact as well, for Arthur exuded the air of one who could command without raising his voice. He wore no-nonsense glasses with heavy black frames, which only heightened the luster of his white hair. Very strong features, sharply focused eyes, prominent ears, strong chin. Big hands and shoulders to match. If ever a man had been born to rule, it was Arthur Wainwright.

He finished reading the brief letter, let his hand drop to his side, and took a long breath before sighing, "Poor Heather." Another shaky breath, then, "Life can be such a dreadful bother."

Brian let the silence of accord rest between them.

"I must thank you for sharing this with me. It is like she has returned to grace these old walls once more." Arthur lifted the letter and mused over the final sentences aloud, "'Yet it was in this place of supposed darkness that she found not only a turning, but a healing. Seek where the darkness gathers, and find wings for your own renewal.'"

"It doesn't make sense," Brian confessed.

"That's because you're not English." Arthur rattled the letter in the space between them. "We Brits are positively mad about mazes and mysteries and puzzles and enigmas. That's why you see us playing all these silly parlor games. Because life's puzzles don't hold enough promise of answers." He reread the letter, then concluded, "My advice to you is, march straight over to Trevor's and ask him to join the merry band. You don't have anything against men of the cloth, I hope."

"No, none at all."

"Excellent. Let's be off then. Sharp as a tack, our Trevor, and he loves a good riddle as much as I do." He led Brian back down the hall and out the manor's front door. "Mind you, the things these religious fellows ask of a chap, well, it's all a bit much. Take that old adage, Bless those who curse you. I say, on my off days I can't even find it in myself to bless those who buy me lunch."

They were brought up short by the sight of two men standing at the corner where the drive branched and led back to the stable yard. Joe Eaves stood beside Hardy Seade, their backs to Brian and Arthur. The realtor was pointing to a boxy vintage Citroen cabriolet, which Joe was in the process of polishing. Seade gestured angrily at the grillwork, while Joe nodded agreement.

Arthur asked quietly, "Any desire to go over and greet the lads?"

"None whatsoever."

"Right you are." As they started down the drive, Arthur said, "I find myself deeply saddened by the thought of that man taking over Heather's beloved home. Gladys keeps telling me that it's only a house, but I find the old place has a character all its own."

"I'm beginning to agree with you."

"Are you now?" Arthur cast him an approving glance. "How interesting."

Brian found himself tasting words he had only begun to

fashion in his mind. "Ever since I've arrived, I've had the impression that I'm healing. More than that. I'm taking a major turn, and somehow this old house is tied up in it. Every day the idea of letting this place go troubles me more and more." When Arthur did not respond, Brian finished, "I guess that must sound pretty crazy."

"My dear boy, not at all. I was just thinking how tragic it is that you've arrived only to be handed the wrong end of the stick."

The drive bent to skirt in front of Rose Cottage, and they looked over to discover that Hardy Seade and Joe Eaves were following their progress with blank expressions. Arthur snorted and turned toward the front gates. "Dear Alex would be rolling in his grave to know Castle Keep is going to be acquired by the likes of Hardy Seade."

"And Heather?"

Arthur smiled. "I find myself amazed at times that even the blessed Saint Peter has managed to hold Heather back."

They did not even have time to cross the vicar's threshold, for as soon as Arthur told him of the puzzle, Trevor demanded to see the letter. It took the vicar all of thirty seconds to come up with, "Have you checked the cellar?"

"The heart of darkness." Arthur snapped his fingers. "Of course. How silly of me not to think of it before." In an aside to Brian, Arthur added, "Didn't I tell you Trevor was a wizard with puzzles?"

"Puzzles?" His wife's head popped through the doorway. "Who has a puzzle?"

"Brian," Trevor replied.

"Several of them, from the sounds of things," Arthur added. "Heather set him up a gift of unraveling mysteries."

"Oooh, I do so love a good poser." She reached out and said, "Be a dear and let me have a look."

Before Brian could think of a reason to object, Molly had taken the letter from her husband's hands, read the contents, and instantly said, "Dear, sweet Heather. Have you checked the cellar?"

Arthur said, "Perhaps we asked the wrong person."

Trevor objected, "She heard me."

"I did not," Molly objected. "Heard what?"

"Never mind." Trevor recaptured the letter. "Come along, lads."

The first things to greet them as they descended the cellar stairs were two giant hippopotamuses.

Arthur followed Brian down the stairs, stepped onto the basement floor, and said, "Great heavens above."

The heads were mounted upon stone pillars and stood as high as a man. The snouts were a full four feet across and opened to reveal stubby fangs the thickness of Brian's wrist. Not even the blanketing of dust could conceal their savage fury. Brian stepped around them to discover a pair of crocodiles twenty feet long, stuffed and mounted with equally ferocious snarls. Beyond that stood a full-grown tiger, a python coiled around a tree trunk, three open-fanged cobras, two vultures, an ibex, a condor, a very dusty zebra, and what appeared to be a full-grown water buffalo. The beasts dominated one side of a chamber that seemed to run the entire length of the manor.

Trevor descended the stairs, took a single look about, and declared, "My old foes."

Arthur rounded on him. "I beg your pardon?"

"These poor animals," Trevor replied, casting a sardonic gaze over the gathering. The beasts silently roared back at him. "What waste. What folly." To Brian he explained, "What you see here is a display reaching back to the Age of Enlightenment. The desire to throw aside the rule of God through human knowledge began here in the reign of George the Third, around the time your nation was formed. The scientists and philosophers of that era decided that if they were to look hard enough at the world around them, they could come to know everything. It may sound silly, I know, but at the beginning of this century a gathering of scientists in London declared that man had almost reached the point of having discovered everything there was to know."

Brian asked, "So they killed animals?"

"Killed, named, dissected, studied, stuffed, mounted. It was the measure of a so-called Renaissance man to go out and name a river and kill a few beasts, bring them back, and display them over his dining table." Trevor dismissed them with an angry wave. "Man's absurd desire to replace God is matched only by his inability to learn from his own past."

"Never mind all that," Arthur said. "I can't imagine Heather meant these ghastly beasts to be Brian's reward."

Brian did not need to look at the letter again to respond, "She said I was to find wings for my own renewal."

"Well, if I know Heather, those dead buzzards certainly don't fit the bill," Trevor agreed. "But the cellar appears otherwise to be empty."

"Let's have a look about, shall we?"

But Brian halted Arthur's forward progress with a hand on his arm. "Have you been down here recently?"

"Me? My good fellow, I'd totally forgotten this chamber even existed."

Brian pointed. "Then whose footprints are those?"

"The light down here is terrible," Arthur complained. "Wait while I go fetch a torch."

The old gentleman made swift progress up and down the stairs. Under the more brilliant beam it was possible for Arthur to declare, "These are recent tracks. Look how the dust hasn't resettled in them."

"Follow them around," Trevor said.

The trio proceeded about the vaulted chamber. Brick and stone pillars dotted the otherwise empty reaches. They found nothing except more dust and footprints leading in a wide circle. By the back wall Arthur sneezed and declared, "If it wasn't stuffed African vultures that Heather meant to surprise you with, it appears someone else made off with your prize."

"I'm not so sure," Trevor countered thoughtfully.

"Well, it's certainly not down here, and all this dust is playing havoc with my sinuses." Arthur sneezed again and started back across the chamber. "Come up and let me make us a pot of tea."

Brian remained standing beside Trevor, staring at the blank wall and wondering what held the vicar's attention. Then he realized, "This wall is newer."

"Not only that. As far as I can tell, nothing has disturbed the

dust other than those footprints, and there are no marks to suggest anything has been removed." The vicar turned to Brian.
"Shall we see if there is another access underground?"

But the day's search proved fruitless and exhausting. Trevor
came and went several times, stopping by on his way to and from
various appointments, offering advice and disappearing again.
Brian finally insisted they stop because Arthur began to flag.
There was little reason to continue, as they had scoured the
ground floor twice, toured all the empty rooms opposite Arthur's
apartment, and circled the house's exterior more times than
Brian cared to count. It was not altogether bad, as he had come
to know the old home better than ever. He had also found a
loose grounding wire that when taped back together increased
the wattage of every downstairs light. Gladys had been so
thrilled she had raced from her apartment to wrap his sweaty
form in a joyous embrace.

Yet after dinner, when he was upstairs and alone with his
thoughts, he still could not halt his restless wandering. Brian
toured through all the northern rooms, so long abandoned he
had to punch the warped and swollen doors open with his
shoulder. The main floor had another two grand salons, the furniture draped in yellowed covers and thick layers of dust. The
carpets were moth-eaten, the walls faded and mottled. Upstairs
he found another two bedrooms and four smaller alcoves, as
well as a sewing room and a study filled with moldy books and
time-wrecked furniture. Apparently no one had disturbed their
quiet slumber for twenty years and more. For the first time,

however, instead of seeing ruin and neglect, Brian surveyed the chambers and began to see *possibility*. The realization did not bring joy, however. As he returned downstairs and prepared for bed, all he felt was pain over the coming loss.

To his utter astonishment, he slept beyond dawn for the first time in what seemed like years. Brian rose and found the sun already up and mocking him from high in a cloudless sky. He made his breakfast and pondered what it might mean, and could only come up with the fact that he was growing ever more comfortable with the place. Dangerously so.

He had just finished dressing when he heard excited voices in the outside stairwell, then a rapid pounding on his door. He opened it to find the vicar standing beside Arthur, who said, "Hope we're not disturbing."

"Of course not."

"Trevor here has come up with a modest brainstorm, if I do say so myself."

"You mean about the riddle?" Brian stepped back. "Come in."

"No time, no time," Arthur cried.

"I only have a moment," Trevor added. "Tonight is the town meeting, and there are a thousand things to take care of."

"Out with it, man," Arthur pressed.

"This morning it occurred to me," Trevor said, "that that dollhouse of yours might not be a dollhouse at all. The Victorians would often build scale models of these grand houses and used them to map out what they called mystery chambers. They loved their mazes and their mysteries, the Victorians did. They built secret passages and hidden chambers, and concealed cubicles behind closets and under staircases."

"Most builders and all the laborers were illiterate," Arthur added. "They wouldn't know a scale drawing from a pentagram."

"Exactly. But work on such passages and additions demanded great precision and a careful understanding of what was required, so they used miniature renditions for the planning and building."

"It sounds to me," Brian said, "like we need to take another look at the dollhouse."

14

Cecilia greeted Saturday morning with great anxiety. It was one thing to volunteer to help with something comfortably distant. But that morning her first thought was one of standing in front of the entire town, and the resulting fear was so strong it catapulted her from bed.

Coffee only added to her nerves. She tried to study the books the vicar had given her, yet every word shouted at her of how that very evening she would be addressing the village.

And to top things off, she could not escape to have coffee with Brian because he never appeared. She set her chair by the kitchen window so as to watch the manor's front doorway. But the morning strengthened into day, and still Brian did not emerge. She found herself unwilling to go to the river's edge by herself, and though the decision made no sense whatsoever, she stubbornly held to it.

Her chair's position granted her a perfect view of Joe Eaves and his battered pickup as he drove through the gates and parked up by the stables. Mug in hand, Cecilia rose and stood by the window, watching as he began dumping tools on the unkempt lawn. She had never been able to see beyond his ready smile, and the man continued to unsettle her mightily.

Which was why she was almost eager to latch onto outrage

when she saw what he was intending, and why she raced from the cottage in her robe and shrilled at him, "What on earth do you think you're doing?"

Brian exited the house, and even before he consciously recognized the voice, he was running. He rounded the far side of the stables to find Cecilia clutching her robe and waving her free hand. Joe Eaves leaned on his shovel and responded with his languid smile.

Cecilia spotted Brian and rounded on him. "Did you know about this?"

"Know what?"

"This man says he has permission to dig a *trench* in my front garden!"

Joe Eaves had the twinkling eyes and ever-present smile of a jester. "Lovely morning for a bit of yard work, your lordship."

Brian surveyed the gouge Joe was in the process of digging in the earth and demanded, "What's going on here?"

"Mr. Seade thought it might dress up the place to put in a line of shrubbery."

"Dress up the place!" Cecilia was so angry she literally spluttered. "Dress up . . . How about maybe starting with repairing the hole in my roof? The one I told him about *last year!*"

"I didn't agree to anything like this," Brian declared.

"Well, sir, I suppose Mr. Seade thought since he was both paying and buying, it'd be all right to do a bit of work around here."

"Well, it's not." Brian heard Trevor and Arthur coming up behind him but kept his gaze fastened upon the sweating young man. "So please fill the hole back in."

A glint of something hard emerged deep within the smiling eyes. "But Mr. Seade specifically ordered me—"

"This is not Mr. Seade's property," Brian snapped. He could not tell which angered him more, the man's lackadaisical attitude or the way he had upset Cecilia. "So pack up your tools and leave."

"Mr. Seade won't be liking this, sir. Very particular about having people follow his orders, Mr. Seade is."

Cecilia snorted. Brian replied, "Now."

"I'd be watching how I cross the man," Joe Eaves warned, the smile slipping away. "He's got the right to push you out sudden or easy, mind."

"As a matter of fact," Brian added, taking mild pleasure from seeing behind that smile. "I don't want you coming back on the property at all."

"That is," Cecilia snapped, "unless it's to repair my roof!"

Joe Eaves gave him a speculative glance. Brian found himself stiffening in response. Then the grin returned to all but his eyes, and he hefted all his tools before turning to Cecilia and saying, "I wouldn't be paying your roof too much mind, miss doctor lady." He dumped the tools in the back of his truck, climbed in behind the wheel, ground the starter, and finished, "Not since Mr. Seade's already booked the 'dozer to come in next Friday and level the place."

Brian watched the truck depart through the main gates, feeling no triumph whatsoever from the exchange. Cecilia seemed equally dispirited as she said, "I suppose I should thank you."

"Good riddance to bad rubbish," Arthur agreed. "I never did care for the chap."

She glanced at her watch and declared, "I have to be getting to the clinic. It's my Saturday half-day."

Trevor called after her, "Ready for tonight, dear?"

To Brian's eye, Cecilia's entire frame seemed to shudder slightly before she said, "I'll be there."

Brian offered, "Show me where the leak is tomorrow, and I'll put a sheet of plywood in to fix the roof at least temporarily."

She turned and rewarded him with a from-the-heart gaze. But her voice was tragic. "I suppose it really doesn't matter."

"It matters a lot," Brian replied.

When she had disappeared inside the rose-covered cottage, Trevor touched Brian's arm and said, "We really must be off."

The church charity shop occupied the ground floor of a building that predated the United States. The bowed front windows remained the focal point of a gaggle of ladies and young girls. Which was why, when the vicar pushed through the door and bid the volunteers a good day and then proceeded to crawl into the display area, a stir enveloped the gathering on the window's other side. Brian slid in beside him, then the two helped Arthur ease himself down and in. But the real clamor began when Brian showed them how the roof and the top floor lifted off.

"That's as far as I got," Brian said, carefully setting down the top stages.

"If the top goes, then so should the rest," Arthur said.

"Look here," Trevor exclaimed, pressing his cheek to the dusty display platform. "There is a three-inch base here below the level of the first floor."

"Of course." Arthur's creaky joints made hard going of getting down to eye level with the base, but he managed. "The front stairs rise a good eight feet to the level of the ground floor."

Brian tried to ignore the little faces jumping up and down and pointing at him from four feet away. "What exactly are we looking for here?"

"A secret passage," Arthur said impatiently. "Now do be a good fellow and help me lift."

A woman's voice approached from behind them. "Can I help you with something, Vicar?"

"Oh, Mrs. Feathers, yes, of course, you must be wondering." The vicar did not turn from assisting Brian and Arthur as they unloaded all the furniture and fittings from the next floor. "Mr. Blackstone here has received another riddle from Heather."

"I beg your pardon?"

"A riddle, Mrs. Feathers. A conundrum."

"From Heather Harding? But Vicar, she's dead."

"Yes, we are well aware of that fact, Mrs. Feathers. Heather set Brian here a series of puzzles. Arthur was good enough to bring me in on the chase. And chase it is, since we only have a few days left to solve them." Trevor squinted down into the now-empty rooms. "Has my vision started to fail, or is the light going bad in here?"

"It's the people," Arthur complained. "The crowd is clogging up the window."

"Mrs. Feathers, would you be so good as to shoo all those ladies away?"

"Shoo the . . . Vicar, you must be joking."

"Well, do be a dear and see if you can find us a torch. There must be one somewhere." He turned to Brian. "Do you see anything?"

"The rooms seem laid out exactly as I remember." Brian

poked a finger into a windowless box. "Right down to the little chamber where I found the dollhouse."

"We might have been wrong to concentrate on the cellar, after all. Darkness could refer to another such windowless room," Trevor mused. "Very well, let's lift up the next segment. All together now."

Three sets of hands pulled off the next floor, and the little girls outside danced harder still. They searched and unpacked and then unsheathed the ground floor, by which time the deck around them was littered with miniature sofas and upholstered chairs and fainting couches and dressing tables and dining room pieces and sideboards and postage-stamp-size Persian carpets and even a pair of Siamese kittens and an intricately carved West Highland terrier.

But the ground floor refused to budge. It was only after they had used the flashlight supplied by Mrs. Feathers and searched every inch for another secret room, then tilted the base on its side, that Trevor and Arthur shouted together, "There it is!"

There from the bottom segment's southern wall was another set of stairs—leading downward and *away* from the house. Trevor said, "Of course, a subbasement."

"These old houses were often riddled with layer after layer of tunnels and vaulted chambers," Arthur agreed.

"But we searched that wall," Brian pointed out. "It was as tight as a drum."

"It was also the most recently constructed." Trevor slid out of the front area, then reached down to help Arthur to his feet. "What we need to do is search around outside the house, making a wider circle than we did before, and see if there is another way down." As they were leaving the shop, Trevor turned back to the openmouthed woman and said, "Mrs. Feathers, would you be so kind as to put the house back together for us?"

It was only as they reentered the front gates of Castle Keep that Brian recalled, "Didn't you have a lot to do today?"

The question only spurred Trevor to greater speed. "Never mind that now. Which side of the house was it?"

"South," Arthur said, holding his own to the pace the vicar set. "I say, perhaps it's out by where the old butler's house used to stand."

He led them to a clump of overgrown ruins lying alongside the manor's boundary wall. Two stubby brick fingers rose to indicate where the chimneys had once stood. The three men separated and began kicking about the rubble, until Arthur cried out, "Here we are, lads!"

Brian and Trevor rushed over to where Arthur was tossing bricks and debris off a rusted metal lid. When they had cleared away the rubbish, they stood upon a metal cover five feet square and perhaps a quarter-inch thick. Trevor started scouting around, saying impatiently, "We need a rod or a crowbar to shift that thing."

"I'll go get us a torch," Arthur said, hustling off.

"There are some old tools by the stable," Brian said, racing in the other direction.

He returned with a rusted hoe and a pickax. Together he and Trevor huffed and puffed and finally managed to shift the steel plate over far enough for Arthur to point the flashlight, peer down, and cry, "Success!"

This was enough for Brian and Trevor to redouble their efforts and finally slide the plate over far enough to reveal steep stairs worn to treacherous curves. Trevor took the flashlight, squatted down low, and said, "I'll light your way; you'll need both hands to grip the walls."

"Take care there, lad," Arthur cautioned.

The steps seemed to go on forever. Brian took them at a wary pace, pressing his hands tight against each wall, testing each stair in turn. Daylight diminished and the air cooled, until even the flashlight's beam was reduced to a feeble glow far overhead. He continued on mostly by feel until the next step broadened beneath his foot, and the wall to his right opened into pitch blackness. He started back up to where he could see the hand holding the light and called, "Drop the flashlight down."

"Here we go," Trevor called, his voice echoing off distant walls.

Brian caught the descending light, then gingerly made his way back down to the cellar. The beam illuminated a low-ceilinged chamber with something long and lumpy beneath a yellowed drop cloth. Brian stepped over, gripped one corner of the canvas, and tossed it aside. Instantly the air was clogged with clouds of dust. It was only when he could stop sneezing and hacking that he realized the two men were shouting down at him. Brian made his way back over to the stairs, and with streaming eyes he looked up to the tiny square of daylight.

Arthur's voice echoed down. "What is it, lad?"

Brian pointed the flashlight back to what lay revealed. "I've found Heather's wings."

15

$\mathcal{I}$t was definitely a very good thing for all concerned that there were no emergencies during her Saturday morning clinic. Cecilia saw to three elderly patients who needed medication and blood pressure monitoring, two young men mildly damaged by a Friday pub brawl, a pair of fretting babies, and an asthma patient who needed an increased dose of summer medication. Yet all the while a portion of her mind remained occupied by what was to come that evening. The closer the hour drew, the less she could believe that she had ever agreed to stand up in front of a crowd of people, no matter what the reason.

As she locked the clinic door behind her, Cecilia was suddenly struck by a welcome memory. She found herself recalling the terror of her medical exams and the way she had prepared. Her walk back through the market square became rapid, her focus tight. A voice called to her, but she did not even bother to respond. She knew now what she had to do.

The day was warm and windless, the air in the narrow lane leading home very close. Cecilia passed a trio of girls skipping in and out of the pillars of sunlight without noting them. She did not even hear one of the girls greet Cecilia with the news that her mother was feeling much better, nor the giggles that followed her as she exited the lane and passed through the manor's entrance.

She let herself into the cottage, put on the kettle, and piled the vicar's books and pamphlets on her kitchen table. She pulled out a pad and a trio of multicolored pens, made a cup of coffee, and seated herself. Until now she had been attempting to treat this upcoming talk as if it were a normal part of her everyday life. But there was nothing normal about it. She had accepted the task, and no matter how much she might dread the prospect, she had to prepare. Make herself ready, just as she would for another dreaded exam. She was not a good speaker, and she tended to come across stiff and jerky. She knew this. The last time she had spoken in public was for her medical license's oral exams. Her answer for the panic she had felt then had been to prepare so well that her knowledge showed through, despite her poor presentation. It was the only answer here as well. Cecilia opened the first book and got to work.

The hours passed in a flurry of concentrated effort. The outside world dimmed to where not even the roar of machinery in the manor's front yard disturbed her. The clanking of metal, the shouts of voices, the calls of people, the driving back and forth through the front gates—none of it reached her. She sat and she read and she wrote. She practiced phrases, she spoke passages aloud to hear how they sounded. And as she had hoped, the grind kept her fear mostly at bay.

At the sound of a rumbling motor and heavy equipment grinding along the manor drive, Brian raced down the stairs and out the front entrance. A huge man in his sixties stepped down from the tow truck and demanded, "Mr. Blackstone?"

"That's right. You must be Bill Wilke."

"The one and only." He was an odd-looking man, not much shorter than Brian but double his weight, big and muscled and fit despite his years. He was dressed in coveralls of denim blue and had bright red cheeks and a graying walrus mustache. He swallowed Brian's hand in a grip like a greasy catcher's mitt. "Vicar tells me you've got yourself a right mess." He looked behind Brian and nodded. "Hello, Arthur."

"You're looking well, Bill."

"Can't complain. Well, I could, but my wife stopped paying me any mind years ago." He started kicking around the grass by the drive and muttered, "Now where is that ruddy thing."

Brian pointed toward the south wall. "The stairs are over here."

"I know where they are, lad, and I don't aim on hauling that lady up any stairs." He took another step across the lawn and kept kicking the untidy lawn. Each blow tossed up another clod of dirt and grass. "Could've sworn it was right here."

Brian exchanged a baffled look with Arthur, then said, "How do you know what's in the basement?"

"On account of me being the one who put it there." His foot connected with something that gave off a metallic rattle, and he grunted, "Knew it had to be here. Couldn't have forgotten something like that." He turned and started walking back to his truck. "Isn't all that often I get asked to bury a prize motorcar in a secret coal cellar."

Brian watched openmouthed as the man climbed onto the back of his truck, gripped the massive hook with both hands, and began pulling the steel cord toward where he and Arthur stood. Bill Wilke explained as he walked, "Miss Heather told me she wanted to enshrine old Alex himself, but the council wasn't having no part of that. So she said she'd have to make do with Alex's favorite toy instead." The mechanic hooked the clasp to what appeared to be a metal ring growing out of Brian's lawn and finished, "I knew from the first instant the lady was joking, but it made for a good telling, and I always did have a soft spot for Miss Heather."

"I don't understand," Brian managed. "The car was her husband's?"

"Just said that, didn't I?" He walked back to the rear of the tow truck, gripped a lever with both hands, and said, "You gents best be backing off. My guess is this thing will be kicking up quite a fuss."

Bill Wilke took up the slack in the steel cable, halted the motor, spit on his hands, gripped the motor handle with one hand, and rested his other fingers on the cable itself. "Here we go, now."

The motor ground, the cable tightened until it hummed taut and shivering. Bill Wilke pressed harder on the handle, and the winch motor began shrieking in protest. The tow truck rose up like a bucking horse, and then Brian's lawn erupted.

Dirt and grass and rocks splattered everywhere as a metal plate twelve feet to a side came bolting up and sliding toward the truck. The steel grate wore a foot of dirt and grass and shrubs like a mantle. Bill Wilke dragged the plate over to the back of the truck, plowing a twelve-foot furrow in Brian's lawn in the process. He halted the winch, jumped down, unhooked the catch, and once again began pulling out the cable.

Arthur said to Brian, "If all of Knightsbridge isn't talking about you already, it soon will be."

"Oh, I don't guess the lad's got much to worry about on that score." Using the cable for balance, Bill Wilke began backing down a steep slope leading into the earth. "Had three people stop by this morning, telling me how Miss Heather's done left the lad here a mess of riddles. Figured it was only a matter of time before I got this call." The deeper the man moved, the more his voice echoed. "Mr. Blackstone, there's a torch behind my seat. Shine it down here so I can remember what I'm about, will you?"

Brian did as he was told, then said, "The name's Brian." He received a thunderous sneeze in response. "How did Heather keep this secret?"

"Had me do it in the dead of night." Another sneeze. Then there was the sound of metal clanking on metal. "Didn't have the heart to tell the old dear she was crazy as a loon. All broke up over losing Alex, was our Heather."

Bill Wilke used the cable to scale back up the slope, saying as he reappeared, "There was some nasty piece of work out to buy the car. Heather finally told me about him once the job was done. She was terrified the bloke would spirit the thing away when she wasn't looking. She had me bring in my brother to wall up the cellar, all done secretlike. Decided the best way to fend off this buyer was claiming she sold it to somebody else. Or so she said. Like I told you, the old dear was dead bonkers."

He hopped back up on the truck, moving nimbly for a man of his size and age. The winch began grinding, and Brian stood alongside Arthur and watched as the automobile was drawn into the light of day.

When the winch was shut off once more, Bill Wilke joined the men in circling the car. The exterior was fire-engine red with layers of sparkling chrome trim. Bill Wilke said in evident admiration, "Nineteen sixty-one MGA. Lovely bit of work, it is. Disc brakes on all four wheels, center-lock wheels. Done up like the D-type Jag. Motor built with a twin-cam head on her."

"Lovely car," Arthur agreed. "Takes me back a ways, I don't mind telling you. Alex loved this machine with a passion."

"Marine ply floors," Bill Wilke continued, beginning to unsnap the cover that fitted over the seats and steering wheel. "Bit of a bone shaker, these ladies. But loads of fun." He flipped off the cover, revealing the walnut steering wheel and seats of stitched Oxford leather. "Typical old British sports car, the MGA. Open roadster, just the tonneau cover you see here. If it rains you hunker down and get wet." He flipped open the hood, revealing a gleaming motor. "Tires are rotted, of course. I'll need to clean out the fuel system as well. And the brakes might have seized up." He ducked his head down and began studying the engine, his stubby fingers moving with the grace of a concert pianist. "But it looks like mice didn't get into the wiring. No rust that I can spot. Valves move smooth as silk." He reemerged to wipe his hands on a dirty rag and announce, "I could most likely have the lady ready to sing this very afternoon."

Brian asked because he had to, though the words hurt to form, "How much do you think I could get for the car?"

Arthur rounded on him. "My dear boy, you can't be serious."

"I don't have any choice," Brian said glumly. "I'm so broke—"

A voice from behind them cried, "That car is *mine!*"

They turned in unison as Hardy Seade raced down the lane, arms up and waving. The man's customary aplomb was in tatters. "We had an *agreement!* Heather promised that car to *me!*"

Bill Wilke observed the man's fury as he would an oil stain.

"I always wondered if you were the goat Miss Heather was talking about."

"You stay out of this, you *meddler!*" Hardy Seade wheeled to shriek at Brian. "This car is not yours!"

"On the contrary," Arthur murmured. "By all appearances and forms, it most certainly—"

"Shut *up*, you doddering old fool!" Seade's voice was one note short of a full-fledged scream. "I should have evicted you and that galling wife of yours years ago!"

Brian felt something snap. He met Hardy Seade's furious approach with a violent shove. "You just back off."

Hardy Seade's arms flailed about, but he could not keep himself from tumbling onto his backside. As Brian took another step toward him, the man shrieked, "Stay away from me!"

"Get off my property," Brian snapped.

"*Your* property!" Seade scrambled up and dusted off the back of his suit. "You penniless mongrel, this time next week I'll see you in the gutter where you *belong!*" He remembered what had brought him over, and he started forward once again. "And that car stays right where it is!"

"Not a chance," Brian said. "I'd drive it off a cliff before I let you get your hands on it."

"You . . ." The man's face turned so red he looked ready to burst. "This isn't some Wild West town where you can batter and shoot your way clear. This is a *civilized* country. We have ways and means of dealing with scum like you!"

"I'm not telling you again," Brian said, taking another step toward the man, balling up his fists in the process. "Get out of here."

Hardy Seade's attempt for haughty authority was defeated by

the way he kept backing off. "I have every right to be here. I'm a lawful tenant!"

"Then I'm serving you notice," Brian said grimly. "Your cars can stay, but if you show up again I'll have Bill Wilke clear the lot of them out of my stables and dump them on the street."

"I'll have the authorities on you for this!" He fanned the air as he retreated from Brian's approach. "*All* of you will be brought up on charges. I'll have you put away!"

His final cry came from safely beyond the main gates. "That car is *mine!*"

Brian waited until he was certain the man was gone, then returned to where the men stood. Arthur greeted him with a satisfied smile and the words, "I thought that went rather well."

"Anything that pushes Hardy Seade one step closer to the edge is a good day's work in my book," Bill Wilke agreed. "Though I warrant that bloke there will top any other cash offer you'll get."

"Hardy Seade is not getting this car," Brian declared. "How much do you think I can get from somebody else?"

"Ten thousand quid or thereabouts. They only made a hundred thousand of these machines. That's a paltry *month's* work for the likes of Ford these days." Bill Wilke granted Brian a look of pure approval. "Word is, the town council's handed you the mucky end of the wicket."

"I guess you could say that."

"Tell you what." Bill Wilke slammed the hood shut. "I'll get the old lady up and running again and arrange for a set of temporary plates. You can enjoy her for a few days at least."

"That's very kind of you, Mr. Wilke."

"Name's Bill to my mates." He shook Brian's hand a final

time. "Instant I set eyes on you, I said to myself, *Here's a bloke with the old head gasket screwed on proper.*" He started back to the tow truck and began winching the MGA onto its rear tires. "Personally, I'd say this whole auction thing is just one big send-up. Won't pack any more bang than a damp squid." He waved a hand toward the front gates. "There's only one bloke interested in this old place, and that's Hardy Seade. Man's been after title and majesty all his life. Nothing he likes better than having somebody give him the old bow and scrape."

Arthur waited until the mechanic had departed with the red MGA in tow to muse, "Now, I wonder what else our dear Heather has in store."

16

$\mathcal{S}$aturday evening Brian met Arthur and Gladys as he was coming down the stairs. They stared up at him for a moment, a question in their eyes. Brian explained, "Cecilia asked me to come and give her moral support."

"My dear boy, such dress might be well and good for an evening out across the puddle," Arthur said reprovingly. "But here in England it just won't do. Not do at all."

Brian looked down at his faded denim shirt, khakis, and scuffed loafers. "It's all I have clean."

"Then you'll have to give me your soiled things tomorrow," Gladys ordered. "I can't have my landlord walking about the village looking like a well-pressed vagrant. It simply isn't proper."

"That won't help us tonight, though, will it." Arthur surveyed Brian's lanky frame. "What size jacket do you wear?"

Brian had to search back two years to recall, "Forty-two long."

"Well, the long's a bother, but we might have something that will do for the moment." He turned toward Gladys. "Be a dear and see if you can find my old duds."

"Really," Brian began. "That's—"

"One of the horrors of joining the ranks of the elderly is that one shrinks," Arthur said, taking Brian by the arm and leading him back to their apartment. "The process of shriveling leaves one unable to recognize oneself some mornings. Truly a horrid moment, I assure you, looking in the glass and having this prune of an apparition there to greet you before your first cup of tea."

"These have been packed away for donkey's years," Gladys said, returning with clothes draped over both arms. "I'm afraid you're going to smell rather mothbally." She handed Brian a shirt and tie and jacket. "Just step into the dining room and give those a try. I'm afraid there's nothing we can do about attiring those long American shanks of yours."

"No one will notice the bottom half if the top is presentable," Arthur said.

Brian decided he had no choice but to do as they said. Through the partly closed door he heard Arthur say, "There's an unwritten code that even eccentrics must attend to in this land. Your dear Heather was well aware of this fact."

"She wasn't my anything," Brian said, slipping his arms into a shirt that smelled of mothballs. "I only met her once."

"Which is your loss," Arthur replied smartly. "As I was saying, the code of an English village states that a person may be mad as a hatter and chase fairies down the High Street so long as one does so well dressed."

Brian knotted his tie and slid it up tight, marveling that he still remembered how, then slipped into the blue blazer. Self-consciously he stepped back into the hallway. "The sleeves are too short."

"Keep your hands in your trouser pockets, and no one will notice," Arthur replied. "He cleans up rather well, wouldn't you say, my dear?"

"Like a Hollywood movie star out slumming for the evening." She gave his lapels an affectionate brush, then drew his tie up straight. "This outfit takes me back, I don't mind saying."

"All right, then, let's be off." As they stepped into the evening, Arthur confessed, "Personally, I don't give a toss about the bells. Banging about all hours of the day and night, it could be a bit wearing at times. But the vicar holds them in high esteem, and one must always stand up for one's mates."

"I miss them," Gladys said. She pointed to the steeple rising beyond the elms. "They've come to be old friends. I'd hate not having them there to mark my days."

The closer they drew to the market square, the more people joined their quiet procession. The soft footfalls and conversation bounced off the ancient buildings, echoing back and forth until it seemed to Brian that the centuries opened and released memories to walk along with them.

The town hall rose from the end of the cobblestone square opposite from the central church. It was an odd structure with a open colonnaded ground floor. Tall pillars surrounded a stone-floored raised terrace. Benches lined the exterior, framing a grandstand space where bands played and children danced and couples courted. This evening all was quiet, however, as the people streamed to the side entrance and climbed the steep stairs to the vast upper chamber. It was tall and broad, the overhead beams smoke-blackened where oil lamps had once burned. And very crowded.

"Arthur, Gladys, so good of you to come." A very nervous vicar rushed over to shake their hands and point to his left. "We're trying to marshal our forces up toward the front."

"Looks like a full house," Arthur said.

"Yes, it's hard to tell how many are here for a night's entertainment and how many to support the cause." He gave Brian a gray-tinted smile. "Very nice of you to take an interest in village life. Though I must warn you, this might be your introduction to our darker nature."

As the vicar was pulled away by someone else, Arthur motioned for Brian to follow. Brian stiffened as he passed Hardy Seade, who was standing with the county finance official and the lady who had accosted him on his own front step. The tweedy woman gave him a frosty glance and sniffed her disapproval before turning away.

"Mr. Blackstone, Brian." A massive figure in an overly tight jacket and walrus mustache slid through the crowd. "Thought I might catch you here tonight."

"Hello, Bill," Arthur said. "How is the world treating you?"

"Better than the doc there." Bill Wilke nodded affably toward where Cecilia sat isolated upon the front stage. She nervously flipped through the white cards she held, her eyes glazed, her features tight. "Looks like she's reading up for her own execution."

"The poor dear," Gladys said. "I'll just go say hello."

Brian debated whether he should go with her until Bill Wilke said, "Just wanted to let you know the motor-car is up and running."

Hardy Seade and the two women slipped around Bill Wilke, heading for the front podium. Brian endured icy glares from all three. "You've already repaired the MGA?"

"Not all that much to fix. Couple of loose wires, set of new wheels and brakes, retuning, that's about it." A few teeth shone behind the mustache. "She sings a sweet tune, that old beauty. You'll want her delivered tomorrow, I warrant."

"I can't thank you enough for all this."

"Think nothing of it." He glanced over to where Hardy

Seade and the two women were sitting on the stage across from Cecilia. "You spot the trio of nasties when you came in?"

"Yes."

"Strip the bloom right off the rose, those three. Shame Miss Heather's place'll wind up in their claws. Which reminds me." He patted his pockets. "Almost forgot. Came across something in the glove box." He handed over a crinkled yellow envelope. "Looks like the old dear left you another note."

"More puzzles." Arthur almost purred the words. "How splendid."

Brian accepted the envelope with numb fingers and noticed the cover was split open and resealed with a fresh strip of cellophane tape. The big man looked mortally shamefaced as he confessed, "Couldn't help myself. Nothing I love better than a good puzzler."

Before Brian could frame a response, a bearded gentleman banged his gavel and announced, "This meeting will now come to order."

Cecilia had almost forgotten just how bad fear could be.

The more crowded the meeting hall became, the louder grew the roar in her ears. Her entire midsection felt ground into a single huge knot, one so tight her heart had to hammer like mad just to force the blood through. When the mayor banged his gavel, she jerked like a rabbit caught between the crosshairs. She could not remember what she was going to say, even with the words written on the cards in her hands. It was just so much scrawl, written by another person speaking a foreign tongue. Someone who was not gripped by terror's fist. Someone sane.

Even the mayor's words seemed caught by the wind's roar. She forced herself to look at him, to watch as he fielded questions and objections. She felt a battery of eyes upon her, many of them hostile. The vicar slipped into the chair beside her and patted her hand. Trevor's touch seemed merely to scald her with all that was yet to come.

She tried to concentrate as first the tweedy Lavinia Winniskill and then the councilwoman rose and spoke to the crowd. All she could catch was how it seemed as though the entire audience seemed to applaud their every word. That and the way the pair loaded their speeches with vehement scorn. Although she could not catch the words, the tone came through loud and clear. Over and over the thought echoed through her mind, *They hate me, and if they don't hate me now, they will soon.*

The second woman seated herself to what sounded like a thunderous ovation. Cecilia searched the room and saw only a few sympathetic faces. For some reason she latched onto Brian Blackstone, seated in a ridiculously tight navy jacket and tie, his hair carefully combed and his tan looking even darker than normal. He watched her with those calm gray eyes, his expression serious. Meeting his gaze left her able to take an almost steady breath and focus enough to hear when the mayor turned her way and said, "Our very own Dr. Cecilia Lyons will speak on behalf of the village church society."

Her momentary gift of calm was washed away in another flood of terror. She wanted to turn and flee. But the vicar was there, standing now to applaud and offer her a hand, as much to help her up as to wish her well. The pale fear in his own features only added to her dismay. She started toward the podium, wishing for nothing more than for the floor to open up and swallow her whole.

Cecilia looked so frail and frightened that Brian had to resist the urge to leap from his chair and go shelter her. But shelter her from what? These were her people, not his. He was the outsider, she the village doctor. And yet she seemed so fragile standing there before the podium, so nervous. She looked up and seemed to search the audience. Then her gaze returned to him, just as it had while the two women had spoken. Brian willed to her all the strength he had to give. She seemed to fasten upon that, or perhaps it was just his imagination. Whatever the reason, she steadied herself with one hand on the podium, the other holding her white note cards, and she began.

"In preparation for this meeting, the vicar gave me several books about Knightsbridge and this region. I have tried to study them with a doctor's eye. My responsibility for this village is to maintain its health. What I have discovered is that we cannot separate its physical health from its spiritual health. Cut out the heart, and the body will die. Cut—"

"What utter rubbish," the tweedy woman snorted. "We don't need an outsider to give us a philosophy lesson!"

The mayor was a hefty gentleman in his fifties with the quiet aura of one used to leading. He was seated directly behind the podium in a high-backed chair embossed with the village seal. He turned and intoned, "Please be so kind as to permit the opposition its time at the podium, Mrs. Winniskill."

"But the woman is spouting nonsense!"

"That is for the people to decide." He turned to the front and said more kindly, "Please proceed."

Cecilia tried to flip the cards, but her nervous fingers could not manage the maneuver, and one fell to the floor. She glanced down, then back at Brian, the fear naked in her gaze.

She took a shaky breath and continued, "Modern medicine is built upon lessons learned in the past. We tend to scoff at the way patients were treated in bygone days. But the truth is, much of what we accept today as modern treatment has its roots in discoveries made hundreds and hundreds of years ago. For instance, da Vinci's description of how the body's musculature is connected to the skeletal structure through ligaments and tendons still holds today. Quinine was first used as a remedy for malaria more than four hundred years ago. And aspirin, or the willow bark from which it is derived, has been used to treat pain and inflammation for more than a thousand years."

Only then did Brian realize how silent the hall had become. They had listened and applauded the two women. But there was a vastly different sentiment now. People were not just listening. They were *intent*.

"The truth is, if we were to throw out all the *positive* benefits that past medical discoveries have taught us because of the errors, we would thwart our ability to treat human illnesses. But no one would think of doing such a thing. At least, not with medicine. And yet we seek to do this all the time with our spiritual life."

"This is *nonsense*." The Winniskill woman bounced a fist on her herringbone skirt. "Mayor, really, I must protest."

"And I must request that you permit Dr. Lyons to complete her remarks."

"But this meeting was called to discuss the bells! Which she has not mentioned one time!"

A man's voice called from the back, "Maybe she would, if you gave her half a chance."

The mayor frowned his reply to the outburst, then said to Cecilia, "Please do go on."

Cecilia searched for her place. The strain was etched deep within her taut features. "We ignore the riches and lessons from Christians in the past, and point only at their mistakes. I know because I have done this myself, and I see my community doing this now."

"*Your* community." The Winniskill woman's voice dripped with scorn. "Why, you silly little ingrate!"

A quiet murmur ran through the crowd. A male voice behind Brian muttered, "She's a bovine in mohair, that woman."

Then Brian spotted the lady who worked as Cecilia's receptionist marching down the side aisle. The Winniskill woman leaned back in her chair, clearly alarmed at her approach. The receptionist was a hefty woman, made larger by the load of anger she bore. She paraded up the stage's side stairs, pulled over a chair, and seated herself alongside the tweedy lady. "There, now," she announced, giving all and sundry a steely smile. "I can sit right here and help you remember to keep your gob shut."

The mayor nodded approval, then turned back to the front. Cecilia shuffled to the next card, breathed hard, and continued, "This village has known some very rich times and some very hard times. Nine hundred years ago, when William the Conqueror made this his first capital in England, Knightsbridge was one of the wealthiest communities in all the land. Records show that by the end of the following century, work on four of our seven churches had begun. Our five monasteries supported three schools and two hostels for wayfarers. According to one historian, these same schools granted our villagers the highest literacy rate in England. The largest of those monasteries, according to rumors, sat where my little cottage is now. As you can see, our village is rich with heritage. And the village bells are part of our heritage.

"So long ago we don't even know when the practice began, people saw the need for regular prayer. The account I read claimed it started in France almost fourteen hundred years ago, and it told how people from all walks of life began halting every hour to give a short prayer. Only a few brief words, but every hour they took time to turn to God."

Brian's attention shifted to the vicar. Trevor seemed to have shed years in the time Cecilia had been speaking. The vicar surveyed the crowd with a small smile upon his lips. He caught Brian's eye and gave a tiny nod. Brian felt a shiver run up his spine in response. Despite Cecilia's nervousness, or perhaps because of it, she had captivated this crowd.

"But how could they do this? How did they know when to pray, since there were no clocks? The answer is, they rang the church bells. Seven churches planted so that their bells could be heard everywhere in the region. And each time they rang, people stopped what they were doing and said a prayer, one that lasted no longer than it took to ring the hour. Those who could read carried a miniature text called the Book of Hours. In it were prayers and short poems, brief words to inspire and direct."

As Cecilia turned over her final card, her voice sounded a new note of relief at nearing the end. "This was not something practiced only during the good times. Records show that the Black Death struck Knightsbridge twice. The second time it killed almost two-thirds of our population. The village became so small that all the believers could fit into just one church. Even so, right through our darkest era, volunteers went every hour to every church, night and day, to ring the bells. Our churches continued to sound out the need for prayer."

Cecilia looked at the audience for the first time since she had begun. "Save our heritage. Remind us of our needs, however dated they might seem at the moment. Let the bells of Knightsbridge ring for centuries to come."

The audience granted Cecilia the highest accolade Brian could imagine. No one moved or made a sound. Cecilia's footsteps sounded overly loud as she collapsed into her seat.

The mayor granted her a quiet, "Well done." Only then did they applaud.

When order was restored, the mayor said, "Vicar, do you have anything further to add before we close?"

Trevor showed the good sense not to approach the podium. Instead he stood by his chair and said merely, "Doctors know that regular exercise and a healthy diet are two vital components of good health. Why should such routine discipline not be true of our spiritual life as well?"

The vicar granted them a moment to ponder that, then added, "The practice of praying the hours stayed with us until the so-called Age of Enlightenment. At that point, for the first time in human history, people began to suggest that they could do away with God and live on the power of science alone. I stand before you tonight to say it is not enough, it never has been and never will be. Every new bit of knowledge we gain leads merely to more questions. There is only one answer that is eternally satisfying. Our ancestors knew this, and our church bells are part of both this lesson and the heritage they have handed down to our care."

The hall filled with scuffling and quiet murmurs as Trevor resumed his seat. The mayor rose once more and announced, "Voting on this matter will take place Monday evening. This meeting is now adjourned."

17

Long after the fear had subsided, Cecilia lay awake, staring at the darkness around her. She remained ashamed to the point of feeling wounded from having done such a poor job. She could still feel the pity pouring about the chamber in waves as she seated herself. The silence that had at first greeted the conclusion of her talk remained as powerful as the night.

Thudding as quietly as her shame was the sorrow over losing her home. Strange that with everything else she had to worry about, the night was filled with coming loss. Her sense of belonging to the village was so tied to her home that she could scarcely think of Knightsbridge without envisioning Rose Cottage.

Yet what had disturbed her sleep the most lay deeper still. She could not escape from the sense that what she had said in front of the town meeting had not just accused her but also left her convicted. She was as guilty as anyone else in the hall of placing science upon a divine pedestal. She had treated her church activities as a part of the village society. She had welcomed the sense of connecting to the town, and the comforting peace most Sundays bestowed. But God had remained a benign father figure, safely ensconced upon a distant throne, watching benevolently as she scrambled about her daily life.

Now Cecilia tossed and turned, knowing it had been a lie. Her smug rejection of God's authority, the unspoken assumption that she could do it all on her own; she had mocked both her heritage and her faith with this conceited complacency.

Brian lay on his pallet in the parlor, defeated by the night. The house creaked and moaned gently about him, the wind whistling about the eaves and drafty windows. Every time he shut his eyes, he found himself watching Cecilia upon the stage once more. The fact that she had been so terrified had been clear to anyone with eyes in his head. And yet she had mastered her fear enough to rise and speak. He remained more than impressed with the woman's deed. He was awed.

Her dedication to the village, and her conviction over what she had said, had pounded him hard. He had spent two years running from everything, even himself. He belonged to nothing and no one. His life held no more meaning than a leaf blown by wayward autumn winds. In the past twenty-four months, he had done nothing not directly tied to his own interests of the moment. Her commitment shamed him such that he could not sleep.

He finally capitulated at four and went around turning on all the lights he could find. He spent another hour studying Heather's new letter, trying to subvert the sense of warning with yet another riddle. But the windswept whispers did not diminish, nor did he find a space where he could escape from the vision of Cecilia there upon the stage. Not, that is, until he found himself staring out at the night and facing his own distorted reflection.

The ancient hand-drawn glass turned him from a man in the prime of life to an ancient crone. His features ran, his hands shivered and flittered as they moved, his eyes looked rheumy, his skin mottled, his hair almost gone. Brian found himself unable to turn away. There before him stood the empty goal toward which he walked. Ahead lay nothing but the final isolation of a wasted life, and beyond that the unforgiving door of death itself. He wiped the perspiration that suddenly beaded his face and stared at an old man whose desperate gaze begged him to look beyond the moment and his own selfish needs. Pleading with him to turn, before it was too late.

Sunday morning, Brian stepped very self-consciously into the manor's front hall. Once again he wore Arthur's jacket and tie. As he walked down the stairs he heard the elderly couple emerge from their downstairs apartment. He said in greeting, "I hope you don't mind—"

"Always glad to have reinforcements," Arthur replied. "Even when the objective is the gates of heaven."

Gladys stepped up to give his lapels another affectionate sweep. "You really must stop by this afternoon, and I'll let out those sleeves."

"Nonsense," Arthur countered. "First thing Monday he'll be able to buy his own gear."

"Not a chance," Brian said, his discomfort rising.

That raised two sets of eyebrows. Arthur demanded, "You are truly that skint?"

"Down to my last couple of hundred dollars," Brian replied,

seeing no need to dress up the news. "Those weeks in the Sri Lanka hospital drained away time and money I couldn't afford."

A silent communication passed between the two, then Arthur said gruffly, "You seem like a good enough sort. I suppose we could loan you the odd bob until you're back on your feet."

"Don't stand on pride," Gladys urged him quietly. "We've all been there at one time or another."

Brian found himself rocked by the strength of his gratitude. "I don't know what to say."

"That's settled then." Arthur started toward the door and cut off further discussion by a swift change of subject. "Our Cecilia did us proud last night, wouldn't you say?"

"It was the bravest thing I've ever seen," Brian agreed.

"All of us have our terrors," Arthur said, blinking as he emerged into the sunlight. "Meeting them alone is the hardest challenge any of us ever face."

Gladys's hands fluttered excitedly. "Was it true, what Bill Wilke said last night? Did Heather leave you another puzzle?"

After their offer of support, there was no way Brian could refuse them the chance to read the letter for themselves, no matter how personal its contents. Especially not since Bill Wilke had opened and read the letter before handing it over. Brian pulled the envelope from his pocket and gave it to Arthur without comment. The old man halted on the graveled drive and eagerly began perusing the pages.

"Oh, come on now," Gladys protested, almost dancing in her impatience. "Either read it aloud or hand it to me!"

Arthur hesitated. "It's rather personal."

"It's all right," Brian replied. "Really."

"If you say so." Arthur adjusted his spectacles and began to read: "'My dear Brian, I have not had a good night. This wasn't at all what I had intended to tell you, but very little of my life is as I would have it just now. Last night I found myself looking back at a lifetime of mistakes, a theater in which you played a starring role. But it was not you who kept me awake. I thought of Alex. He was a good man, Brian. A very good man. You would have liked him immensely. He was kind and thoughtful and gentle as only a strong man can be. And I loved him. We had four years, two months, three weeks, and two glorious days together. Then he died.

"'I know you understand what that means, to love someone more than your own life and then lose them. So I will not dwell upon the horror. He left me. I desperately wanted to go with him, but I was too much of a coward to take my own life. Part of me still wishes I had done so, as the years between then and now remain filtered by his absence. But some deeper portion of me clung tenaciously to what no longer held any meaning. And so I went a bit mad.'"

Overhead a warm breeze tossed the trees about, tall fingers pointing toward a cloud-flecked sky. The sound was musical, a constant sigh of quiet sympathy. Arthur's quiet voice melted into the day and the song.

"'Two things saved me from going entirely off the deep end. The first was coming to God. I had no time for matters of the spirit before Alex left me. After, I clung to God with the desperation of a mad Englishwoman. And then there was your beloved Sarah. She was God's greatest gift to my remaining years. She is the one reason I can turn to God even now, and give Him thanks for my lifetime after Alex.

"'But last night brought me face-to-face with what I never

wanted to accept, not even to see before now. And that was, God had been ready to heal me. I don't mean that He was ready to see me through my remaining days. I mean, He was prepared to *heal* me. But I did not let Him.

"'I have never permitted myself to look so deeply at my past and my burdens as I did last night. But I know the truth now, and perhaps at some secret level I have known it all along. I was afraid that were I to permit God to heal my sad and wounded heart, I would forget Alex. Not forget Alex the person, but rather forget the power of what we had. And perhaps I would have, in some small way. But I see now, Brian, that in turning away from the chance to be healed, I also turned from whatever life God might have prepared for me. I not only turned from a full healing, I turned from God's intended future. It was *my choice* to dwell in sorrow all my remaining days. It was *my choice* to go a bit mad. In the dark recesses of my addled mind, I thought this might hold Alex a bit closer. And perhaps it did. But it was the closeness of the shroud, one I should have set aside after a proper time of mourning. But I did not. And the result was, I did not heal.

"'We are pushed ever closer to the eternal door and the question, How will we be received? I dread this meeting. I shall be brought before the throne of light, and I shall fall prostrate in shame to the floor. The fact that I know I shall be forgiven counts for little just now. I have failed to serve my Master as well as I should. Oh, the gentle hand turned aside, the gentle invitation ignored. Oh, the chances lost. Oh, my Lord, my Lord, forgive me.'"

Gladys sniffed loudly and rubbed at her eyes. "Poor, dear Heather," she murmured.

The day's quiet song took the words and joined them with the whispering wind, weaving it into the fabric of light and Sabbath peace as Arthur continued reading, "'Brian, I share with you as only one can who knows the cost of lifetime mistakes. Do not do as I have done. Do not bind yourself to what is now finished and buried. God will heal you, if only you allow. What you lose, in terms of closeness to your beloved Sarah, is in truth already gone. In God's time, you will be rejoined. Until then, accept what God has in store for you. Accept His healing. Accept His future. Do this for Sarah, for God, for yourself, and for me.'"

Arthur halted there, removed his glasses with the hand holding the letter, and wiped the edges of his eyes. The gaze he gave Brian was full of all the things that from necessity would remain unsaid.

Arthur fumbled a bit as he replaced his glasses, cleared his throat, and continued, "'Here, then, is your next riddle. There are times when only by facing one's greatest fear can one grow. Remember Sarah's own time of woeful childhood fright. Remember the treasure trove she found by growing beyond, by searching where was hardest, by learning to do what did not come naturally. And heal, my dear sweet boy. Find the treasure of a worthwhile tomorrow.'"

18

As they approached the front gates, the sound of Rose Cottage's front door halted them again. Gladys offered Cecilia a smile tinged by unshed tears and said, "Good morning, dear."

Cecilia held to the same sense of smallness and fragility that had shadowed her the previous night. Her voice sounded tiny as she asked, "Do you mind if I walk with you?"

"My dear, it would be an honor," Arthur replied. "I can't tell you how impressed I was by your—"

"I'd rather not talk about it," she replied quickly.

"Of course, of course," Arthur said, casting Brian a questioning gaze before gesturing toward the waiting day. "Shall we be off?"

Brian walked alongside the village doctor and listened with one ear as Gladys spoke with forced vivacity about the continuing spell of good weather. Cecilia responded with single syllables, her face etched and drawn. As they approached the market square, all Brian could think to say was, "I'll come by this afternoon and try to cover that hole in your roof."

The words only seemed to deepen Cecilia's tense gloom. "It's not worth the effort, is it?"

"From the sounds of things, the weather around here can change at any time," Brian replied lamely. "Anyway, I'd like to do it for you."

Hesitantly she lifted her gaze, only to flinch as she spotted the town's meeting hall. But she nodded and said, "If you want."

"Very much."

Brian was halted from saying anything further by the sight of Bill Wilke approaching. The mechanic's massive girth was inserted into a suit purchased at an earlier, leaner time. The mechanic pulled him aside and muttered, "Wanted to take a quieter chance to apologize for reading your personal mail."

"It's all right."

"Thought I was going to be reading a riddle, didn't I." Fingers darkened by years of oil and grime fumbled with his jacket, his sleeves, his tie. "Didn't have no business in prying, as my dear wife has spent half the night reminding me."

Brian watched helplessly as Arthur and Gladys ushered Cecilia into the church without him. "You've called me a good mate. I can't help but consider you the same."

The mitt-size hand reached across the distance. "Do us all a favor. Find a way to hang about, will you?"

The service was already beginning when Brian stepped inside Knightsbridge's central church. He slipped into a pew at the back and nodded to the young couple seated alongside. The church was not large, yet it overflowed with heritage and beauty. The polished stone floor dipped and weaved, a tapestry of muted colors. The nave was separated from the rest of the church by a hand-carved frieze dated 1319. The pews had the same rough-hewn look as the latticework of beams high overhead, with seat backs stained and polished by seven hundred years of hands gripped in supplication.

Brian sat and rose and pretended to follow the ancient litany. In truth, his gaze remained fastened upon a dark head seated toward the front, sheltered on either side by Gladys and Arthur. Cecilia Lyons was all that he was not. She was deeply committed to her work and her life. Even her attitude toward the crumbling Rose Cottage was that of a devoted friend.

All the words of Heather's letter and the thoughts of his restless night bound together with the service, the choir, the Bible readings, and finally with Trevor's sermon. The longer Brian remained seated there, the greater grew his sense of being goaded toward a future, and all the fear the unknown contained.

He did not know what Heather's riddle was about, but there was no question of his own greatest fear. He was terrified of having a future. Planning for tomorrow meant committing himself to a place and a course. Commitments meant the risk of sacrifice, of being called to give and do and go beyond the comfortable. Shadows of soul-racking pain remained draped about him, so close he could feel them even within these hallowed walls. Brian knew he had no choice but to go forward, yet doubted his own strength to do so.

The sun was chased by a windswept cloud, and suddenly the church hall went gray and dark. Brian found his attention drawn toward the only electric light in the chamber, the one that shone upon the pulpit.

The preacher's rostrum was reached by a spiral staircase of

intricately carved marble that wound its way around a vast central pillar. The podium itself was sheathed in polished granite and inlaid carvings of saintly knights, and from it Trevor's voice rang with quiet authority. "In the sixteenth chapter of Matthew, we read that when Jesus entered the region of Caesarea Philippi, He asked His disciples, 'Who do men say that I am?' There were a number of responses, from a reborn Elijah to a modern prophet. Jesus then asked them, 'And who do *you* say that I am?'

"Jesus asked His disciples because He wanted them to go beyond opinion. He asked them for a *verdict*. He was telling them, 'Now is the time to declare yourselves before God and man alike.'"

Trevor looked out over the congregation and quietly demanded, "Who do you say He is? Are you able to stand before the world and declare that the Lord dwells in your heart? When voices throughout the land are raised in criticism and condemnation, can you stand fast and say that you are living for Christ?"

For Brian it seemed as though he listened to two voices. The vicar's tired, drawn features added as much dignity and weight to his words as the shining robes. Yet behind this voice there echoed another, one carved from the same timelessness as the chamber, one that whispered to Brian's heart, and beckoned, and challenged.

"It was Simon Peter who answered for all the generations to follow. He was the very first to declare in openhearted certainty, 'You are the Christ, the Son of the living God.' Jesus responded with the same direct certainty that marked all His statements, 'Blessed are you, Simon son of Jonah . . . You are Peter, and on this rock I will build My church.' Peter said the blessed name twice in that sentence—'You are the Christ, the Son of the living God.' He had removed himself from life's spectators. Jesus rewarded Simon Peter for being courageous enough to *declare*."

The sun chose that moment to strike the stained-glass window, casting the vicar's features in a golden glow. "Jesus did not reward Peter with an authority to erect earthly structures. Let us be perfectly clear about this. The word Jesus used, which today is translated as 'church,' was the word for *community*. Jesus was saying, 'You, in all your frailty and humanness, shall be remade into something so strong that not even the gates of darkness shall prevail against you. You, and others like you who commit to the truth of salvation, will be bonded together by the Spirit's gift.'"

It seemed to Brian that the vicar's own frailty spoke to him. There before him stood a man wearied to the point of fatigue. Yet he spoke with a confidence that rose beyond his exhaustion and his worry. He spoke with an authority that *defied* how he felt and what he feared. Brian found himself able to listen and accept, because there before him stood the power of a living example.

"Jesus does not expect perfection," the vicar continued. "He does not welcome you because you are either strong or whole in your own right. He *knows* you are weak, flawed, sick, worried. He is fully aware that you are human. And His response to all of us, no matter what our condition or our needs, is the same: 'Come home.' We also shall become part of this rock, this community, this herald to a dark and confused time. Find the hope, the healing, the peace, the power to face tomorrow—whatever you need, it is here in the Lord's open arms."

19

Cecilia's head poked up through the attic hole and said, "Gladys tells me you've found another letter."

"That's right." Brian shifted the final board into place and dug in his shirt pocket for another nail. "At least, Bill Wilke did."

"Are you sure I can't help you up there?"

"There's not room for two." Every pound of the hammer meant almost clobbering himself in the forehead, the crawl space was so narrow. "There's hardly room for one."

When he stopped hammering Cecilia said, "I can't thank you enough for helping out like this."

"I'm happy to do it." Brian tested the board, found it secure, and started sliding out on his back. "To tell the truth, I needed to find something like this to do."

She backed off the ladder to let him down. "What do you mean?"

"The way you stood up there in front of the crowd, it . . ." He was stopped by the look on her face. "What's the matter?"

"I was a miserable failure!"

Brian's laugh was halted only by the distress in her expression. "You were a lot of things, but a failure was not one of them."

"Oh, please." She collapsed the ladder with an angry clatter. "I was so nervous I couldn't even recognize my own voice. I dropped my cue cards. I sounded like a loon."

"Cecilia." He waited until she had turned to face him. "I don't know how to make you believe this, but I spent all last night convicted of all the mistakes I've made. And it was because of you."

She studied his face for any hint of mockery. "Because of all the blunders I made?"

"No. Because you did what you believed in, despite the fact that you were afraid."

"Terrified out of my skin," she woefully agreed.

"Right. And everybody saw that. And they admired you for doing it anyway."

"They thought I was nuts." She kicked the wall. "Not to mention the fact that I let Trevor down."

"Nobody could have done a better job," Brian replied with conviction. "Of that I am absolutely certain."

"You're . . ." She was halted in mid-flow by the sound of an engine revving just outside her cottage, one loud enough to rattle the windows. A horn sounded impatiently. Cecilia walked over to the window and said, "It's Bill Wilke. Whose car is that?"

"Mine, at least for a few days." Brian walked over to stand beside her and looked down. The car positively gleamed in the afternoon light. "Would you come for a ride with me?"

The walrus mustache parted in a wide grin as they emerged from the cottage entrance. Bill Wilke revved the engine another couple of times before cutting the motor. In the sudden silence he called over, "Grand afternoon for a spin."

Slowly Cecilia approached the car, then turned back to where Brian stood. "This is yours?"

"Miss Heather left it to the lad." The mechanic grunted with the effort of squeezing himself out from behind the wheel. He rose to his feet, whipped a clean cloth from his back pocket, and began stroking the already-gleaming hood. "Goes like a rocket, she does. Alex never took her out more than once a week or so, and only in summer. Clock doesn't have but four thousand miles."

"I can't thank you enough," Brian said.

"Think nothing of it." Bill Wilke gave Cecilia an affable nod. "Grand performance you put on last night."

Cecilia cast Brian an uncertain glance before timidly responding, "Thank you."

"Left a lot of us thinking perhaps we ought to do more. Spent a good few hours pondering on just that last night. That is, when the wife wasn't getting on me for opening somebody else's mail." Bill turned to where Brian was circling the car. "Any luck with the riddle?"

"Nothing so far."

"Well, sleep on it, that's my motto. Anytime you can't see heads from tails, have a kip. Wife says it's on account of my lazy nature, but I've solved more of life's puzzles flat on my back than I ever did deliberating."

Brian knew it had to be said. "About the bill for the repairs. I'll have to wait until you sell it to pay—"

"Like I said yesterday, lad. Think nothing of it. You're good for what you owe, of that I have no doubt." He squinted into the sunlight. "Lovely day, ain't it."

"Fantastic," Brian agreed, wishing there were some way to offer real thanks. "Been like this ever since I arrived."

"Then you're lucky. Rained all but three days last month. We often get a nasty June. And July. Mind you, August can go right

179

off. Had snow one August, 1963 it was, the year I repaired my first E-type. That was one nasty job. The fellow got halfway down the street, and the motor blew right off the frame."

Cecilia asked, "What did you do?"

"Took off for parts south, what do you think?" The twinkling eyes surveyed the two of them, and Bill Wilke seemed to nod his approval. But all he said was, "Foot of snow we had that August day. Eighty degrees two days later. That's England for you. All the weather, all the time."

Brian asked, "Anything I should know about driving this car?"

"Turn the key in the ignition, press on the gas, put it in gear, aim, and shoot. That's the way most motorcars work this side of the puddle." He nodded once more. "Guess I'll be off, then."

"Can I give you a lift?"

"Thanks, lad, but I live just past the good doctor's clinic. Been within sound of the village bells all my life." His look to Cecilia was one of deep affection. "Almost forgot how much all that clatter meant to me, or what it stood for. Guess too many of us did."

In the silence of his passage, Brian found himself smiling at Cecilia's look of utter confusion. When she finally turned his way he asked, "Ready to go?"

~

Cecilia found herself unable to hold back the smiles. The wind pushed and buffeted and rushed in her ears. The sun warmed and tickled the edges of her mouth. The car roared and bounced her about upon the stiff springs and hard leather seat. Every corner threw her one way or the other. She could see how Brian was forced to grip the wheel tightly and use real effort to make the turns. He kept to the small country lanes, roads so narrow he had to slow and pull to one side to allow oncoming traffic to pass. The lanes were bordered by high hedges and even taller trees, opening only when they entered hamlets of a dozen houses and a church and a pub, then closing back again to fragrant green burrows.

He halted at a sign posted on a squat stone marker with hand-painted names. She was relieved to see he could not seem to contain his smile, either. Brian asked, "Any idea where we are?"

To Cecilia it suddenly seemed as though the entire day had been leading her to this point, where she could look at a medieval road marker and realize it was time to share with this stranger one of her closely guarded secrets. And feel in the process only a rightness as gentle and comforting as the afternoon. "Take a right."

Brian squinted through the narrow windscreen and read, "Wittenham Clumps."

She directed him down one country lane after another, until the road ended at the base of a hill so strange Brian could only gape and say, "Is this natural?"

Cecilia opened her door and asked, "Feel like taking a walk?"

A narrow path cut a swath through fields of ripening grain, leading up a steep-sided hill that looked like a perfectly fashioned golden cone. As they walked, she pointed ahead and explained, "This is a dwelling area that dates back to the time of Stonehenge. Back before the Roman era, a tribe cleared the hillside and planted their crops. They founded their village in the forest you see at the top. They built two walls—an outer barrier of thorn bushes that still grows today, and an inner one of stone. Their final defense was the forest. They left the trees standing close and tight, protecting them from invaders and the weather."

She led him up and into a crown of trees so tall and dense neither sun nor wind could enter. Cecilia found herself tempted to halt here, where the loudest sound was birdsong and the strongest sensation was of peace. But this was not why she was here, and to do anything less than complete the task would be to leave unfinished a truly fine day. She pointed to the path leading out the forest's other side. "Let's go this way."

The sun seemed doubly warm after the forest's cool embrace. Brian followed her along a path too narrow for them to walk side by side, and drank in a view so complete it seemed as though he could see to the end of this fair isle and beyond. Fields stretched out to join the misty gray horizon, dotted with little villages and church spires and stone border walls and tree-lined lanes. The River Thames cut a mirror-green swath through the land. Clouds flittered overhead, painting the landscape with cool shade before racing away. They took the path on the hill's opposite side from where they ascended, down toward a narrow, tree-lined valley.

The day was so quiet, the air so warm, even the raven's caw seemed content. Cecilia did not speak as she led him along the steep path, through meadows resounding with the lowing of cattle. Up ahead, the hay rippled and waved a golden welcome. Thistle lining the pathway bloomed chest-high and filled the air with summer snow.

The wind sang a distinctly English tune, cheerful and warm.

It chanted a myth, promising only fair days to come, neither rain nor chill nor blustering dark days of foreign seasons. And because the sun and the birdsong and the fair lass beside him found answering chimes within his heart, Brian smiled his pleasure of the fable and the teller both. Because he could give himself fully, because the chains of past seasons did not hold him in the here and now, he found it possible to call this day eternity, and so the fable became real.

They reached the base of the hill and entered a narrow cut. A copse of ancient chestnut and oak closed in about them. Cecilia led him to where the tiny valley took a sharp right turning, and halted before a church. It was a tiny structure, so old the stones seemed to have melted and run together. A thick mantle of moss dressed the slate roof. The same green adorned the waist-high stone wall, within which grew five massive trees. Tombstones dotted the church forecourt, markers from which all traces of names and dates had been washed away, as though to say that here such minor things no longer mattered—these people rested easy, and that was all one needed to know. Cecilia led him to the single stone bench which was still upright and level. Overhead two trees had grown to be so intertwined it was impossible to say where one stopped and the other began. The expression on her face said this was a long-standing habit. Brian settled down there beside her and felt the silence seeping into his very bones.

Finally she spoke, her voice as quiet as the wind. "I found this place my first year in medical school. We're only about twenty miles from Oxford."

He found himself unwilling to disturb her flow and the moment with words of his own. So he leaned upon the stone wall and let her go forward alone. She breathed a pair of long sighs, then continued, "My parents were never happy. They seemed to enjoy quarreling. My mother was English, I've told you that. My father was in the military. She hated America; she moaned constantly about how much she missed her little English village. It was only when I graduated from college and won a scholarship and came back . . ."

She halted once more, and this time the silence was long enough for the birdsong to speak in her place. Brian felt no desire to push the conversation in any particular direction. The day had its own course, certain as a river's. His task was to chart it and follow it as well as he could.

"Everything was so different from what I expected," she finally continued. "I was so alien and so totally alone. Then I met Mark. He was doing his residency in cardiology at Radcliffe, that's the Oxford hospital. That year we became engaged to be married. This was my second try at commitment; I also got engaged as an undergraduate. His name was Steve, and the only thing he shared with Mark was an absolute confidence that if he loved me deeply enough and argued long enough, he would turn me from my dream of becoming a country village doctor. That is the clearest memory I have of both my engagements, the quarrels. It seemed as though I was doomed to the same kind of life as my parent's. So I broke off both engagements. But each time it seemed as though I had cut off a part of my dream, and my own soul as well."

A pair of gray doves fluttered down, their wings gentle summer thunder. They waddled before the bench, cooing in sympathy as Cecilia went on, "This place became my refuge. I would come here and cry and try to sort through the mess I was making of everything. I knew part of what drove me was my mother's own unanswered dream of returning to live in an English village. Even so, it was *my* dream now. And I didn't want to give it up. Even if it meant having to live my life out alone." There was another long sigh, this one so harsh it rattled her throat. Then, "When I first came to Knightsbridge, I made the worst mistake of all, at least as far as the men in my life. I started up with a local. A dashing fellow, village born and raised, so handsome and charming." She cast him a shamefaced glance. "You know him."

Brian guessed, "Joe Eaves."

"Did somebody tell you?"

"No. I just thought there was more to the argument I saw you have with him than a hole he was digging in your front yard."

She nodded glumly. "What a disaster that was. I never figured out the real man behind his bright smile and his glib tongue. After a while I just stopped caring. But by then I was Joe's girl. Everybody in the village knew about us. So when I broke things off, I just accepted that I was fated to spend my life here alone. I worked, I had my few friends like Trevor and Molly and Arthur and Gladys, I had my little cottage. Most of the time it was almost enough."

"I'm so sorry, Cecilia." It was not much, but it had to be said. "Both about the problems you've had and about your losing Rose Cottage."

She studied the sun-splashed church and abruptly asked, "Do you have a strong relationship with God?"

"No. I did, though. For a while." At any other time, it would have seemed an odd question. But here there was nothing forbidden, no secrets that were to remain unshared. "Sarah and I attended church. When she became ill, we started taking religion a lot more seriously. We prayed for her healing, and then after a while I found myself just praying for comfort. After she died, God and religion were left behind with everything else."

"Were you angry with God?"

"To be perfectly honest, I really can't say. We were both pretty ready by the time it finally happened. She had been sick long enough, and I didn't want to see her suffer any more."

The words came easily, without pain, almost without regret. It seemed as natural as the day and the wind to confess, "Maybe I was angry with God, but I was so hurt and so lost I couldn't really say for certain one way or the other."

Cecilia asked in a gentle voice, "And now?"

Brian continued to look out over the tiny tousled courtyard and the church and the trees and the day. When he spoke, it was not in regret, but in peace. "Sarah would have loved it here."

They rose then, their time done. Brian walked over to the nearest tombstone and found his heart inscribing his own words of parting upon the time-washed surface. Written this time with the clarity of passage and the strength of healing. He reached down and patted the stone, then turned away.

Halfway back up the hillside, Cecilia reached behind her, and it seemed the most natural thing in the world for Brian to lean forward and take her hand.

20

They pulled into Castle Keep's gravel drive and cut the motor. Brian felt as though his body still rocked and hummed in time to the now-silent engine. Cecilia turned to him and said, "I can't thank you enough for a lovely day."

"Sharing that church with me was very special. I wish I knew how to tell you . . ."

She stopped him with a hand on top of his. "You've done just fine."

They sat in companionable silence, the narrow cockpit forcing them into intimate closeness. Then he heard voices outside the front gates and the treads of several feet start down the drive. He was pleased to see Cecilia frown, for that was how he felt as well. As though the outside world was encroaching on them and their special day all too soon.

She leaned closer still and said, "Let me cook you dinner tonight."

He could not help but smile. "That would be fantastic."

"I wouldn't call it that so swiftly, if I were you. I don't know what I have in the fridge, and it's Sunday, so all the shops are closed."

"I'm sure it will be fine." He rose from the car to greet Arthur and Trevor as they hurried toward them.

The two men bore worried expressions. Arthur halted and announced, "Bad news, I'm afraid. Someone's broken into the charity shop and stolen the dollhouse."

21

Together with Trevor and Arthur, Brian and Cecilia rushed down the narrow lanes and crossed a market square dappled with late afternoon light. A single police constable stood outside the charity shop's main entrance, making notes in a leather-bound book. Together they made a cursory examination of the exterior, which yielded nothing. The back door had been jimmied, then apparently the thief had waited in the shadows for a moment when no one was looking through the window. As they inspected the shop's interior, a chorus of wails rose outside the shop as word spread and more young girls arrived to bemoan the loss.

As the police finished up, Trevor surveyed the shop with tragic eyes and complained, "Seven hundred and nineteen pounds."

"What's that, Vicar?" the constable demanded.

"How much we've raised through the sale of raffle tickets. Seven hundred and nineteen pounds."

The policeman asked, "You're certain this dollhouse was the only thing stolen, Vicar?"

"As far as I can tell."

"Let those who want have a refund, but I doubt there will be many takers," Arthur said kindly.

Trevor led them out the back, and with the constable's help secured the door as best he could. "The dollhouse was the biggest moneymaker of all. We planned to draw the winning ticket as the highlight of our celebration when the bells are rededicated." Even from behind the shop they could hear the chorus of woe rising from the market square. "Those poor children."

"If we turn up anything, we'll be in touch." But the policeman's tone suggested that he very much doubted it would happen. He touched the rim of his cap. "Evening, all."

They trod back around the shop and bid the dejected vicar a farewell. As Brian, Cecilia, and Arthur started back toward the manor, the old gentleman mused, "You know, we may be missing something here."

Brian continued to watch the vicar's departing back as he asked, "What's that?"

"What if the burglars weren't after the dollhouse at all?"

Cecilia pointed out, "But that's all they took."

"Exactly!" Arthur looked from one face to the other. "What if it wasn't the dollhouse they were after, but another hidden hoard?"

"You took the entire dollhouse apart," Cecilia reminded him, "and didn't find any other secret compartment."

Brian realized he could not let the vicar go off alone, so he hurried to catch up. Trevor heard his approach and turned to greet him with a questioning gaze. Brian stammered, "I just wanted to thank you for the message at church this morning."

"How kind of you."

"No, really." He struggled to find a way to express what his heart was feeling. "All day I've felt, well, enriched."

Trevor straightened gradually. "My dear chap, what a nice thing to say."

"I'd appreciate being able to come by and talk with you sometime."

"By all means. Shall we say tomorrow evening?"

"Perfect. Thanks." Brian could find nothing else to say that seemed adequate, so he merely offered his hand. "For everything."

As he dressed for Cecilia's dinner in his cleanest khakis and shirt, Brian's eye fell upon the letter. Heather's latest note lay crumpled and yellowed upon the dresser by the parlor's center window. He reread Heather's words, then carefully folded the letter and slipped it into his shirt pocket. Standing by the window, his eyes open and staring out over his back garden, he spoke aloud, "Thy will be done, oh Lord. Amen."

He turned away, immensely satisfied. It was not much as prayers went, but he had two years of rust to remove.

Sunday dinner was a cheerful affair, salad and omelettes and freshly baked bread. Over a basket of fruit for dessert, Brian shared with Cecilia the latest letter from Heather. It seemed the most natural of acts, a gesture of thanks for the blessings of that soft day. Midway through the reading she reached across the table for his hand. Brian sat and studied the way the kitchen's lighting softened her features. Even in repose she was very intense, this petite lady, with an air of intelligence so brilliant it turned her eyes to fiercely dark jewels. He noticed for the first time how a few freckles sprinkled the highest points of her cheeks. Almost as though she could feel his gaze, one finger of her free hand rose to stroke beneath her eye, then moved over to slip a strand of hair back behind her ear. He found himself wishing there was a way he could lean forward and trace that same line with his lips.

Cecilia chose that moment to look up. She sat there, staring back at him, a new depth to her gaze. "I wish . . ."

When she did not go on, Brian quietly pressed, "What?"

She rose to her feet. "How about some coffee?"

He leaned back in his chair, watching her still. "Sure."

"All I have is instant, I'm afraid."

"That's fine." He asked a second time, "What do you wish, Cecilia?"

"I wish I had been able to meet Heather." She filled the kettle and set it upon the stove. "What she said there was beautiful."

"I thought so, too. But that's not what you wished, was it."

Cecilia's movements halted abruptly. When they restarted, everything was in slow motion, as deliberately she poured hot water over the instant coffee and brought over the two cups. "How do you take it?"

"Black is fine, thanks."

When she reseated herself, she did not meet his gaze. "Any idea what Heather meant in her clue?"

Her sudden shyness kindled a pleasant warmth in him. "I've been thinking about that."

"And?"

Brian reached across and captured her hand, forcing her to lift her chin and reveal the confusion in her gaze. "Cecilia, I wish I could stay here at Castle Keep."

She breathed as though suddenly her heart was too large for her body. "I suppose that will have to do."

They sat there a long moment, drinking coffee and holding hands, the overhead light bathing them in a glow as yellow as freshly churned butter, granting a gentle intimacy to the tattered room.

When Brian finished his coffee, he rose and pulled her up with him. "Would you come over to the house with me? There's something I need to check out."

As they walked the gravel path beneath a star-flecked sky, Brian explained, "I remembered something Sarah said once. I think it was after one of her long conversations with Heather, but you know how it is, things get mixed up in your head."

"You can say that again," Cecilia murmured, and the night wind caught her words and tossed them skyward.

"The thing about the house that scared her the most was the attic and the stairs leading up. She described the top floor as a long, narrow hall, not much taller than Heather and running the entire length of the house. The stairs were tight even for her, and so steep she had to use her hands to climb. The place was full of dust and strange noises. She used to have terrible nightmares about monsters coming down from the attic to get her."

As they crossed the front hallway and started up the main staircase, he continued, "Whenever it rained or the wind blew hard, her bedroom ceiling creaked and rattled like beasties were racing back and forth overhead."

Together they walked down the middle floor hallway and started up the steps to the third floor. "What I just remembered was Sarah describing how Heather had turned this into a game. She and Heather spent an entire weekend making a list of all the things that scared her. Then Heather took the list up into the attic, and she said that if Sarah could face up to her fears, meet them head-on, the rewards would be greater than she could ever dream."

The attic stairwell stood behind a door that merged with the hallway, a crack and a keyhole the only signs of a door being there at all. Brian twisted the rusty skeleton key, pulled back the door, and went on, "Whatever it was Sarah found, she said it was like entering an Aladdin's cave."

But Cecilia did not start up the stairs. Instead she looked up at Brian and asked, "What is it that frightens you the most?"

He started to explain the thoughts of the previous night and how he had spent two years running from anything that hinted of commitment or responsibility. But the night seemed years ago now, back on the other side of all he had experienced and learned that day. He stood there in the dimly lit, dusty hallway, and realized that his entire world was changing. Altering so greatly that he had to search to find something new to be frightened of. And when he realized what it was, he wondered whether he should say it at all.

Cecilia cocked her head to one side. "Why are you looking at me . . ."

They heard the sound together. A scraping and a knocking from up above. Cecilia's eyes grew round. "Was that one of Sarah's beasties?"

Brian launched himself up a stairwell so narrow that his shoulders brushed each wall. The steps were almost as steep as a ladder, and he used his hands to climb faster. "Stay there!"

"You're not leaving me down here alone!" Cecilia scrambled up behind him.

He fumbled at the catch to the narrow door, slammed it back with his shoulder, stepped into gloom, and shouted, "Who's up here?"

Then stars erupted in his head, and suddenly his legs could no longer support him. He did not even feel the floor when it rushed up to catch him.

*

"Brian? Please wake up!" The voice worked its way through his fog and growing pain. "Can somebody hear us? Help!"

It was the near-panic in her voice that gave him the strength to fight off the blackness and the agony that took its place. Brian rolled over, groaning softly only because anything louder threatened to lift the top of his head. "Cecilia?"

"Over here." She almost sobbed the words. "I was so worried."

Brian could not rise to his feet. Pushing himself to his knees was enough for the entire world to thunder with pain. Cecilia's frightened face swam through the gloom, and he crawled toward her. "What happened?"

"I don't know. Somebody hit . . . Oh, you're bleeding." She leaned over, revealing hands tied behind her back. "Can you release me?"

"I'll try." Every word heightened the pain in his head. He

squinted and brought the knots into focus, but his fingers seemed unwilling to work. It took forever to loosen the cords enough for her hands to slip free.

Cecilia swiveled back around and cradled his head in both her hands. "Look at me—can you focus?"

"Hurts."

"I'm sure it does." She held up a bloodied finger. "Follow this, please. Good, good." The hand returned to probe his head, so gently that the fingers soothed the agony, at least momentarily. "Your skull seems intact."

He mumbled, "Did you see who hit me?"

"Nothing. Tilt your head back. Good." The probing continued. "I heard you fall, I rushed up, and I saw this shadow. Then I was hit, but on the shoulder and not my head. I fell and somebody fell on top of me, holding me down. Then he tied me up and left."

"He?"

"Had to be a male, he was too strong and heavy for a woman." She used her good arm to push him up. "Can you stand?"

"Yes." But only because she was there to support him. Even so, the steep attic stairs almost defeated him. Twice he swayed and thought he was going to fall. But together they made it down both sets of stairs and into the central parlor. With a groan of relief Brian collapsed onto his pallet.

"Stay right there."

Brian had to laugh at that. As if he were going anywhere at all.

"I'll go call the police and get my bag. That cut needs a couple of stitches."

Brian lay and listened as a doorbell rang and voices drifted up from downstairs. He could make out Gladys and Arthur's rising worry. Then he must have drifted off, for the next thing he knew the pain seemed fresher, and Cecilia was bending over him again. But at least now he could focus more easily, and he saw that there were three figures behind her—a very worried Arthur and Gladys, and beside them the same constable Brian had seen at the charity shop that afternoon. Brian murmured, "We meet again."

"Hold still," Cecilia said. "I'm going to give you a local. This will sting a little."

The policeman waited until Cecilia withdrew the needle to ask, "I don't suppose you observed any more than Dr. Lyons?"

"Less." Brian watched her thread the hooked needle. "I didn't even see a shadow."

"I've had a good look around upstairs. It appears the intruder used a high stepladder to scale your side wall and broke in through the ventilation slats. There are footprints all over the place. Any idea what was stowed up there?"

Brian felt a faint queasiness as the skin of his forehead was poked and tugged by the needle. "None at all."

Cecilia must have caught the change, for she paused and asked, "Are you all right?"

"So-so."

"Really, Officer," Gladys complained. "Can't this wait until tomorrow?"

"If we want to catch the assailant, we need to be on this immediately." But he wore the same skeptical expression he had shown at the charity shop. "Though to be perfectly frank, sir, unless you can tell us what was up there we have nothing to go on."

"He can't help you, and neither can I." Cecilia slipped a hand behind Brian's head, raised it up, and held a plastic cup to his lips. "Drink this."

The viscous liquid seemed to soothe even before he swallowed. He felt the warmth flow directly from his belly to his head. He sighed, "Better."

"Good." Cecilia smiled at him before turning to the constable and continuing, "We were actually going up to see what might be stored there."

Brian forced his suddenly sluggish mind to function. "Did you see any secret compartments?"

"Secret . . . I beg your pardon?"

"Oh, so Heather's clue was behind this little escapade of yours, was it?" Arthur brightened. "I say, that means I must have been right about the dollhouse."

The policeman turned toward the old gentleman. "You are referring to the house that was stolen today?"

But Brian found it impossible to stay around any longer. His eyelids drifted lower, and he fell asleep to the sound of Arthur's excited voice.

It seemed he was only asleep a moment, for he returned to the same excited voice. Even before Brian was released from the drug-induced slumber, Arthur's words took form in the dream. Which was perhaps why his first truly rational thought was the answer to Heather's riddle.

"Oh, look what you've gone and done," Gladys scolded. "He's waking up."

"I haven't bothered him a bit." Arthur prodded him with one finger. "Am I bothering you, old chap?"

"Do stop being such a booby." Gladys waved his hand away. "Cecilia told us to let him sleep."

"Can't sleep his whole life away." Arthur was immensely cheerful. "Can you now, dear boy? I say, would you care for some tea?"

Brian nodded, focused on his watch, saw it was just after one. "What are you two doing here?"

"I spelled Cecilia a few hours back." Arthur's grin was immense in the parlor's gloomy half-light. "Gladys insisted on keeping me company. How's the old noggin?"

"Hurts."

"Well, of course it does!" Arthur seemed to find great satisfaction in that bit of news. "You just had yourself a lesson in the school of hard knocks!"

"I really wish I knew what has gotten into you," Gladys erupted.

"Brian knows precisely what's kept me up the better part of the night, don't you, sport?"

He nodded and instantly regretted it.

"We know they stole the dollhouse because there's something more hidden away!" Arthur's voice brimmed with triumph of the chase. "And they broke into Castle Keep to find it!"

Gladys huffed but said merely, "I suppose I'd better go put on the kettle."

Brian took the opportunity to say, "Could you go get Cecilia?"

The old man's gaze sharpened further. "I say, you haven't come up with where it's hidden, have you?"

"Just go wake her up, okay?"

22

$\mathscr{A}$ few minutes later Cecilia's plaintive voice arose from downstairs. When she stepped into the parlor, Brian had to smile, though every movement of his face stretched and pulled at his wound. Cecilia wore a college sweatshirt so old the stitching had come out and the letters fallen off. Her jeans were washed to a chalk color, and her sneakers came from two different pairs. Her hair was tousled and her face lined with the sleep that was still in her eyes. Brian croaked in greeting, "Here we have what the fashionable doctor is wearing this season."

"I'm not on duty tonight so I didn't lay out any clothes." She knelt beside him and opened her bag. "I knew I should have given you an injection. That oral solution wasn't going to keep you out all night."

"The stuff you gave me was almost like an old friend after my time with the kidney stones," Brian said. "It wasn't the pain that woke me, either. It was Arthur."

The gentleman's gaze turned furtive. "I say, old chap. That's telling."

Before Cecilia could speak, Gladys appeared in the doorway and fussed, "Poked the poor man in his ribs, Arthur did. Ought to be taken outside and horsewhipped."

"Really, Gladys dear, that's a bit much."

Brian interrupted, "If he hadn't done it, I might have missed the dream."

"There, you see!" Arthur cried in relief. "Just as I said, the man was ready to get up."

Cecilia's gaze narrowed. "You told me he was in pain."

"Well, of course he is. All you need to do is—"

"Arthur," Gladys warned.

Brian said, "I asked him to go wake you."

"You asked . . ." Cecilia rounded on him. "In case you didn't know, I have to be at the clinic in less than seven hours."

"Which means we've got to hurry." Brian stretched out a hand to Arthur and another to Cecilia. "Help me up."

"You can't be serious," Cecilia objected. "You may have a mild concussion. You certainly aren't acting sane."

But Arthur was already hauling on his other arm. Brian grimaced, swayed, but held on to his balance. Arthur inquired, "Are you quite certain you're up for this?"

"Absolutely." To Cecilia, "It was a dream, but it was also a memory. Something Sarah said after one of her talks with Heather. It wasn't the attic at all."

"And all it took was a bump on the old noggin to sort things out," Arthur said, rubbing his hands in glee. "I say, perhaps we should write a note and thank the thief for—"

"Arthur, stop it, please. You're acting your age." Gladys appeared with two steaming mugs and handed one to Brian. "Drink this, dear. Tea is proper treatment for almost anything that ails you." She handed the second mug to Cecilia, cast Arthur a stern look, and added, "Except perhaps senile dementia."

Cecilia continued to stare at Brian in utter confusion. "Why did you wake me up?"

Brian took a sip, then sighed a sweet, milky breath. "I didn't think you'd want to miss this."

"Miss what?"

He took another noisy slurp, and a third, then set down the mug and replied, "Let's go see."

Brian led them along the upstairs hallway, turned the key, and opened the door leading to the attic stairs. He stepped aside, and let Arthur and Gladys crowd in for a look. "I say, they're rather steep."

"Exactly," Brian agreed, watching Cecilia over the two gray heads.

"You've lost me," the doctor said, but the excitement was catching, and sleep was a long-lost memory. "So?"

"So it's not as if they're exactly cramped for space around here, is it," Brian replied. "Why on earth build stairs so narrow you have to climb sideways, and so steep you've got to use your hands?"

"Unless," Arthur exclaimed, "they were intending to mask something behind it!"

"What I remembered," Brian said, beginning to tap his way down the hall, "was how Sarah said it was never the attic that scared her the most. It was the stairs. That was what she had the worst nightmares about."

"So what are we looking for?"

"I don't know," he said. "Just start looking."

Arthur banged his way noisily down the wall, saying, "Trevor will be absolutely livid when he learns what he's missed. Do you suppose I should go—"

"Arthur, do stop your nonsense." Gladys did not pause in her own banging to scold. "And really, what you intend to hear with your bad ear pressed against the wall is utterly beyond me."

"It's not out here," Brian decided. He left them to their soundings of the walls and began searching the hall door itself. When that proved fruitless, he started on the stairs, the walls, even reaching up on his toes to bang on the ceiling. All he uncovered was years of dust. He reached the top step and went back into the attic, his head throbbing now in time to every knock of every hand down below.

Arthur called up, "Find anything?"

"Nothing but a headache." He sat down on the landing. "I was so sure—"

"And you were right," Cecilia exclaimed.

He almost tumbled in his haste to join her. She was down on her knees, feeling at something a few inches above the first step's baseboard.

"You were looking at the height of an adult," she explained. "But it was a child who made this discovery."

Cecilia fitted a fingernail into a small crevice, and out popped a door about ten inches square. Four heads struggled for position, and Brian bumped his head against Gladys's, which caused him to moan as the others cried, "A secret handle!"

"Go on, Arthur dear, give it a tug."

"Wait, let's get Brian down."

Three pairs of arms pried him out onto the landing and propped him against the wall. They were all far too excited to comment on how he held his thumping head, nor did he himself particularly care. Arthur pulled on the handle, but could not make it budge. Impatiently the two women sandwiched him in, the three of them so tightly packed Brian would have laughed out loud if he thought his head would stand it. Together they heaved, paused, huffed, then heaved again. The handle gave with a reluctant rusty groan.

Brian watched in amazement as the stairs disappeared.

One moment they were sturdy and as solid as the house itself. The next, they flapped down like oversized shutters to reveal a dark rectangular hole.

The four of them peered down in astonishment until Arthur cried, "Stay right where you are, I'll go fetch a torch. Don't anyone dare go down without me."

The wait was just long enough for the thunder in Brian's head to subside. The old gentleman puffed his way back down the hall and breathlessly announced to Cecilia, "It's good you're here, I might have need of your services."

"Sit down on the floor, you great ninny," Gladys scolded. "You won't do any of us any good having a heart attack."

"If you say so, dear." Arthur eased himself down, then handed Brian the flashlight. "I suppose you'd best take over from here."

The light revealed another series of oversteep stairs, six of them leading down to a between-floors level. Gingerly Brian lowered himself until he was standing on the floor and shoulder-level with what had before been the first step. He ducked down, shone the light around, and said, "There's a tunnel."

"The excitement is definitely getting to me. Move over, dear," Gladys said as she collapsed alongside her husband, who had slid up to dangle his legs over the ledge of the opening.

Brian leaned over and duckwalked down the tunnel's ten feet. At the other end was a rough wooden door. He worked the latch, pushed, and the door swung open. Dust and musty air puffed out to greet him. He waved at a few scattering cobwebs, squinted against the dust, shone his light around, and found himself utterly beyond words.

"Don't just stand there," Cecilia called down to him. "Say something!"

Brian turned and shuffled back out to where three huge pairs of eyes waited. Arthur demanded, "What did you find?"

"Just like Sarah said," Brian replied. "An Aladdin's cave."

23

$\mathcal{B}$rian inquired, "Shouldn't you be getting to the clinic?"

"Don't make me feel any more guilty than I already do." Cecilia shifted the box to gain a better grip, causing the contents to jingle. "How's your head?"

"Okay, as long as I don't think about it."

Cecilia halted before a door with hand-etched gold letters proclaiming it to be an antique and curio shop. "This is the place." When she pushed against the door, somewhere in the depths of the shop a chime sounded. "Mr. Miles?"

"Well, if it isn't my favorite visitor." A little man with an oversized head and oddly cocked spectacles entered from the back. "Are you here to not buy something again?" To Brian he offered his hand and the words, "And you must be the famous Mr. Blackstone. How do you do? I'm John Miles."

Brian gingerly set the box he carried down on the counter and shook the man's hand. "Nice to meet you."

"The honor is mine, I assure you." He adjusted his spectacles, or tried to, which merely left them cocked at a different angle. "You look a bit knocked about. I say, is that thread dangling from beneath that bandage on your forehead?"

"Afraid so."

"Well, life in Knightsbridge has been far too dull since poor

Heather left us." John Miles stood only an inch or so over five feet, possessed a distinctly pear-shaped body on stumpy bowed legs, and had a way of cocking his head that left his glasses looking almost level. "I suppose the village should be glad to have you around. Though from what I hear, it won't be for long. More's the pity, I say."

Cecilia had set her own box down on the floor and wandered to the far end of the room. "Brian has something he'd like to sell to you."

"Well, of course, I couldn't pretend to believe you'd actually bring someone in here wanting to *buy* anything." To Brian, he explained, "Dear Dr. Lyons has been stopping by for, how long is it now, dear?"

"Almost two years."

"She treats my shop as her personal museum, you see. She latches onto the most valuable items in the place, moons and sighs about for a time, then turns distinctly hostile when I happen to find someone able to acquire them."

"You're supposed to keep them for me."

"Of course I am." He explained to Brian, "She has marvelous taste and no money whatsoever. Are you rich?"

"Am I . . . Definitely not."

"Pity. I am certain this young lady will prove extremely adept at spending someone else's money."

"I just happen to like nice things," Cecilia countered. She traced her hand along the lines of an inlaid cupboard. "This is pretty."

"It's also very expensive, I'm afraid. Rosewood with ivory and ormolu inlaid. French. Eighteenth-century." As an aside to Brian, he added, "Impeccable tastes. Are you sure you're not wealthy?"

"Bone dry." Brian reached into the box. "Cecilia says you might be able to help us find a buyer for these."

"Oh, well. This is quite splendid." The gentleman deftly took the glass object from Brian. "Instruments designed for a Catherine wheel, are they?"

"You tell me."

"Ah. Not a connoisseur of Victorian glass, are you?"

"I couldn't even tell you what you said."

"Quite. Well, the mainstay of these items is what they called a Catherine wheel. Named after a firework, which in turn was named after a rather obstinate saint who refused to recant her beliefs, even when she was tied to a great wooden wheel with rockets strapped to her body. Or so the legend goes. The baddies set her alight, and she began to spin, and as she spun she sang. Converted an entire nation with her passage." He offered Brian a quick smile. "I suppose that's where they came up with the expression 'Going out with a bang and not a whimper.'"

"You're a very terrible person," Cecilia declared from her corner. "Is the glass valuable?"

"Depends on one's definition of value, I suppose. It won't allow you to acquire the cupboard you're eyeing there, but certain collectors will be delighted." To Brian, "Did you find this stumbling about the manor?"

"In a manner of speaking."

"How astonishing. Mrs. Harding had me over a few times to value items. But all she cared to show me were some rather frayed carpets, two huge horrid hippo heads and a moth-eaten alligator." John Miles refocused upon the article, which was a long, slender glass pipe with a definite bulge at one end. "This is what we call a Crookes' tube. See the little object hanging in the middle of the protrusion here?"

"It looks like a butterfly."

"That's precisely what it is. These were very popular in Victorian times, made in huge quantities. It was hooked up to the Catherine wheel, which was really just an electric spark machine; I don't suppose you found one of those as well. It would have looked like a great wooden wheel on a stand, probably with a brass or ivory handle attached to one side."

"I saw two or three," Brian replied.

"Oh, excellent. The spark machines are actually rarer than the glass, and thus more valuable. Well, you would attach cables to either end here, then spin the wheel and create a spark. Not enough to kill you if you held the tube wrong, but it would certainly make you go numb for hours. The tubes light up, you see. Depending upon what gas was trapped inside, and what they used to paint the decorative item like this butterfly, it would turn a variety of colors. Cobalt blue, potassium red, and so forth. Back before the invention of the Edison light, these tubes were all the rage."

Cecilia walked back over. "Sort of the Victorian equivalent of our lava lamps."

The antique dealer took on a pained expression. "I very much doubt our ancestors would appreciate your comparison."

Brian demanded, "How much are they worth?"

Carefully he set the glass down on the countertop. "Oh, possibly as much as two hundred pounds for a nice one. And five or six hundred for the spark machine, if it's in working order." Mr. Miles adjusted his spectacles once more. "How much of this glassware do you have?"

"A whole roomful."

"You don't say. How splendid. I suppose I could take as many as a dozen."

Brian had to ask, "Until they sell, could you maybe front me some money?"

"Things are that bad, are they?" Mr. Miles peeled back the towels they had used to wrap the glass and began lifting others out of the boxes. "I don't see why not. I have a couple of collectors in mind who would probably take the lot. Shall we say five hundred pounds?"

Brian signed over the glass articles, accepted the cash, and held the shop door for Cecilia. Once they were back on the street he asked, "Why do you look so glum?"

"It's silly, I know. But I was hoping we'd found something valuable enough that you could save the manor."

"So was I," Brian confessed. "And it's not silly at all."

"How much do you need?"

"The death duties are six hundred thousand pounds." Just saying the amount depressed him. "Over a million dollars."

"I wish . . ." Cecilia spotted something behind Brian, and abruptly her face turned to stone. She demanded coldly, "Have you been following us?"

"Got better things to do with my day." Joe Eaves stepped up and gave Brian his ever-friendly smile. "Morning, your lordship. Looks like somebody took a swing at you. Don't say I didn't warn you about messing about with Hardy Seade."

Cecilia demanded, "What did you hear, Joe?"

"Not a thing. Didn't need to. I know all there is about the likes of our Mr. Seade." He slid between them. "Better watch out for the doc here, your lordship. She may not look it, but the lady has expensive tastes."

Brian said nothing as the handsome, lanky gardener stepped into the shop and called out, "Morning to you, John. How's tricks?" The dealer's response was cut off by the door slamming shut in Brian's face.

He asked Cecilia, "What is he doing here?"

"Oh, Joe knows everybody. He probably makes deliveries for the shop." She glanced at her watch, and said tiredly, "I have to go. I'm an hour late already." She started down the street, her earlier gaiety lost and forgotten. "I never told you why I finally broke up with him."

"It's none of my business," Brian protested. "And I'm not sure I want to know."

She acted as though he had not spoken. "Joe let it be known that he felt like Rose Cottage was his by right. Every time he came over, he would walk around the place like he was surveying it, just waiting to get his hands on it and start remodeling."

"That's another reason for me not to like him," Brian said, walking alongside her. "As if I needed any more."

"Joe claimed it had been the gardener's house for generations. That was why Heather had let him go; he had insisted to be allowed to move in. She refused and then fired him. Two years after Heather's death, he was still arguing with her. It was the only time I ever saw him angry, whenever he'd start talking about Heather stealing the cottage from him."

Brian continued up the street with her and softly declared, "If there was any way for me to keep the manor, I'd give you Rose Cottage."

She turned toward him, started to speak, then abruptly spun and walked away. Ten paces farther along she turned back, revealing a struggle in her eyes that kept her from speaking. Cecilia stared at him a moment longer, then walked on alone.

24

$\mathcal{C}$ecilia was barely through the clinic's front door before Maureen gripped her arm and tugged her down the passage. "Will you let go of my arm?"

"Just come along here, dear," Maureen sang, pulling her into the kitchen alcove and shutting the door. "Well?"

"I wanted to apologize to the patients for making them wait."

"Never mind that," Maureen snapped. "What did you and Brian find?"

Cecilia gaped at her assistant. "How did you hear about that?"

"My dear sweet innocent doctor, this entire village is talking about Mr. Brian Blackstone and his mysteries from beyond the grave. Gladys told somebody and that somebody told another somebody, and now the whole town wants to know what you've unearthed." She crossed her arms and leaned against the door. "You are not going anywhere until you tell me what you found."

"Alex's secret study."

"Alex, as in Heather's long-dead husband?"

"He had a study hidden underneath the attic stairs. Or at least he used this secret room for his collection of Victorian glassware." Swiftly Cecilia recounted their visit to the antique shop. "Now may I please see to my patients?"

Maureen pried herself away from the door. "This just keeps getting better, doesn't it?"

"I'm not so sure," Cecilia replied, only to be halted in the process of opening the door by Maureen's hand. "Now what?"

The older woman gave her a careful inspection, then opined, "You're falling for him, aren't you."

"Will you please let me get to work?"

"I can certainly see why," Maureen went on, staying right where she was. "From all accounts, he's not only handsome, but sweet and caring and eccentric enough to make for an interesting time."

"There's something else about him you forgot to mention." Cecilia managed to pry open the door, then as she slipped through the opening she turned back to say what was sweeping waves of sorrow over her heart. "He's also leaving."

Cecilia's first patient of the week was the tense business-woman, who paraded in and declared, "I am not accustomed to being kept waiting for over an hour."

"I am very sorry."

"I was forced to cancel two appointments, and this was after having my secretary call *twice* to make sure I would be seen first."

"Something unexpected came up. I do apologize," Cecilia said. "How are you?"

"Busy." She planted herself in the chair opposite Cecilia's desk and set her briefcase in her lap, using it as a shield. "You said you wanted to see me again this week."

"That's right. Are you over your initial case of nerves?"

"Oh, absolutely. This is a grand job. Almost as though it was tailor-made. I'm so happy."

But the woman did not look happy at all. "So you don't need a refill of the tablets I prescribed?"

"Well, yes, I suppose . . ." The woman's hands clutched the top of her case like talons. "Perhaps it would be best if I could have them just a bit longer. For insurance."

"I see." Cecilia inspected the taut features, the gray tint ringing her lips and eyes. She leaned across her desk and asked quietly, "How are you really?"

The woman's lips were pressed so tightly together they barely emitted the word, "Terrible."

"Why is that?"

"I don't know!" The internal struggle sent tremors through her entire frame. "It's absurd, really. I've fought all my life to get precisely where I am now. I should be ecstatic."

"But you're not."

The tremors rose to shake her head. "There's so much riding on my every act. I had no idea it would be so intense. And everybody is waiting for me to fail. They watch me like vultures."

Although they had nothing in common, and Cecilia could not even recall the woman's name without glancing at the chart, still she felt a sudden bonding. "Everybody expects you to have all the answers, and you can't show any weakness."

"Not for an instant."

"And you're so alone."

The tremors formed a nod.

"I'm afraid I can't help you. Not in my role as a doctor,"

Cecilia said, as inwardly she listed all the problems she faced herself. The impossibility of treating a child whose illness she could not diagnose. The threat of losing her home. The utter shambles she was making of her private life. Even so, she felt a strong inner urging to continue, "But I can offer you some advice, woman to woman, if you're interested."

"Yes. That is, of course."

"Accept that you are not perfect, that you don't have all the answers, and that you can't make it on your own." She trod carefully forward, glad indeed her own sense of rightness was strong enough to overcome the sense of sudden vulnerability. "I am finding God to be a very good friend to have at times just like this."

She waited for the woman to condemn her for meddling, but she said nothing at all. Instead, the tension seemed to ease slightly.

Cecilia took the silence as a signal to go on. "I am constantly being faced with my own inadequacies. There is nothing I can possibly do to correct so many problems in my world. I am finding more and more that I must have a source of support who is both more powerful and far wiser than I can ever be."

The woman stilled entirely, sat for a long moment, then said quietly, "I shall think upon what you have said."

"Fine." Cecilia scribbled on her prescription pad, tore off the sheet, and handed it over with a smile. "And this is just in case you need something else."

"Thank you." She rose to her feet, and when Cecilia rose with her, the businesswoman offered her hand. "I appreciate . . . well, that you care."

"To be honest," Cecilia replied, "I feel like I was talking as much to me as to you."

She waited until the door closed behind the departing

patient, then returned to her chair, bowed her head, and offered a few silent words for the both of them. And felt the turning grow stronger still.

"Trevor? I say, Trevor!"

The vicar's face appeared at his living room window. "Most people find it more polite to knock on the door."

"Never mind that," Arthur snapped. "Open the door, will you? We have an injured man out here."

A moment later the vicar appeared in the doorway. He inspected Brian's forehead and said, "It really is as bad as they say."

"Of course it is. And here you are, making your gift-bearers stand out here in the hot sun."

"How are you, lad?" Trevor stepped forward. "And what on earth is in the wheelbarrow?"

"A replacement for the dollhouse," Brian replied. "And I'm doing okay. My head hurts."

"A replacement?" Trevor's gaze flittered from the blanket-covered object in the wheelbarrow to Brian and back. "My dear chap, you've given too much already."

"Which is exactly what I told him," Arthur cried. "But would he listen to common sense? No, he would not. 'Load up the heaviest thing we can find,' he ordered. 'And cart it right down to Trevor's for the raffle.'"

"But—"

"None of that," Arthur interrupted. "Brian's mind is made up. What's left of it, that is. And the item is far too heavy for us to take back."

"I can't believe we got it down the stairs without dropping it," Brian agreed, grinning through his thumping pain. He had never seen the old man so happy. "Not to mention Arthur's puffing like an old steam engine."

"Cost me a few years, this trip. And I don't have that many left." Arthur gripped one edge of the blanket and bellowed, "Prepare to be amazed!"

He flipped back the cover, and Trevor gawked at what lay revealed. "What on earth is it?"

"We don't have the foggiest idea!" Arthur declared proudly.

"But it's heavy," Brian added.

"And old. And there's something written in what looks like Latin down there on the brass plate at the bottom. See that?"

The apparatus was a good four feet high, and made up of a variety of components. Thick handblown glass grew within a series of brass rings as broad as Brian's waist. Brian said, "I took some of the smaller ones by the antique store this morning. He said they were Crookes' tubes. They connect to something called a Catherine wheel."

"Victorian—of course, I remember seeing one in a museum." Trevor straightened and protested weakly, "It's too much, really. I can't accept this."

Arthur menaced the vicar with a ferocious frown and a clenched fist. "Don't you dare try your humble nonsense around me today! I've had just about all I can take, having this lad wake me at one in the morning to go hunting down secret compartments!"

"You were the one who woke me," Brian pointed out.

The mock anger was instantly forgotten. "Oh, I say, that's right, isn't it." Arthur dropped his fist and revealed the smile once more. "Take the gift, Trevor, that's a good chap."

"But . . ."

"It's like this," Brian said. "I feel indebted to all of you. Arthur, Gladys, Cecilia, you, the church, the village, I can't tell you how much it's meant to be here." He searched for the proper words to say, then sighed his defeat and confessed, "I've spent two years either running away or running toward, I never could figure that out. And then I came here, and now it feels like Knightsbridge is where I was headed all along."

"My dear chap," Arthur murmured.

"I'll probably be leaving in a few days, but while I'm here I want to help out with your troubles, just like you've helped me with mine." Brian sighed with the relief of finishing. "So please take it and raffle it in place of the dollhouse."

Trevor dropped his gaze to the huge device, spent a long moment searching for something to say, and could only manage, "What on earth do we call it?"

It was Arthur who swept a hand over the wheelbarrow and its load and announced in a grand voice, "Aladdin's lamp! That should set the village hens to clucking, wouldn't you say?"

25

$\mathcal{B}$rian enjoyed a merry lunch with Trevor, Molly, Gladys, and Arthur. They were the object of attention from every other table in the market restaurant. One villager after another stopped by to shake his hand and discuss the latest find. He talked little and in the middle of the meal found it necessary to take another half-tablet for his thundering head. Even so, he found the atmosphere melting barriers he did not know even existed, opening him to a group and a way of life he had thought lost to him forever. Not even the glares cast by the table in the far corner, where Hardy Seade sat with the woman from the village offices, could dispel the moment's glow.

He returned home to sleep much of the afternoon, waking to an improved head and a day more gold and soft than he would have ever thought possible. He dressed and left the manor. In the late afternoon light, the vicar's cottage looked drawn from a Renaissance painting, the ancient stone splashed with a light too pure to exist upon this earth. The noise, however, was very real. The market square was filled not only with stalls but also argument, as people talked about the bells. Everyone seemed to have an opinion, and all of them were loud. Brian felt eyes upon him from every quarter. Some of the faces offered friendly greetings; others glared and muttered before turning away. As he started down the tiny lane leading beside the church, a dozen bell-ringers passed him walking in the other direction, chiming a merry tune on handbells and wearing placards begging all to turn out and vote that evening for the sake of their village and their heritage.

Trevor's house was a hive of activity. Brian was greeted and ushered inside like a conquering hero, everyone either sympathizing over the break-in and the knock on his head, or blessing him for the second gift and speculating over its original purpose.

When Trevor opened the doors to his study, Brian offered, "I could come back another time."

"Not at all." He pulled Brian into the room, started to shut the door, then called loudly, "Mr. Blackstone and I are not to be disturbed."

A woman protested, "But Vicar, there's the pamphlets to be proofed and distributed."

"See to it yourself, will you, Agnes? And no calls, please. Take all messages down on the pad by the phone." He shut the door, and in the sudden quiet continued, "As if these last-minute gyrations will solve a thing. There is not a single soul within a hundred miles who hasn't already heard about these bells and formed an opinion."

"I really should come back another time."

"Your visit is a blessing," Trevor replied firmly. "I've been worried sick over this coming vote. I've spent far too much time agonizing over the might-becomes, and not paying any attention whatsoever to the here and now."

"I don't think I've ever been called a blessing before."

"You have earned that accolade a dozen times and more."

He pointed Brian into a seat by the empty fireplace, settled himself, then continued, "Now tell me what's on your mind."

Brian had hoped for a chance to ease himself into the act of confessing, but the tumult filtering through the closed door pressed him to launch straight in. "There has been a lot pressing down on me lately. Cecilia's talk the other night, gaining the manor only to lose it again, Heather's letters, your sermon, a lot. Everything seems to be forcing me to look at how I've drifted away from God since Sarah died."

He watched as Trevor settled deeper into the sofa, and saw how the tight furrows around the vicar's eyes and mouth and across his forehead began to ease. It was the greatest sign of rightness Brian could have found. "Sarah came to faith in college. I think . . . No, that's not right. I *know* I became involved with faith because of my love for her. After she died, I ran away. From my job, my life, my world, everything. Including my God." Brian released a breath he had not even been aware he had been holding. "Now I don't know if I can find my way back."

Trevor nodded slowly, back and forth, waiting patiently to ensure that Brian had finished speaking. Then he said softly, "And in her illness, she drove you to prayer."

"So hard I could feel the blood dripping from my forehead," Brian agreed, remembering those harrowing times, yet feeling safe in the here and now. "So hard I could carve my prayers on stone by thought alone."

"White-hot prayer. Desperate prayer. Fervent prayer," Trevor continued quietly. "And your Sarah came, and your Sarah went. And you are the better for it."

Brian felt the doors of his heart creak open, the disused portion of his life flicker with a light he had forgotten had ever been kindled. "So much," he murmured.

"And now the season for mourning is over," Trevor went on. "You won't forget her. She is a part of you always. But the question you face now is, What will come next?"

"It's a question," Brian confessed, "I wasn't ready to ask myself until I arrived here."

"The fact that you are asking at all is the greatest sign we could find of your healing. The fields have lain fallow for their season. Now you are asking yourself, What should I plant?" Trevor leaned forward, clasping his hands upon his knees. "You have already seen for yourself that the darkest depths are not too distant for God to find you. You have called upon Him in your own dark night. Now learn to greet Him in the light of day."

Brian hesitated, then confessed, "I don't know what to say to Him anymore."

"The strongest prayer is not one of asking for earthly needs, though too many people feel that is the only reason to pray at all. The greatest petition we can place before the holy throne is the request to be brought into the presence of our Lord. Seek Him, and in your seeking find your own way forward. Let Him show what is to come next, not by asking for guidance, but rather by begging Him to enter and dwell within you." Trevor's eyes glowed with a light that defied his weariness. "If you can only find your way back to your knees, you will discover that step-by-step you are moving ever closer to holy ground. Of this I am absolutely certain."

26

The sense of peace from the vicar's words and their ensuing prayer was so strong that Brian remained untouched by the commotion as he bid the volunteers farewell and promised to return for the vote that evening. Trevor walked him outside, stood upon the landing, and said, "May I share with you a rumor?"

"Sure."

"Well, more than rumor, actually. You would be surprised what one learns in my position. It seems my bells and your manor are more closely tied than either of us expected."

There arose a heightened clamor behind them. Trevor's face gradually settled back into his tired pinched lines. "It appears that Hardy Seade will offer the only bid at Wednesday's auction, and his is backed by a very large chemical firm." Trevor went on. "They want to keep the manor intact for offices, you will be happy to hear. But all the outbuildings will be destroyed, if my information is correct, which I fear it is."

"We've heard something about that from the gardener." Brian shook his head. "Poor Cecilia."

"Yes, I have dreaded passing on that bit of information." Trevor squinted toward the tumultuous market square, then continued, "Apparently, all this quarreling over the bells began because the lab asked for them to be silenced."

"You've got to be kidding."

"I agree, it sounds quite absurd. But I have it on very good authority that they intend to use animals for the testing of certain chemicals, and they fear the bells will disturb them. They decided it would be less expensive to silence the bells to than add additional soundproofing." The vicar's smile was too tight to hold any humor. "Naturally, they don't want to let this out, for fear of alerting the animal rights activists. And Lavinia Winniskill's husband has won the contract to construct the laboratories."

"The tweedy woman?"

"None other." Trevor walked Brian down to the end of his garden, and opened the gate leading through the stone border wall. "It is a pity, really, that Heather's manor has such a checkered past. She spent quite a bit of time and money toward the end, trying to have it declared a historical monument. But the place is such a mishmash; the records clearly show that it has been built and torn down and rebuilt five or six times. The original structure was supposedly a monastery dating back to the time of William the Conqueror, erected where Rose Cottage currently stands if the tales are true. The problem is, no hint of this remarkable heritage remains."

"Which means that without some kind of special historical restriction, they're able to do whatever they like to the place." Brian stepped into the lane. "I can't thank you enough for, well, everything."

"You are more than welcome." Trevor offered his hand. "Pity how you've arrived only to be tossed right into the thick of things."

"I really don't mind," Brian said, shaking the vicar's hand.

"I only wish there was some way to keep hold of the place."

"As do we all," Trevor replied. "There is no doubt in my mind that you would make a worthy master of Castle Keep."

Brian returned to the manor and prepared his evening meal, sorrowing over the coming loss. He could not help but feel as though he were failing Sarah by losing Castle Keep. Nor could he deny the powerful attachment he was forming for the house and for Knightsbridge. It was within these tattered walls and this stone-lined village that his life was becoming transformed. Here he had begun to turn away from the past, and started the struggle of learning to focus on what lay ahead. His entire being felt the desire to hold on to Castle Keep, to make it his own, to establish this as the place where his future would unfold. Brian ate his meal and stared out the kitchen window, marveling at how he could feel so sad over losing something he had known for such a short while.

When he finished eating, it seemed the most natural thing in the world to push his plate aside and bow his head. The words came with no more fluency than the last time, the plea more felt than formed into true words. But when he opened his eyes and saw anew the final faint splash of gold upon the western horizon, it was with a very clear sense of what needed to be done.

The strength of purpose was enough to carry him back into the parlor, where he lifted the telephone receiver and dialed the number from memory. As he listened to the ringing, he marveled at how easy it had been to dredge up the number, as it was to remember the voice who answered with, "Blackstone residence."

"Hello, Steve."

"Brian?"

"Yes."

"Is it really you?"

"What, you don't remember your own brother's voice?"

"Good grief, man, don't do this to me. Wait a second." There was the sound of a chair scraping across the floor. "All right. Is this really Brian?"

"I just said it was."

A woman's voice sounded in the background. Steve said, "It's Brian." The woman's voice rose an octave. Steve said into the receiver, "Where are you?"

"England."

"He's in England." To the receiver, "The last card we got was from somewhere more exotic, wasn't it?"

"That's right. Sri Lanka."

"He was in Sri Lanka." When the woman pressed on with something more, Steve said, "We've got more than one phone in the house, Carol. Go get on another line."

An instant later a woman's voice said, "I have to hear this for myself."

"Hello, Carol."

"I don't believe this. Brian, shame on you, you're making me cry."

"It's good to hear your voice again."

"Wait a second." There was the sound of rustling and someone blowing her nose. "How are you? Did you already ask him that?"

"You didn't let me," Steve replied.

"How are you, Brian?"

"Fine. Really."

"Your cards have sounded, well . . ."

"Grim," Steve finished for his wife. "Worse than awful."

"I'm good and I'm getting better."

"I almost believe you," Steve said.

"Your brother calls for the first time in two years. Believe him," Carol said, then went on to Brian, "Sarah had that relative in England, didn't she? The one she said was like a second mother to her."

"That's right. Her Aunt Heather." He decided his first call home in two years was not the time to go into details of what he found himself facing here, so he asked, "How is the family?"

There came the expected pause, then Steve replied, "Carol and I are doing great."

"How's Judy?" Judy was their daughter. She was a model kid, beautiful and sweet and a joy to be around.

"Judy is a godsend," Carol replied.

"And Rick?" Rick was their son. He had been fine until his teenage years had catapulted him into serious rebellion.

"No change," Steve replied flatly.

"Well, there's change," Carol added, her voice matching her husband's. "But nothing you want to hear about."

"Yes, I do."

"We're involved in something called crisis intervention," Steve said, "and that's all we're going to say for now."

Brian found the urge to give something in return for all their caring and their constancy so great it pressed like a fist into his middle. "I never realized how strong you guys had to be to just hang in there."

There was a moment's silence, then his sister-in-law said, "You need something important enough to keep you caring."

"And God to keep you strong," his brother added.

"I'm beginning to see the truth of both those lessons," Brian replied.

"Man," Steve sighed. "You really are getting better, aren't you."

"All the time," Brian agreed. "Just know I'll be praying for you. Every day."

On Monday afternoon Maureen slipped in between patients to tell Cecilia that the senior physician, Dr. Riles, wanted to see her. It was not uncommon for them to go days without more than a few words, dashing in and out, coming together only for their weekly briefing. With her nerves already jangling, Cecilia could not help but worry her way through the rest of her day.

After seeing the final patient out the door, she walked to Grant's door and tapped softly. When he called from within, she stepped inside and said, "You wanted to see me?"

"Come in and have a seat." He finished making his final case notes and carefully inserted the gold Cross pen back into the top. "I suppose you're off to the village meeting about the bells?"

She stiffened. "You don't think I should be involved?"

"I don't have a problem with it in the least. We're running a caring service here. Taking sides in a village dispute is a very healthy sign of settling into Knightsbridge, as far as I'm concerned."

She relaxed a trifle. "I might have made some enemies."

"That's their problem," he declared stoutly. "You are as fine a doctor as I've ever worked with, and you are showing every sign of making a solid name for yourself in the community. We're not in the business of firing and laying off and correcting life-long attitudes. All of which is why I was so concerned about taking you on." He smiled. "I can't tell you how happy I am to discover that I worried over nothing."

"Thank you, Grant. Both for the words and the sentiment."

He pulled a pocket-pendant from his vest and opened it to reveal a tiny pair of scissors. He pared a fingernail, inspected it, and finally said, "It has come to my attention that you might be having more than what might be considered normal feelings for one of your patients."

The denial was formed almost before Cecilia could stop herself. Shame and exposure left her voice shaky. "I'm sorry, Grant. It's, well, I'll need to correct things."

He showed an elder doctor's powers of perception. "Come on rather sudden, has it?"

"Totally unexpected," Cecilia agreed, swallowing to relieve the trembling in her throat. "I think I was more surprised than anybody."

"The medical faculty would tell you that such a thing as a doctor becoming involved with a patient is simply not done." He pried out a tiny file and began buffing the wayward nail. "Of course, one must be careful not to drop him in the midst of ongoing treatment and leave the poor bloke on the hob."

"Maybe so, but the sooner I stop being his doctor, the better."

"It's a minefield, of course. But we're not immune when it comes to falling in love, are we?"

Cecilia found it necessary to blink hard, merely to cover the sudden heat that filled her eyes. "No."

"The greatest risk, of course, is falling in love with a chap who's still grieving." He tossed a glance her way, there and gone in a flash. "Have you given thought to that?"

"All the time."

"Never met the fellow myself. But Mr. Blackstone seems stable enough, by all accounts. Kind. Intelligent. Handsome in a roguish way, if Maureen can be believed." A smile almost as swift as his glance. "Can't hurt that the bloke is rich."

"He's not, though." Cecilia found she had no choice but to show her misery. "And when he loses the manor there's every chance he'll be leaving Knightsbridge."

"Ah." A careful inspection of his nails. "And would you be planning to leave with him?"

"No," she said, both to him and herself, the misery exposed. "I've fought too hard to call this place home."

"That's a relief. We'd hate to lose you, Cecilia."

She rose from her chair, feeling that her self-made decision had blasted a hole through her heart. "Was there anything else?"

His look said he understood all too well. "I'm sorry, lass. Truly."

27

$\mathcal{C}$ecilia returned home from work utterly drained from the day and the fractured night before. She dumped her doctor's bag and papers and keys and purse on the kitchen table, then just sat there, staring at the sink and the dripping faucet, too tired to rise and make her own dinner. Her thoughts were a jumble of worries and half-formed fears, some centered around her patients, others about her house, and more still about Brian. None of her motives seemed clear anymore. None of her goals appeared worthy of the life she was spending to realize them.

Finally she managed to walk into the parlor, where she collapsed on the sofa and closed her eyes for what she thought would be a quick fifteen minutes. But when she awoke it was to discover she had conked out for two full hours, and the voting was to end in less than ten minutes.

Cecilia bolted from her house, raced down the lane, and was vastly relieved to find the throng gathered about the town hall still in noisy disorder. She waited in line, trying to make herself as small as possible, cast her vote, then joined the tide moving upstairs. As soon as she slipped through the door she spotted Arthur and Gladys seated beside Brian. They waved her over, pointed her into the chair next to Brian, then Gladys demanded, "Where on earth have you been?"

"Asleep. I got home from work and crashed." She inspected Brian's head. "How are you doing?"

"Fine."

He didn't look fine. He looked morose. "No dizziness or serious pain?"

"It feels more like a bad bruise." Gingerly he felt the bandage over his stitches. "How long do I have to wear this?"

"A few days, not more." Cecilia started to ask what the matter was, when the mayor climbed to the podium, banged the gavel for quiet, and announced, "Voting is now closed. We will count the ballots as swiftly as possible."

Trevor slipped into the row behind them and muttered, "There is nothing I hate worse than waiting."

"My dear fellow," Arthur exclaimed, "you look positively ghastly."

"I keep repeating that it doesn't matter," Trevor answered, clenching his arms across his middle. "But I can't seem to convince myself."

"It matters," Brian said grimly. "All of it does."

The comment caught them all by surprise. Gladys commented, "You scarcely look any better than the vicar."

"They're holding the auction the day after tomorrow," Brian reminded them.

A second pall settled over the little gathering, isolating them further from the tumult. Finally it was Arthur who straightened and said sternly, "See here, do you want to hold on to Castle Keep?"

"More than I've wanted anything in a very long time," Brian answered.

"Then it's settled." The old gentleman pounded his fist on

the seat beside him, and for an instant he shed his burden of years and once again became the general leading his troops into battle. "I knew Heather better than anyone alive, and I am absolutely certain she would not have neglected the issue of death duties."

"It has been bothering me all along," Gladys agreed. "But what are we to do?"

"Six hundred thousand pounds is six hundred thousand more than I have," Brian agreed.

"Oh piffle!" Blue eyes clear as winter's first frost glared at them. "What are we, a bunch of whiners?"

"No, dear," Gladys chided gently. "But we are rather poor."

"Nonsense. I for one am not willing to sit around and let Hardy Seade and his ilk walk away with my home!"

"But what are we to do?" Cecilia demanded, drawn to hope despite herself.

"The answer is in the riddles," Arthur said. "I'm convinced of it. And where have the riddles been found?"

"Inside whatever the last puzzle revealed," Brian said, a spark of interest flaring in his voice and his eyes.

"Precisely." Arthur used his fist as a gavel, pounding it a second time. "Then we must go back and tear apart that laboratory." He stared at them, one at a time. "Who's with me?"

Before they could respond, the mayor climbed back up and hammered the gavel. "The meeting will come to order. Silence, please." When everyone had settled as best they could, and those who remained upon the stairs had entered and found spaces around the back wall, the mayor continued, "We have arrived at a final count. Bailiff, do the honors, please."

A portly man with the bearing of a retired policeman mounted the side stairs. He dragged out the moment long enough for the people to begin stirring impatiently, hunting for his spectacles, coughing and fiddling with the page, dearly loving his moment in the spotlight. Cecilia found herself clenching the chair in front of her as the man finally began, "We are here to decide the matter, which reads as follows: 'Should the village churches have their bells restored, and the habit of chiming the hours be resumed?' The villagers were asked to vote for or against."

"Get on with it, man," someone muttered, and was swiftly joined by a restless chorus of assent.

The bailiff lifted his gaze and frowned the gathering to silence. Beside her, Trevor shifted nervously in his chair.

Finally the bailiff admitted to himself he could tarry no longer and released the news, "The ayes have it, five hundred and nineteen votes to—"

His final words were drowned out by the pandemonium that filled the chamber. The crowd on their side of the hall leaped to their feet with a great shout, and Cecilia found herself hugging everyone about her. From across the hall there were angry shouts and accusations, but the merriment that surrounded her was so great Cecilia could ignore them all. Her back was pounded by people she did not see, she shook a dozen hands in as many seconds, she laughed, she cheered.

Then she found herself staring into Brian's eyes, seeing the happiness and the melancholy mixed there with such tender openness that it was the most natural thing in the world to sweep him into her arms, and offer the comfort of a heartfelt embrace. Brian stood in stunned immobility for a long moment, then slowly brought his arms up and around her. And the feeling was so good, so complete, she could do nothing save close her eyes to the world and the commotion, and give herself over to the comfort she had expected to give, yet found herself receiving.

They were finally forced to release one another when Arthur stepped in close and cried, "One battle down and one to go! All right, who's with me?"

"Count me in," Cecilia said, running her hand down Brian's arm, squeezing his hand, releasing it, and stepping back, feeling still the embrace and the strength of the man.

The old gentleman lifted his fist in defiance to the crowd and the tumult and the night. "Tallyho!"

28

$\mathcal{B}$ut the search of the secret study proved futile. More than that, it was depressing. They began in the best of spirits, joined by Molly and Trevor, laughing and calling to one another, buoyed by the recent victory. Yet the hours ticked by, and with them their gaiety and energy drained steadily away.

Finally at midnight Gladys chided her husband, "You really must have a lie-down, dear."

"Nonsense." Arthur fumbled about, fatigue increasing his burden of years. "Has anyone checked the corner over here?"

"I did," Brian replied, using Gladys's words as an excuse to sit down. "Twice."

"I'm afraid I can't keep my eyes open any longer," Trevor admitted. "This hasn't been the easiest of weeks."

"There, you see," Gladys scolded. "And he wasn't up half the night like you were."

Arthur's shoulders slumped in defeat. "My dear chap, I feel like we've let you down horribly."

Brian's face mirrored the weary resignation in his voice. "You've done all you could."

"We'll start again first thing tomorrow." Slowly Arthur bent over to accommodate the tunnel. "Come along, my dear."

Cecilia and Brian were the last to leave, walking down the

stairs together, standing outside the old place beneath a star-chased sky. Too tired and too beaten to speak, she reached over and gripped him in another tight embrace. Only as she turned away, this time it felt more like a farewell.

Cecilia managed to make it upstairs and disrobe before sleep overcame her. The next thing she knew, the first faint tendrils of dawn were gracing another clear-blue sky. She rose from bed and dressed hastily, suddenly ravenous. She scrambled three eggs and ate them with two pieces of toast. Only when her stomach was full could she sense the same sorrow she had known the night before.

Her mind went back to the talk with the businesswoman, Monday's first patient. How clear it had all seemed then. How vivid the sense of turning. Cecilia found herself hearing her own words as though spoken by someone else. About the vulnerability and the need for answers she did not have. Her body began rocking back and forth, gentle motions driven by unseen winds. Her eyes closed, and her heart whispered words that seemed drawn from outside her, speaking far more clearly than she could herself, expressing thoughts she had never given voice to, until now.

Brian was glad he was alone when he found the letter. Very glad indeed. He had awakened an hour before Tuesday's dawn, eaten breakfast, and returned to the secret room because there was nothing much else to do. It was as he was packing one of the spark machines, turning the ivory crank and polishing the great wooden wheel, that he had heard a sibilant rustling.

Squeezing in close to the contraption, he had squinted and poked and prodded and finally pulled out yet another yellowed envelope.

"My dear Brian," Heather began, "I do so hope you enjoy my latest little surprise. Well, Alex's, actually. He discovered this place and these contraptions in our early courtship days. On our rare bad moments I would accuse him of marrying me just so he could claim them as his own. But never mind that. I hope they bring you as much pleasure as they did him."

Brian used the cloth to wipe off a low bench, then tested it cautiously before easing himself down. By the light of Arthur's flashlight he continued reading, "My hands are better today, perhaps because I spent half the night talking with your dear wife. These contacts with her remain the most brilliant light in my dimming vision. Sarah is truly an earthbound angel. But of course, this you know. What you most certainly have not heard from me before, my newfound friend, is that she deserved you, and you her.

"I spoke at length about this particular missive with your dear wife, and it has left me feeling restored. Not in health, but in confidence. I hope you will forgive me for mentioning Sarah here, but I feel it important to establish credibility. I have shared with you my mistakes. Now allow me to pass on some of Sarah's own wisdom.

"'The treasure you seek is not here in this room, of course. And I am hoping you have already begun to discover it for yourself. That is my hope for you, Brian. That this lovely village and this marvelous house will bestow upon you the most precious treasure of all, that of knowing God.

"'Prayer is the answer, dear one. Prayer gives us the strength to go beyond the boundaries of fear and pain. In order for you to heal, in order to live the life I refused myself for so long, you must learn to dwell within the refuge God grants us through prayer. Prayer then becomes a doorway to what lies *beyond* the pain and the fear and the past. Prayer will reveal to you the wonder of life in Jesus.

"'To arrive at this deeper purpose, you must develop prayer as a regular discipline. You must make it a constant in your life, and not just a sometime act. Prayer will grant you a very special distance, allowing you to step back from life and view everything more clearly—both the internal and the external, both the good and the bad. So my challenge to you this day, my dear, is to see prayer as a continuing surrender. Little by little, relinquish all that separates you from God. Your grief, your woes, your fears, your worries, your unfulfilled desires. Not every time of prayer will provide consolation or fulfillment. But only through the preparation of this discipline will you become ready for that holy moment when it *does* arrive. You must be brought face-to-face with the shadowy vista within yourself where God is not. Then you shall be ready to climb the glorious Jacob's ladder toward the miracle of a heart renewed in God.

"'Step-by-step you shall be brought to the pinnacle where you are smitten with bliss, where God shall implant within you His own holy desire.' Those are your dear Sarah's own words. I wrote them down as she spoke, knowing the message was intended not for me, but for you. Use the testimony of her own departure, and the strength she found in the midst of her greatest tragedy, to drive this point home. And grow beyond where I find myself."

Brian had to set down the letter there. He did not know how long it was before he was able to clear his face and begin anew.

Here in this windowless alcove time mattered little. The silence and the isolation only heightened the force he found there upon the page.

Eventually he was able to refocus upon Heather's words. He turned over the page and read, "I must apologize for the state of Castle Keep. I am not so far gone as to be unaware that it is a dismal wreck. I never much cared for the worry of maintenance, which is a full-time occupation with such a house. I was born here, you see, and tended to treat it with the same matter-of-factness that I viewed my arms or feet before they started going off on me. Castle Keep was simply a part of who I was. Big houses do that. They are either friends so close you scarcely see them at all, or your worst enemy. I am pleased to say that Castle Keep and I were on the best of terms, and I am certain the old dear has long since forgiven me for forsaking her so.

"Alex was the one who loved the task of keeping the old place up. After he left me, well, I dared not do anything that might fill the hole he had left in my life. It was a mistake, I realize that now. A dreadful one, and I have paid for it with half a life only half lived. Part of why I was so eager to be a part of Sarah's little plan was to save you from repeating my natural mistake.

"Now then. I expect you to set things right about the place, Brian. I leave all my possessions to you, with the express command to retain only what you truly care for, and burn the rest. I expect you to begin your destruction with the hippo heads, which were brought back from Africa by my grandfather, a ne'er-do-well who cost the family half its fortune seeking the lost treasures of Zin."

Brian dropped the letter to his lap, utterly confused. Heather did not speak with the tone of someone who was so addled as to forget the matter of death duties. And Sarah was bound to have informed her of their own financial state, particularly after the horrendous costs of Sarah's illness.

"So here is my next clue, dear one. On your knees you will need to search, falling prostrate as was done in ages past. Seek what is ancient and yet timeless. Beg from lowliest point for the highest gain. The most ancient places contain the newest wisdom. Seek on your knees with the hunger of a questing heart. Ask for the divine spark to ignite the fires of holy passion. And find more answers than I can ever give you alone. Yours ever, Heather."

Brian sat staring at the dark shapes and the glinting glass, mulling over the words and the riddle. It was only when the distant door creaked that he was brought back to reality. He heard a voice call down, "Brian?"

"In here!"

A few moments later, Cecilia's shape emerged in the tunnel. The instant she saw his face she exclaimed, "You've found another letter!"

"We're missing something," he said, lifting the yellowed page. "Something big."

$\mathcal{T}$ogether Brian and Cecilia rushed downstairs, where a knock on the ground-floor apartment door produced a very irate Gladys. Cecilia began, "I know it's early—"

"It most certainly is," Gladys declared, planting fists upon her hips. "It's barely gone seven!"

"I'm so sorry. But this is important."

"And so is a man of Arthur's age having a proper rest and a decent breakfast!"

"Could we . . . Are you saying Arthur's not here?"

"That silly old codger left ages ago! I didn't half give him a piece of my mind, let me tell you. Him rising at the crack of dawn, calling the vicar, the two of them shouting over some nonsense or another. Another call, somebody from Arthur's regiment, I didn't catch the name, I was too upset. Then off they go, headed for London of all places." She shook a finger in Brian's face. "This will not do, sir. Not do at all!"

"I didn't have anything to do with it," Brian protested.

"You most certainly did! Your—"

"We're so sorry to have disturbed you." Cecilia grabbed Brian's arm. "We'll stop by later."

The door slammed shut with a power to rattle the front

windows. Cecilia said to Brian, "I guess we'll have to do this on our own."

Together they descended into the basement. The vast chamber and its assortment of dusty beasts looked very daunting. Brian said, "We'll have to search the walls, I guess."

"On our knees," Cecilia glumly agreed. "Look for something low."

But two hours of grubby searching produced nothing but two pairs of sore knees and a number of very loud sneezes. Finally, Cecilia announced with guilty relief, "I have to go to the clinic."

"First you'll need a shower," Brian said, rising and stretching and walking over. He sneezed powerfully, then added, "So do I."

"You look like a dirty snowman," Cecilia observed. "Stop by and I'll give you a surgical mask. That will keep the worst of the dust at bay."

"And some goggles," Brian added. "I feel like clawing out my eyes."

They climbed the stairs, weary and resigned. At the front door, Cecilia took a deep breath of fresh air and said, "The others might have an idea of something we've missed."

"At least we've found another clue," Brian agreed. He took a step closer, then added, "You're a good friend, Cecilia. The best."

She started down the stairs, saying over her shoulder, "I'll come back at lunchtime, and don't you dare forget to come get me at the clinic if you find something exciting." She crossed the lawn, not minding in the least that she must have looked very foolish, smiling a filthy, dirty greeting to the dawn.

Brian was finishing an early lunch when he was drawn downstairs by the tinkling of the front doorbell. Gladys appeared in her doorway long enough to make sure that it was not Arthur returning, then slammed her door so loudly it resounded through the front hall like cannon fire.

The bespectacled little antique dealer looked nervously about as he said in greeting, "Great heavens above, what on earth was that?"

"Nothing serious. Nice to see you, Mr. Miles." But the warmth of his greeting was tempered by the sight of Joe Eaves standing on the next stair down. "Did you find a buyer for my glass?"

"I did indeed." He adjusted his spectacles to another odd angle, reached into his pocket, and offered Brian a pen and paper. "Sign here, please."

Brian inspected the figures and exclaimed, "Nine hundred pounds!"

"I did rather well on our mutual behalf, if I do say so myself."

"This is fantastic."

"Quite." The dealer accepted the paper back and inspected the signature before stuffing it in his pocket and drawing out an impressive roll of bills. "Here you are, the remaining four hundred quid. Naturally you are welcome to count it."

"I'm sure it's all there." The money made a comforting bulge in his pocket. "I don't know how to thank you."

"That's very simple, actually. Allow me to have more of that excellent glassware."

Yet as Joe stepped up to join the eager dealer, Brian found

himself reluctant to allow the men entry. "I'm not sure I want to go that route yet."

"But I thought you told me there was more."

"There certainly is."

"I've heard about the village that you're on the verge of losing the place."

"That's right. I am."

"Then there's not a moment to lose!"

But there was something about the way that Joe Eaves crowded forward, or perhaps the way he seemed to mock Brian with his easy smile. Or maybe it was just the memory of him and Cecilia. Whatever the reason, Brian said, "Just the same, we're going to have to wait on that one."

"But . . . But . . ." John Miles's hands fluttered about, touching his glasses, his skewed tie, his frayed collar. "I've already arranged for Joe here to help cart the articles back to the store!"

"I'll give you a call if I change my mind," Brian said, closing the door on the little man's protests. He reclimbed the stairs, feeling illogically pleased with his decision. The house and its contents and its secrets might not be his for much longer, but they were his just the same.

Cecilia spent most of her lunch-break completing paperwork she had planned to do that morning, then rushed down to the market for a sandwich. As she crossed the central square to return to the clinic, she spotted four figures standing in front of the charity shop, peering through the front window. But it was not a group of young girls this time, though they seemed to share the same strained excitement. She walked over and said, "Arthur, what on earth?"

"My dear, this is positively marvelous!" Arthur waved a hand toward a pair of dark-suited gentlemen standing between him and a grinning Trevor. Proudly he proclaimed, "May I have the pleasure of introducing Percival Atkins and his associate, Gerald Frost. Gentlemen, this is the famous village doctor I was telling you about, Cecilia Lyons."

The older gentleman was polished and handsome and as smooth as money could make. He gave a fraction of a bow and said, "Charmed, I'm sure."

"Percy was a member of my regiment, back when His Majesty had need of such wastrels and was willing to prod them into service with the sharp point of a saber."

"I say, Arthur, that's rather harsh." The man had eyes the color of a winter meadow, palest hazel and clear as glass. "He's never forgiven me for waiting to be called up."

"He was drafted, I believe that's the term you Yanks use," Arthur said cheerfully. "Not that he wasn't brave when push came to shove. He simply held to an odd notion that he'd rather stay at Cambridge than fight for king and country. Percy always was one for poking about dusty tomes and sorting stuff from other people's attics."

"Never mind all that," Trevor said, almost dancing in place with impatience. "Tell Cecilia what you've found!"

"Ah, yes. Well, this is all rather thrilling." Percy turned back to the display and the brass-rimmed apparatus on the window's other side. He motioned to the man peering through the window and said, "Gerald here is our in-house specialist on antique scientific instrumentation."

The young man was beside himself with excitement. "Could I possibly get into the shop and have a closer look?"

"Percival is one of the directors at Christie's Auction House," Trevor explained. "Arthur and I drove into London this morning with a Polaroid I snapped of the contraption. That's why they're here."

"I'll let you in there when you've told our young ladyfriend what it is you think we have on our hands," Arthur told the young man, then explained to Cecilia, "Stroke of genius, really, if I do say so myself. It occurred to me in the depths of night that if Heather failed to leave us another clue, it was because she had something rather special in store right here."

"But she did," Cecilia interjected.

"Did what?"

"Leave another riddle. Brian found it at dawn."

"I beg your pardon," Percival interrupted. "Who is Heather?"

"Never mind that," Arthur snapped. "What did you find?"

"Nothing. A lot of dust." She waved her hands in impatience. "What is it you've discovered?"

"Go on then, Gerald," Percival said. "I suppose you might as well tell them what you suspect."

"It's rather stronger than that." The young man was caught up in the thrill of discovery. "I am fairly certain what we have here is a very rare example of a medieval vacuum pump."

"Ether extractors, they were called," Percy explained. "The philosophers of that day were determined to draw out the invisible matter they called ether, and in so doing come to understand the basic workings of the imperceptible universe."

Cecilia protested, "But we were told it was Victorian glass!"

Percy and the young man exchanged a glance. "By whom?"

"A local antique dealer."

"Well, all I can say," Percy replied, "is that you are very lucky you didn't give him anything."

"But we did!"

For the first time Percy's aplomb was shaken. "You don't mean to tell me there's more."

"A whole room full!" Arthur announced with pride.

"A room?" The young man looked stunned. "Of glass like this?"

Cecilia demanded, "How much is it worth?"

Percy resumed the measured tones of a cultured auctioneer. "Hard to say, really. First we must establish the piece's provenance and see if we can determine who actually made it."

"Never mind that twaddle!" Arthur gripped the arm of Percy's suit. "Give us a figure!"

"Arty, really, this is Savile Row's finest you're wrinkling." Percy extracted Arthur's grip, then said to Cecilia, "I would estimate somewhere in the neighborhood of ten thousand pounds."

But Cecilia was already moving back across the market square. Trevor called, "Where are you going?"

She continued to gather speed, calling back, "I've got to warn Brian!"

By the time she passed through the manor gates, Trevor and the young auctioneer had caught up with her. Arthur and Percy's protests rose from the distance as they scooted down the gravel path, pounded up the front stairs, crossed the hall, and climbed the main staircase. By the time they arrived at the landing, Brian was already in his doorway and demanding, "What's going on?"

Cecilia puffed through two hard breaths, then gasped, "Do you still have the glass?"

"The stuff in Alex's study? The antique dealer came by for more, but—"

"Don't give him a thing!"

"I didn't . . ." Brian watched in astonishment as Arthur and Percy wheezed their way up the staircase. "Are you all right?"

"Never had any idea riddles could be so exhausting," Arthur huffed.

Percy whipped an immaculate handkerchief from his lapel pocket and dabbed at his forehead. "What riddles are these?"

"Never mind that," Trevor said, then demanded of Brian, "Do you still have the devices?"

"I just said so."

"My dear sir," Percy said, stuffing his handkerchief away and stepping forward. "Could we please trouble you for a look?"

The sight of the secret chamber and its contents rendered the two auctioneers speechless. As they walked dumbfounded about the windowless cubicle, Cecilia and Trevor explained who they were and how they came to be here.

Brian looked in utter astonishment from one face to the next. "Ten thousand pounds?"

"Possibly more." Percival completed his tour and halted in front of Brian. "Would you permit us to photograph this room just as it is?"

"I guess so. But—"

Gladys chose that moment to pop through the tunnel opening. She spotted Arthur and cried, "There you are! Shame on you!"

"Gladys, please, we have guests."

"Never mind that!" She brushed at her skirt and stalked over to glare up at her husband. "Where on earth have you been?"

"London. My dear, this is—"

"I don't care if he's the queen's own messenger! You have no business tearing about the country like this. Really, Arthur, a man of your age should have better sense."

"It is all my fault, and I offer you my most abject apologies." Percy stepped forward and offered Gladys his hand. "Percy Atkins. You may not remember me, but we actually met at several of the regimental balls."

She eyed the hand as she would a rotten mackerel. "Then you should have more sense as well."

"My dear, it appears that Brian has stumbled upon something of genuine value. The articles you see before you here—"

"Not all of them," Gerald interjected from the chamber's far corner. "Most are exactly what the antique dealer told you. Victorian glass. But several others are quite unique." He lifted what appeared to be a brass fan, opened it out entirely. "Take this, for instance."

"Oh my, yes," Percy murmured. "Quite remarkable indeed."

Gladys looked from one suited stranger to the other. "Arthur, what on earth are they going on about?"

"Money, my dear," Arthur replied.

"This appears to be a gilt-brass proportional instrument." The young man drew it closer, squinted, and continued, "Yes, you can see here the Latin inscriptions, '*linea tetragonica, linea subtensarum, linea circularis.*'" He looked up and explained, "It is one of the earliest models for calculating spatial relationships. Early seventeenth-century, probably Dutch in origin. They were the best at this sort of thing, and this is quite a remarkable piece."

"And the price," Arthur demanded, preening for his wife.

"Somewhere in the vicinity of five thousand pounds."

"There, you see!" Proudly Arthur waved his arm around the chamber. "A veritable Aladdin's cave."

"You needn't go on so," Gladys scolded, only partly mollified. "It's not like you made the things yourself."

Percy stepped closer to Brian. "I say, about taking those photographs."

"Help yourself," Brian said. "Long as you can do it today."

"Ah yes, Arthur mentioned your problem with the death duties. How tragic." Percy turned back to the chamber. "Well, we shall move with all possible haste. Gerald?"

The young man was already headed for the tunnel. "I'll get on it immediately."

Arthur demanded, "What's this I hear about another riddle?"

Gladys looked stricken. "*Another* one?"

"Brian found a letter in the spark machine," Cecilia said, then glanced at her watch and felt a chill run through her. "I have to go back to the clinic *now*. Promise you'll come get me if you find anything?"

"Promise," Brian answered. "And thanks."

The last thing she heard as she passed through the tunnel was Percy's voice echoing, "I say, I've always enjoyed a good puzzle."

30

The afternoon slowly resigned itself to a tedious evening, filled with nothing but frustration and grime. Cecilia returned to Castle Keep after work, supplying them with surgical masks and plastic lab-goggles. The articles helped, but the strain showed on all their faces. Percival Atkins and his young assistant came and went, anxiously returning to the search when not occupied with photographing and cataloging and packing the glass. They finished with the basement and moved to the cellar where the car had been found. When that proved fruitless, they made a careful inspection of the grounds, then walked through Rose Cottage and the stables, searching for a door or catch of any kind that might lead to another cellar. Despite their best efforts, however, they found nothing at all. Gradually their sense of urgency slipped into grim resignation. When Gladys finally called them to dinner, no one had the strength to argue.

They entered the ground-floor apartment, a grubby and weary lot. Percy did not even have the strength to complain over the state of his Savile Row suit, and the dust in Gerald's hair aged him twenty years. Their eyes were red-rimmed, their knees bruised, their fingernails broken and blackened by searching for cracks and levers in the walls. They all had weak coughs from the dust. Over dinner they held a desultory discussion of the riddle, but no new ideas were formed.

As they tarried over coffee, all of them reluctant to return to what seemed a useless search, the doorbell rang. Brian walked across the front hall, only to discover himself confronting Hardy Seade. The man wore a natty blue blazer and striped shirt with a stiff white collar and a kerchief to match his bright yellow tie. Joe Eaves stood on the bottom step, showing nothing but his ever-present smile.

Hardy Seade eyed Brian's rumpled form with disdain and said, "I see you're preparing yourself for a return to the gutter."

Brian found himself unable to even care, much less respond. He started to shut the door, but was blocked by Hardy's foot. "I just came by to let you know that I have received unofficial word that my bid for Castle Keep has been accepted."

"Get your foot out of my door."

Hardy Seade pushed on the door, and when Brian did not budge he shouted through the opening, "I'm a generous man! I'll give you twenty-four hours to clear off before I call in the bailiff!"

Brian reared back and heaved, wanting to strike the door hard enough to break the man's foot. Hardy Seade sensed the motion just in time, and pulled his foot to safety. The door boomed closed, then Hardy shouted from outside, "Twenty-four hours! Tell that geriatric pair and your meddling doctor friend they have the same, and not one minute more!"

Wearily Brian crossed back to where the group crowded about Arthur's doorway—Gladys and Trevor and Molly and Cecilia and the auctioneers. "I say," Percy drawled. "He's rather a bad sort, wouldn't you agree?"

"Oh dear, oh dear," Gladys murmured. Cecilia's look was so potent Brian reached over and took her hand for comfort, not caring who noticed.

Arthur blew out his cheeks, then said, "I suppose you could look on the bright side. At least you won't be going away empty-handed."

Brian did not remove his gaze from Cecilia's tragic features. "But I don't want to go at all."

Cecilia went to bed because her exhausted body cried out for rest. But sleep came and went in fitful snatches, and the hands on her clock seemed to crawl their way around the night. Her mind remained a tumultuous muddle. Brian and the riddle and Hardy Seade and her beloved little home—thoughts and worries tumbled and tangled until she could scarcely tell one from the other. She found herself returning to the conversation with Angeline Townsend, doubting now that she had done the right thing in telling her not to take Tommy to the Reading hospital. Every choice seemed wrong now, every avenue ahead fraught with peril.

Helpless frustration welled up until she could no longer lie there. Cecilia rolled from the bed, fell to her knees, and prayed with a fervor so strong that her mind not only began to calm, but the worries began to unravel. They had to, for the only way to pray over them was one at a time. She knelt there so long her legs went numb, yet she was blessed with a comfort she would have thought impossible to find in such a dismal night.

She stood by pressing up with her hands because her legs

would not support her. At that moment the final words in Heather's letter seemed to rise up before her eyes, flaming there in the dark night. Cecilia saw them for the very first time, with such clarity that the answer might as well have been illuminated by the night.

The dream was soft in coming. It seemed to have been waiting for Brian just on the other side of sleep, waiting for him to stop with his prayers and slide into his pallet and give in to his exhaustion and his defeat.

It was as much a memory as a dream, really. Yet a dream just the same, for the image's vivid clarity held no pain whatsoever. Brian found himself seated once more beside Sarah's hospital bed. It was during one of her final stays; he knew that as soon as the dream took form. She had the look of one hollowed by her illness, all the life and all the energy and all the joy that had made her who she was just scooped out such that she was left an empty gourd.

Sarah looked at him and once again said words Brian had thought lost and gone forever. "I'm ready to go home now."

At that moment, the dream seemed to split in two, part of him recalling what had happened on that day, the other part living it anew. That day he had protested as he had done so often before, but his objections had been as hollow as her gaze. Now, however, he sat and nodded, and said simply, "I know you are."

"Grieve for me a while," she had said then, and now said again. Only this time she was not crying, and the defeat and the coming farewell were no longer in her voice. There was only calm, only love. So much, so very much love. "Then I want you to get on with your life."

Though he dreamed, still he remembered that day very well. At the time he had confessed with a broken and remorseful spirit, "I don't know if I can." But now it was different, for he was held by the same love and peace he felt pouring from his dead wife's gaze. Now he was able to say in utter honesty, "I'm trying."

Sarah smiled at him, and in so doing took him back to another time, back before the illness and the strain had robbed them of so much. She said, "I know you are."

Then she said what she had said that day, yet this time it was with the joy of eternal light, a flooding so powerful Brian found himself being pushed back to wakefulness, though he wanted to remain. Oh, he wanted so very much to stay right where he was. Sarah said to him, "Just remember I will be in the company of all the saints." And the joy and the love seemed to rise up and take him along, like a bubble being lifted from the darkest depths, up into the light of endless day. And the last thing he heard before waking was his beloved wife saying, "I'll be waiting there to greet you when your own time arrives."

He awoke and opened his eyes not to sorrow or loss or loneliness. No, instead he bounded from the bed and shouted to the gathering dawn, "I have it!"

Brian slipped into his clothes and raced down the stairs. He was midway along the gravel drive when he heard footsteps hurrying toward him. He knew it was Cecilia even before he rounded the trees and saw the slight, shadowy form. Knew because there was an illogical rightness to her being there, caught in the same power that sped him along. He rushed up, gripped her hands, and half shouted, "Rose Cottage!" Yet she could not hear him, not entirely, for at that very same moment she shouted back, "Joe Eaves!"

He said: "You told me the old monastery wasn't situated at Castle Keep, it was at your cottage!"

She said: "He pops up everywhere we turn! He's here with Hardy Seade, and he's pacing off the garden and digging holes that don't make any sense."

They stopped, then started off together once more. Brian said, "Joe—of course, he was here with John Miles yesterday." And Cecilia said, "The cottage—of course, Joe was always stamping around, looking under the carpet. I just assumed it was because he wanted to get his hands on it and rebuild."

They stopped a second time, so excited they could only gasp a little laugh, not wanting to miss anything else the other said. Cecilia pressed, "You first."

"No, you."

She gave Brian's hands an impatient shake. "I don't want to talk about Joe anymore. Tell me!"

"Heather said we had to get down on our knees."

"And look in the oldest place."

"Right. You told me, and then I think it was Trevor who also said something, about a thousand-year-old monastery on the grounds."

"Castle Priory—that's what the legend claims it was called." Cecilia gave his hands another shake, this one from irrepressible excitement. "And the old-timers say it was built where Rose Cottage stands now."

"Then that's where we have to look."

"But the cottage doesn't have a cellar." Even so, she was already turning and hurrying back down the drive. "And if there had been, Joe would have found it."

"There has to be . . ." Brian had to stop. He had no choice. Cecilia halted because his arm reached full stretch and pulled her back. "What's the matter?"

"That smell," Brian said, breathing deep. "It's incredible."

"Oh." Cecilia returned to stand beside him. "You haven't been here at night before, have you."

"Those are your roses?" To his mind the night had drawn a perfumed veil across a star-swathed sky, revealing a secret mystery kept for a select few.

"They give off their strongest fragrance after dark. This was the first thing that I fell in love with, the way the aroma reached out and greeted me even before I could see the old place. I'm glad you like it."

"I love it." Brian sensed a change to the night then, a different fragrance, one that drew his gaze down to where Cecilia was looking up at him. Her dark eyes had captured the starlight. He felt drawn down by their power, closer and closer until he kissed those soft lips. Arms warm and strong rose up to envelop his neck and tighten so that he felt he would never be let go, nor would he want to be. When they finally released, as he traced a hand down the side of her face and neck and then kissed her a second time, he felt as though the night and the world surrounded them with sweet-scented approval.

31

This time the two hours of searching did not dispel either the happiness or the excitement. Wednesday's dawn arrived and strengthened into another sunlit day. Brian and Cecilia used the light to tramp about the cottage's exterior, making wider and wider circles, kicking at the grass and rummaging under shrubbery, looking for another ring or opening. When that proved fruitless they stopped for coffee and toast. Neither needed to ask whether they should go and gather the others. This was their discovery, their morning, a gift too precious to share.

They drew their chairs close together and lingered long over the final cup of coffee, holding hands and listening to the birdsong drifting through the open window. Finally Brian said, "What we should be searching for is some corner of Rose Cottage where Joe Eaves couldn't have looked."

Reluctantly Cecilia lifted her head from where it had been resting on his shoulder. "A place he couldn't have gotten to without making me suspicious."

"Someplace hidden," Brian agreed. He felt her stiffen beside him. "What is it?"

She rose slowly, as though pulled by invisible strings. "Probably nothing."

He watched the tense excitement play upon her features. "You've thought of something."

"Maybe." She walked over to the kitchen pantry, pried open the reluctant door, and pointed at the ancient shelving in the corner. "Come give me a hand."

"With that?" Brian cast it a doubtful glance. "The thing looks planted."

"Which is exactly what Joe would have thought." Cecilia was already worming her way to the corner by the rusty fuse box. "But the only way to get to the house's wiring is by shifting this thing around. It can be moved, though. Arthur and I did it together the day you arrived."

"Right." He tried not to give in to the rising excitement. They had been disappointed so often before. But as they heaved and scraped the heavy shelving back out of the way, he could not completely stifle the thrill gripping his gut. As soon as there was space, he dropped to his knees and tapped the floorboards. Instantly he knew. "They're hollow!"

"Wait right there!" Cecilia flew away and returned with a foot-long screwdriver and a flashlight. "Try this."

He inserted the screwdriver between the boards, pushed, and the board slipped up into his hands. He stopped and looked up at Cecilia, whose eyes were so comically round he had to grin and ask, "Don't you need to be getting to work?"

She gripped the flashlight with both hands and cried, "I'm going to have a seriously afflicted patient on my hands right here if you don't get a move on!"

He turned back and pulled up another board. The next ones came with hard tugs of his hands, and soon the opening was large enough for him to take the flashlight from Cecilia, peer down, and exclaim, "There's a ladder!"

"You go first and check for creepy-crawlies," Cecilia instructed, crowding in behind him.

Gingerly he tested the ladder, which was good, because the first step cracked and gave before he had placed half his weight on it. "The wood is rotten."

"How deep is it?"

Brian pulled himself out. "Hold my legs." He slipped his head and shoulders through the opening and shone the flashlight downward. Below was a shallow hold floored with grimy close-cut stone. "It's only about eight feet down."

Brian gripped the boards as tightly as he could, and with Cecilia offering extra support to his upper arms he started sliding downward. When he was at full stretch, he released his hold and dropped to the floor. The stones were so slippery he instantly lost his footing and fell with a clatter.

"Are you all right?"

"Yes." But his head was thumping from the fall. He pushed himself erect, set his feet as best he could, then reached up and said, "Okay, easy does it."

Cecilia first handed him the flashlight and waited until he had set it on the floor before sliding through the opening legs first. He helped her down, waited until she was certain of her footing, then picked up the flashlight. As soon as he had glanced about, he knew.

"This is it," Cecilia said, her voice trembling. "Isn't it?"

Brian found himself unable to do more than nod.

32

"Here." Cecilia handed down a small shovel and the screw-driver. "Help me down again."

Brian found pleasure in letting her slip through his hands. He steadied her on the slippery flooring, then found himself unable to release her. "What took you so long?"

Her smile had a way of recasting her features into younger lines, as though the little girl she had once been remained there just below the surface, eager to be set free. "I had to call the office. I told them I was coming down with a case of the never-get-overs. Which isn't all that far off. I'm so excited I think I might be sick."

"Grab that screwdriver and come help me."

"What are we looking for?"

"I don't have any idea." He kept his hands outstretched as he half walked, half slid across the mossy floor. It was more like gliding on ice than walking. The walls were even more over-grown than the floors. He scraped the shovel across the wall, and the dank goo rolled back like ice cream in a scoop. "Anything that might suggest an—"

He was halted by the shovel clanking over some protrusion. Cecilia gingerly made her way over to stand beside him. She took the flashlight so he could use both hands on the shovel.

First an iron ring was revealed, then a wooden cover about three feet square. So excited his breath sounded like bellows in his own ears, Brian chipped away at the moss and grime around the cover's edges. He watched as Cecilia slipped the screwdriver through the ring. His voice sounded hoarse as he said, "Brace your foot where the floor meets the wall. Okay. Ready? On three. One, two, pull!"

The cover groaned, shifted, then popped out like a cork from a bottle. They released the screwdriver and let it fall with a resounding clap to the stone floor. Brian shone the flashlight down a long, stone-lined tunnel, and suggested, "Maybe I should go down there alone."

"Not on your life." She pushed him eagerly. "Hurry!"

The tunnel was as fetid and grubby as the cellar. With every crawl forward, his hands and knees sank in a boggy mire inches thick. Brian tried to keep himself from thinking what might have grown in the centuries of dank grime. But Cecilia did not complain as she followed behind, so he pushed on in silence.

Twenty feet forward, however, he halted with a groan. Cecilia demanded, "What's the matter?"

"Dead end." He felt the edges, pushed hard, could only moan in defeat, "A stone wall."

"I thought we were headed toward the property's border," she said. "We must be below the estate's outer wall."

"We'll have to back out," he said. "I don't have room to turn around."

The return trip seemed ages longer. The goo worked its way up his trouser legs with each backward shuffle. With vast relief his feet finally slipped over the edge of the opening. Brian eased himself upright and banged on the floor with one foot, then the other, to work the crud out from around his shins. His socks and shoes were filled with sludge. He turned the flashlight back to the cellar and observed, "You look like you've crossed the Everglades on your hands and knees."

"Never mind that." Shovel in hand, Cecilia was already sliding her way across to the opposite wall. "Shine that light over here."

"What are you looking for?"

She paused long enough to give him a look reserved for extremely dumb questions, then began scraping long swaths down the mire-encrusted wall. Brian hefted the screwdriver and went over to help.

On her sixth sweep, something clanked beneath Cecilia's shovel. Eagerly they attacked the wall. This time, the aperture was larger, beginning at the floor and rising almost four feet high.

Brian found himself too breathless to speak as he slipped the screwdriver through the ring and waited as Cecilia gripped the other end and wedged her foot against the wall. She nodded, and together they pulled. The door did not budge. They took a firmer grip, nodded again, and heaved.

The portal creaked and groaned and fell with a resounding boom. Brian sent the light cascading down the tunnel, then turned back to her grime-streaked face. "This is incredible."

"Go on, go on," she cried, pushing and prodding him impatiently through the door. Cecilia stepped in behind him, keeping one hand on his back and walking so close he could hear her excited breathing.

The tunnel was tight and fetid, but rose to a stone-lined peak so that Brian could angle his shoulders and walk upright. On and on it went, making two narrow turnings, and finally ending before another door. This one took several hard punches from both their shoulders before finally groaning open. When it gave, it spilled Brian onto the dusty floor. The flashlight clattered from his hand and rolled across the stones. His head began thundering from the rough treatment, and he was slow rising to his feet. By the time he was upright, Cecilia had picked up the light and walked to the chamber's far end.

"What is it?" She did not look up. All he could see through the gloom was the top of her head and the grime in her hair. "Cecilia?"

When she raised her gaze, it was to reveal wonder-filled eyes. She breathed, "Come over here."

33

Still in his pajamas and house slippers, Arthur opened his front door, took in their grimy forms, and immediately realized, "You've found it!"

Gladys's voice echoed from the kitchen, "Found what, dear?"

"Call Trevor," Brian said.

"Put on your oldest clothes," Cecilia added.

"And we need a ladder," Brian said.

Gladys appeared in her robe, gaped at them and demanded, "Whose pigsty have you been rolling around in?"

"Never mind that," Arthur barked and headed back down the hallway to the phone. He picked up the receiver and began stabbing at the phone. "Whose bright idea was it to make the numbers so small only a child can dial?"

"Let me do that, dear." Gladys hurried back to join her husband. As she dialed she cast another doubtful glance to where they waited in the doorway. "I'm afraid I can't invite you in."

"No problem," Brian assured her. "But I'd love a cup of tea."

"Trevor? Hello, it's Gladys. I'm sorry to bother you so early, but Brian and Cecilia are standing in my doorway dripping the most horrid green slime all over—"

"Here, give me that." Arthur took the receiver and shouted, "We've got an emergency on our hands! Get over here fast!"

Then he slammed the receiver down.

Gladys protested, "No need to be rude, dear."

"Nonsense." He gave one and all a fierce grin. "I merely gave him a neat summing up. Now where are my galoshes?"

"In the cupboard where they always are." To Brian and Cecilia she inquired, "Are you hungry?"

"Starved."

"I'll put on the kettle and make some toast." She hurried away. "Don't you dare come any farther."

Arthur's head popped out of the back room. "Percy and his assistant stayed over last night at the Red Lion Inn so they could continue with the cataloging this morning. Should we give them a call?"

Brian felt the dried mud on his face crack as he smiled. "Absolutely."

Gladys objected, "Shouldn't we find out what all the fuss is about before we go waking up the entire world?"

"Nonsense!" Arthur was busy crashing drawers and doors in his bedroom. "One look at their faces tells you everything you need to know!"

Gladys managed to sit them on the front stairs and feed them bacon sandwiches and mugs of steaming tea before Percy and Gerald and Trevor and Molly clattered down the drive. It was only when Brian rose back to his feet that he realized just how weary he was and how much his head hurt.

"My dear boy," Arthur observed, "You've gone all green."

"It was that bacon," Gladys fretted. "The butcher assured me it was fresh."

"I'm fine," Brian said. "Just tired."

"Then we'd best be off," Arthur declared, marshaling his troops. "Here, Trevor, give me a hand with this ladder."

Together they marched down the drive. At the turning to Rose Cottage, however, Cecilia halted Brian with a touch on his arm and the words, "Look who's by the gates."

Standing just outside the entrance to his property, Hardy Seade fumed alongside a butter-yellow Bentley. Brian called out, "Get out of here, or I'll call the police."

Hardy Seade stiffened as though slapped. "This road is public property!"

"Then I'll have you arrested for loitering," Brian shouted, his pulse punching hard knots of pain through his forehead. "And if that doesn't do, I'll accuse you of breaking and entering!"

The man's face went purple as he shouted through the gates, "What utter nonsense are you talking about now?"

"Come on, you lot," Arthur pressed. "He's a nuisance and nothing more."

"I heard that!" The man was almost dancing in place. "Tomorrow morning you'll see how much of a nuisance I can be! Mark my words, this time tomorrow you'll all be on the street where you belong!"

As they trooped through the front door of Rose Cottage, Brian caught sight of Hardy giving the Bentley's fender a savage kick.

The kitchen seemed overly cramped with all of them inside. Brian and Arthur manhandled the ladder into place, then with Gerald holding the top they made their way down into the stone-lined cellar. Five flashlights flickered and scattered light about the grime and gloom. Gerald was the last down, and he instantly pulled a camera from his pocket and began flashing pictures.

When Percy walked over to the smaller opening and peered

inside, Brian warned, "You're going to ruin that nice suit of yours."

"It's all I brought." The words bounced and echoed about the stone cubicle. "Never mind. Where to?"

"This way." Brian led them back down the taller tunnel, feeling the thrill tighten his chest all over again. They entered the chamber, and Brian turned back to watch their expressions as they passed through the ancient portal. To his immense satisfaction, Percy and Gerald looked utterly stunned.

Percy walked straight up to the front altar and said, "Do you have any idea what you've uncovered?"

"Suppose you tell us."

"A secret medieval chapel," Gerald breathed, pointing his own flashlight at the peaked stone roof. "I've read about them, but never seen one before."

"That's because so few of them survived," Percy said. To the others, he explained, "Some very early monasteries built hidden chapels that the brothers could retreat to in times of turmoil. Armies, battles, and brigands passed with tragic regularity. The monks would bring in their texts, their chalices, and the sacramental pieces, and wait out the troubles."

Gerald thunked his hand upon a narrow portal behind the altar. "My guess is this would lead on to the crypt."

"It does," Brian affirmed. "Shelves filled with bones and rags."

"Only three of these underground chapels are known to exist throughout the length and breadth of the British Isles," Percy breathed. "And none of them are as intact as this. It's our good fortune that no one has been down here for centuries." He glanced back to where Brian and Cecilia stood holding hands by the entrance. "I suppose the chapel was empty?"

"Not entirely," Brian said, glad he had held the best for last. He asked Cecilia, "Do you want to do the honors?"

"It's your discovery," Cecilia replied.

"But it's under your cottage."

Her eyes widened, and as the power of Brian's words hit home, she bit a trembling lip and whispered, "My cottage."

"That's right."

Percival exclaimed, "Will you please make up your collective minds before I burst from the strain?"

Reluctantly Brian released her hand and walked forward. He fumbled beneath the altar's stone top for the catch he had spotted, and once more a corner of the altar top popped open.

"I say," Arthur exclaimed, moving forward. "You're getting rather good at this, aren't you."

Brian lifted off the lid and pulled out the two items. Everyone crowded forward. Brian cast a look back to where Cecilia watched him, then he unwrapped the top item and stepped back.

"Oh my dear sweet word," Percival breathed. "Gerald, your camera."

"Step back please, everyone." With shaky hands Gerald focused and began shooting pictures.

Percy's hands were no steadier than Gerald's as he pulled off the tattered cloth covering. He blew softly at the dusty binding, then lifted the book's cover. He did not seem to mind in the least that the jacket came away in his hands. He set it to one side and ran one finger down the first page. He looked up, but seemed incapable of focusing on Brian as he declared, "This is the monastery Bible."

Trevor crowded in beside him, and exclaimed in a shaky voice, "Look at the illuminations."

"They would have spent years on this work," Percy agreed, turning back another page, then another. "Years and years and years."

"Take a look at what's underneath," Brian said.

The vicar and the auctioneer gave him an astonished look. "There's more?"

"We saved the best for last," Brian affirmed.

"Give me a hand here, please." Gingerly Percy and Trevor slid the book to one side. Underneath was not another book, but a rather slim box. One whose inlaid surface had dimmed until it was scarcely possible to see that gemstones had been set into the surface, in the shape of a cross.

Percy spent a long moment staring at the surface and tracing a trembling hand around the edges, before saying softly, "Gerald, if you please."

The young man understood instantly, for he reached into his pocket and handed over a pocketknife. Percy unfolded the blade, and delicately fitted it into one side as his assistant continued to take pictures. Cautiously Percy pried open the lid, set it aside, and breathed, "I am well and truly amazed."

"What is it?" Trevor demanded.

Percy gently lifted out what appeared to be a cloth-wrapped bundle. "This is the reason I have spent my entire life dedicated to the past."

Percy held up the cloth's top facing so that Gerald could snap another picture, this one of jewels sewed with what appeared to be solid-gold thread, again making the form of the cross. "What this is," Percy repeated, his voice none too steady, "is every historian's dream. The discovery of a lifetime."

He finished unfolding the cloth, and lifted up the tiny contents for Gerald to photograph. "Ladies and gentlemen, I give you a Book of Hours."

34

"When the great William arrived in 1066," Percy explained, "he seeded this land with a number of habits born and bred in his native France. The square Norman towers you see on many of our oldest churches are an adaptation from medieval French bell towers. The habit of praying the hours—I don't suppose you've ever come across that practice."

"On the contrary," Trevor demurred, glancing with pride at Cecilia. "The whole town is aware of it."

"How extraordinary. Well, those patrons who could read would carry with them miniature texts known as the Book of Hours. When the bells chimed, they would read from them a short prayer or spiritual poem, directing their thoughts momentarily toward the divine."

They were gathered in Gladys's spotless dining room, all thoughts and concerns of the grime they tracked in momentarily forgotten. They were seated in a cramped little circle, all save Gerald, who was busy talking softly at the hall phone. Percy fondled the rotting fabric with its jewel-stitched embroidery and continued, "It will take some very careful investigation to know anything for certain. But I would like to hazard a guess, if you will permit me."

"Go on, out with it, man," Arthur commanded. "This isn't the examination board at Cambridge you're facing."

"Very well, then." The auctioneer took a long breath, touched for a tie that was no longer there, then said, "My guess is that this belonged to a member of the royal family."

The table emitted a collective gasp. Percy nodded his agreement. "William made Knightsbridge his first capital, as you know. And only someone of his standing would have been able to afford such an elaborate text."

Percy picked up the book itself, which was only slightly larger than his hand. "I would venture to suggest that this was never actually used. The cover and the box and the ornamentation you see here in the cover, not to mention the illuminations themselves . . ." He swiveled the book around so Brian could see the page, which showed a woman in a long robe kneeling beneath a tree, from which sang a dozen golden birds. "Look here, you see how brilliant these colors remain? This indicates that the illuminators used not dyes, but precious metals and ground-up gemstones. These birds, for example; I would wager they are actually gold leaf, and the green of the tree might well be crushed emeralds." He set down the book and declared, "All this suggests that the book was designed as an offertory from the king to his first monastery in the kingdom."

Gerald settled the receiver back into the phone, and appeared in the doorway. "It's all arranged," he announced. "They should arrive in under two hours."

"Good show." Percy turned back to Brian. "With your permission, I have arranged for an armored car and a security detail to transport this to safety. You're under no obligation to deal with Christie's, of course. But I would urge you to let us stow this in the company vaults until you decide precisely what course you wish to take."

There was a moment's stunned silence, then Brian ventured, "This is valuable?"

"My dear sir, this find is absolutely priceless." Percy could not keep his hands off the book. "There has not been one of these on the open market in over a decade. Once authenticated, I would hazard to say it could fetch five million pounds, and possibly much more."

Brian turned to Cecilia and felt her shining gaze down to the core of his being. He looked back to Percy and asked, "Could you loan me a million dollars?"

The flurry of explanations and strategies rose to such a point that Arthur had to stand and shout to be heard. "I say, one moment please. *Quiet!*" He waited for silence, then continued, "That's better. I hate to put a damper on everyone's fun, but I regret to inform you that money alone will not be enough to retain Castle Keep."

"He's right," Trevor worriedly agreed. "The time for receiving bids has closed."

"Good grief, I forgot," Percy said anxiously. "Today's the day of that auction nonsense, isn't it."

"It's not nonsense, but it is this afternoon," Brian said. Then he turned to Arthur and asked, "What do we do?"

"A frontal attack's no use," the retired commander declared. "The council's lined up with the enemy. Thick as thieves, that lot."

"This is not good," Percy fretted. "Not good at all."

"Quiet, man." Arthur commanded. He pondered a long moment, his entire face furrowed. Then he straightened and demanded of his former peer, "You have connections within the Ministry of the Interior, don't you?"

"Of course, but what—"

"And friends in the antiquities departments of various museums?" Arthur pressed on.

"Of course!" Trevor's cry pushed him to his feet. "Arthur, you continue to astound me."

Percy looked from one man to the other. "Sorry, you've lost me there."

"We must plan a flanking maneuver!" Arthur's jaw jutted out, ready for the assault. "If we manage to have this manor and its grounds declared a historical monument, what happens to the plans for their ruddy lab?"

"They'll drop all their plans in an instant," Trevor declared ecstatically. "They'd have to, because such a monument would be untouchable."

"They'd never be permitted to place a lab on the grounds of Castle Keep," Arthur announced. "Not in a thousand years."

"With the discovery of that chapel," Gerald excitedly agreed, "having this place declared a Grade One listed building will be an utter cinch."

"I say, old chap, that's positively brilliant," Percy said. "My hat is off to you."

"The critical issue here is one of timing," Arthur warned.

"Quite right. We don't have a moment to lose." Percy rose to his feet. "Gerald, our car."

"Right away." The young man nodded a farewell to the room and vanished.

"You arrange for the museum muckety-mucks to write up what we need," Arthur said, already moving for the front door. "Brian here will drive us to the Ministry, and we'll await you on their doorstep."

"Just one minute!" Gladys cried.

"Not now, dear, this is important—"

"I'll tell you what it is, it's an outrage!" She planted herself in her husband's path. "If you think I'm letting any man of mine make a journey to the Ministry in muddy trousers and galoshes, then you've got another think coming!"

"She's right," Brian agreed. "I feel like my hair is cemented to my head."

"We'll stop by the hotel for a quick cleanup, then fly off to process the photographs and assemble the allies," Percy said, sliding around the table. "You meet us at the Ministry."

"I'll go lay out your regimental jacket with all the nice medals," Gladys said, somewhat mollified. "You've always said nothing could move the bureaucrats to action faster than a bit of spit and polish."

35

The road from Knightsbridge to London wound its way across the Chiltern Hills, rising and falling through forested hilltops and carefully tilled valleys. Over the rumble of the MGA's deep-throated engine Brian could hear the calls of cattle and sheep, urging him to ever greater haste. Traffic was light, trees caused the sunlight to play flickering games overhead, and the wind sang a merry tune. They arrived at the foot of the steepest hill of all; Brian downshifted, the motor's drumbeat took on a deeper boom, and not even Arthur could resist the urge to laugh out loud.

The hilltop was heavily forested, and the car crested the ridge and drilled a noisy hole down a long green straightaway. The walls and roof of their living tunnel tossed the motor's growl back at them, until it seemed that all the world was shouting with them to fly, to hurry, to reach their goal.

The first indication Brian had of anything amiss was when a second roar joined his own, and in the rearview mirror he spotted a battered truck bearing down on them. He watched in disbelief as the distance between them closed, and it was only when he recognized the face behind the steering wheel that he shouted, "Hang on!"

"What's that?"

But the truck answered for him, as it ground its gears and the motor hit a shrieking high-pitched note, then struck.

Brian floored it at the last moment, pulling away enough so the truck pounded his rear fender and not the side door as Joe Eaves had planned. The MGA slewed violently, but Brian managed to keep hold of the road and not wrap himself around a tree. The closeness of fleeting death raised his voice a full two octaves as he yelled, "What is he *doing?*"

Arthur swiveled about just as Joe barreled in for a second try. He gripped the top of the windscreen and the doorjamb and yelled back, "It's that idiot gardener!"

"Hold tight!" Brian's foot was pressed down so hard it threatened to ram the gas pedal through the floorboard. But the truck was both newer and more powerful, and it roared forward like a shrieking metal beast with hoes for horns.

At the very last moment, Brian swerved as much as the narrow lane allowed. Once more he saved the car from enduring a full-on strike. Even so, the impact was enough to send him careening off the side of the road and onto the cramped ribbon of grass. Tree trunks hurtled by, the limbs reaching out to draw them to oblivion.

Finally the tires caught hold, and he slithered back onto the pavement. Immediately the truck's motor roared, and a snarling Joe Eaves drew up parallel to the much smaller MGA. He took careful aim through the side window, deathly determined that this would be the killing strike.

"Don't just hang about," Arthur howled. "Here he comes!"

At the last possible instant Brian slipped his foot from the gas and hammered both feet down on the brake. The four wheels locked in a smoky scream of burning rubber, and the car slewed sideways. But the sudden change in acceleration was enough to jerk them back out of reach.

Joe Eaves caught the action, but not in time. He whipped his wheel about, but his acceleration was so great the top-heavy truck whipped up on two wheels. He hit the grass verge just as his two near-side tires returned to earth. The truck disappeared between two large trees and vanished into the forest. Over the sound of their own idling motor they heard the noise of rending metal and shrieking blows and finally a vastly satisfying crash.

Brian's legs were shaking so hard he found it difficult to remove them from the brakes. Arthur demanded hoarsely, "Are you able to drive?"

"I—I think so."

"Let's see if you locked the brakes. Put it into first gear and ease down on the throttle."

It took a long moment to fit his hand around the gearshift and work the clutch. Arthur pretended not to notice Brian's trembling motions. The old man seemed utterly unfazed by the attack. The motor purred and the car moved forward as though nothing untoward had ever happened.

Brian found he had no choice but to drive over to the side of the road, pull on the brake, and open his door. Arthur asked in genuine astonishment, "Where on earth are you off to?"

"I have to make sure he's okay."

Arthur cast a soldier's disdainful glance back to where the deep furrows plowed across the grass and into the forest. "Joe Eaves received precisely what he deserved, wouldn't you say?"

Brian answered by walking back on shaky legs and entering the woodland's cool depths.

He could have followed this particular trail on a moonless

night. The truck had uprooted three young saplings, scraped the bark off several trees, and in so doing had clearly slowed itself to a safer speed. For when Brian finally found the attacker, the motor was idling quietly, the truck wedged between two mammoth oaks. Joe Eaves had swiveled himself up on the seat and was using both feet to push with savage fury at the front windscreen. When he spotted Brian's approach, he redoubled his efforts. The sight was enough to turn Brian around and hasten him back to the car.

Arthur greeted him with, "Well?"

"He's alive and kicking," Brian said, climbing in. "Let's go."

36

$\mathcal{T}$revor met them at the entrance to Castle Keep with a strident, "What in name of all under heaven kept you so long?"

"You try rushing a bureaucrat," Arthur replied querulously.

"But the auction begins in less than an hour!"

Arthur extended his arm. "Hold off on the complaining and help me out of this motorcar. You're worse than Gladys."

"I've been twice to the mayor's saying you were on your way." He eased the old man erect, then spotted Brian's side of the car and demanded, "What happened to your lovely machine?"

The pair of journeyers responded together, "Joe Eaves."

Trevor walked around for a closer look. "You had an accident with the gardener?"

"Never mind that," Arthur snapped, brandishing his folder. "That battle's over, but victory still hangs in the balance!"

Brian matched his stride to that of the gentleman, whose medals and shoulder-stars glittered magnificently in the light. Ever since Joe Eaves's futile attack he had felt utterly protected, sheltered even from the tense moments with the Ministry bureaucrat. For a time Arthur had looked as though he would explode from the frustration of dealing with a recalcitrant official. Even though Brian knew full well his occupation of Castle Keep and the future he saw unfolding was edging ever closer to the cliff of abandon, he remained utterly disconnected from the swirl of argument and tension. Once in a while he had sensed the tide of anxiety approaching, only to be pushed away by a single swift thought, one that seemed to arise from outside him: It was truly in God's hands.

Percival Atkins had finally lost patience with the bureaucrat's endless objections, and strode off in search of the Minister himself, who happened to be a frequent visitor to Christie's hallowed chambers. Brian had sat and watched as if from a great distance while their meeting had then been moved to a vast and ornate conference room. There two crusty historians on annuity from Christie's gave unequivocal backing to Percy's strident demand for immediate action. Over the objections of his own underling, the Minister agreed to extend a temporary reclassification of Castle Keep, pending a final decision to elevate the property to Grade One historical significance.

As they raced down the cobblestone lane toward the council offices, Brian began to have swift glimpses of a future beyond this moment and this day. The jolting surges of hope left him feeling as though he were seeing Knightsbridge anew. Not even his rising excitement and the pressure of time could keep him from appreciating what they passed. Their way took them along a medieval estate wall so old it billowed like brick-and-flint sails. Beyond that were centuries-old homes of Cotswold stone, held up by metal stays connected to iron cables that ran through the house. It was only when he passed beneath a row of ancient willows forming a tunnel of light-flecked green that Brian realized what caused him to see everything anew. For the first time since his arrival, he was seeing the village as home.

They halted at the entrance to the council offices for a quick breath. "Steady on, chaps," Arthur puffed. "Who's to do the talking here?"

"You are," Brian directed.

"Give them both barrels," Trevor agreed.

"Right you are." Arthur squared his shoulders, pressed through the door, and said, "Once more into the breech, dear friends."

It was the final word that cast a glow over their passage down the hall and into the mayor's outer office. *Friends*. Even when there was the thunder of footsteps behind them, and Brian turned to confront a furious Hardy Seade, the glow remained. It was true, so genuine that not even the man's boiling wrath could diminish the realization. He was not alone. He was flanked by friends, and this was home.

Seade demanded, "What's this claptrap about delaying the auction?"

Arthur waited for the mayor to rise from his desk and join them to declare, "Today a temporary injunction has been issued against both the auction and any possible development of the property."

The county finance manager stomped up alongside Hardy Seade and screeched, "By whom?"

"The Minister of the Interior himself," Arthur announced smugly.

"That's a bald-faced lie!" Hardy roared. "The auction is going ahead as scheduled!"

"Afraid not, old chap." Arthur opened the file and presented the papers to the mayor. "You'll see the minister's chop down at the bottom of the page."

Hardy Seade pushed Arthur aside. "Let me have that!"

The old man would have gone down had Brian not been there to catch him. "I say, steady on," Arthur protested.

"Yes, do get a hold on yourself." The mayor used his body to fend off Hardy's clawing for the papers.

"But my buyers are already *arranged!* The deal is finalized!"

"Not according to these papers." The mayor read aloud, "'Any intended disposal of said property is hereby postponed until after a review of its historical significance and appropriate heritage classification can be assigned.'"

The tax woman cried, "That is absolutely preposterous!"

Hardy Seade added, "A government survey could take *years!*"

"Indeed so." The mayor looked up, and offered Brian a genuine smile. "Well, Mr. Blackstone, it appears that you are now an official resident of our little town."

"But he *can't* be!" The tax woman appeared on the verge of coming undone. "This man is a vile, treacherous, irresponsible—"

The mayor revealed a hard edge to both his gaze and his voice. "Perhaps you could tell me why you seem so personally involved in this matter."

"I . . . He . . ." The tax woman foundered, then gave Hardy Seade a glance of desperate appeal. "Hardy, dear . . ."

"I asked *you*, not Mr. Seade," the mayor barked.

She could only manage, "That man owes us back taxes."

"Which he is now in a position to pay," Arthur proclaimed. "With interest."

"Then our involvement in this matter must be strictly limited to upholding the minister's ruling," the mayor grated. "Wouldn't you agree?"

"I . . . That is . . ."

"You can't do this!" Hardy Seade waved his fist within an

inch of Brian's nose. "I had enough of this treachery from Heather Harding! Well, I won't stand for it from you, I can promise you that!"

"You accuse *us* of treachery?" Arthur's laugh rang out, as strong as the afternoon sunlight. "My dear chap, after the tricks you've pulled with Joe Eaves, that goes beyond the pale."

"Eaves? What does the ruddy gardener have to do with anything?" Seade's hair sprouted wildly, his eyes bulged. The man looked on the verge of exploding. "We're talking about Heather Harding and her vile tactics. And now yours! Well, you won't get away with it, I can tell you that! I'll—"

The mayor glanced behind their little throng and said, "Ah, bailiff, there you are. Please be so kind as to escort Mr. Seade from the building."

"Come along, sir."

"You haven't heard the last of this!" Hardy Seade attempted to grip the doorjamb as he was pulled from the room, but the bailiff was ready and blocked him neatly. As he vanished down the hallway, he shrieked, "Castle Keep is *mine!*"

The mayor waited until the outer doors had shut to offer Brian his hand. "Mr. Blackstone, allow me to welcome you to Knightsbridge."

37

$\mathcal{T}$heir dinner that night was a subdued affair. Cecilia sat across from Brian, stunned to immobility by the sudden reversal. The old couple were clearly exhausted. Trevor and Molly tried gamely to keep the conversation going, but the effort was too much even for them. Brian sat and marveled at his growing sense of belonging somewhere. He studied the faces about Gladys's dining table, cast by the overhead light into softly wearied lines. Brian looked from one face to the next, indulging in the joy of knowing that here indeed were friends. Here were family.

The phone's ring seemed to jangle them all. Arthur returned to the dining room to announce, "That was Percy. His in-house experts have passed tentative judgment over both volumes. The Bible is in sad shape, but he thinks many of the illuminated pages can be restored and mounted as individual prints. The Book of Hours, on the other hand, has the entire house agog. It appears, Brian, that you are now a wealthy man." He waved his hand across the table and announced grandly, "Ladies and gentlemen, I give you the new master of Castle Keep."

"Here, here," Trevor said.

"You know, something continues to niggle at me," Arthur went on, fumbling his way back into his chair. "Why on earth would Joe Eaves attack us after the book was safely stowed away?"

"Revenge," Cecilia suggested.

"Doubtful," Arthur murmured. "Hardy Seade must have mentioned our excitement this morning, and he could well have followed us out of town. No doubt he sought what we might have been carrying with us."

"Who's to understand the workings of such a mind," Gladys said. "I for one will sleep better when I hear the police have him under lock and key."

"There's something else," Brian said, releasing the doubts he had found surfacing all day. "You know how Percy said the chapel had been untouched for centuries?"

Trevor nodded thoughtfully. "If so, how did Heather know about those tomes?"

Arthur fiddled with his coffee spoon. "Percy's not the sort of chap to make such a declaration unless he was absolutely certain."

"I've found myself wondering about that as well," Gladys added reluctantly. "It wouldn't be like Heather to find such a glorious book and just leave it sitting there in the gloom for years and years."

"Quite right," her husband agreed.

Cecilia looked from one face to the next. "Are you saying what I think you're saying?"

Trevor shared her disbelief. "You mean there's more?"

Arthur demanded, "Search on your knees in the depths, isn't that what the riddle said?"

"In the manor's oldest part," Brian agreed.

"Well, barring the cellar," Gladys observed, "our kitchen is the oldest portion of the house itself."

Trevor stared at her. "I don't recall hearing anything of the sort."

"Heather told me that on several occasions, I remember it distinctly," Gladys countered. "Our kitchen was at one time the original scullery of the first Castle Keep."

Arthur surveyed the gathering, and gave one and all a grand smile. "I suppose you know what that means."

"Shouldn't we leave off until tomorrow, dear?"

"Nonsense." The old gentleman was already struggling to his feet. "The tide of events and all that rot. Come along, let's get to work."

38

An hour later, all the pots and pans had been plucked from Gladys's shelves, all the cupboards laid bare, all the stains and age revealed. Gladys alternated between helping them stack and standing in the middle of the floor, wringing her hands over the dust and the decline.

After a first circuit of the room proved futile, Brian walked out the front door and seated himself against the pillars. A few moments later, the door opened and Trevor's voice asked, "Mind if I join you?"

"Not at all." He waited for the vicar to slip down beside him, and said, "I just had to come out and appreciate the night."

"A momentous occasion," Trevor agreed. "Our hearty congratulations. We're all happy for you."

"I know. And that makes it all the sweeter."

The vicar hesitated, then asked, "Might I pry for a moment?"

"Fire away."

"My wife would most certainly say that I was meddling where I did not belong. But it is a pastor's habit to snoop about at times." Another momentary vacillation, then, "Cecilia has become something of an adopted daughter. And not just by me. Many of the locals about here take quite an interest in her."

Brian folded his hands in his lap and waited. Overhead the sky was awash with silver.

"You lost your wife two years ago, and began traveling almost immediately, is that not correct?"

"Left the day after the funeral."

"And you've been traveling ever since?"

"Haven't been back to America a single time."

The voice was gently English, but the gaze direct, the words cutting. "It has left me wondering, you see. Have you experienced two years of healing, or two years of avoiding your grief?" When Brian did not respond, Trevor went on, "I understand that you might *think* you have feelings for our Cecilia. But are these feelings merely a result of unresolved grief? Your judgment might be all over the place, really. Grief affects people in so many ways. Not to mention anger. There's bound to be some anger in such a situation. We must guard against passing on a dose of this unresolved wrath to someone else."

"Like Cecilia," Brian offered.

"She certainly deserves better, wouldn't you agree?"

Brian found himself caught by a sudden rush of memories, so vivid now he had no choice but to speak of them out loud. "Sarah died in June. On a Tuesday. Her eyesight had failed about two weeks earlier. It was a crushing blow for both of us. It tore at me to see her imprisoned within her own body. She had always loved the colors of springtime." He stopped, took a breath, and seemed to smell the perfumes of petals lost and gone forever. "So I started going out and walking around gardens and studying the sunlight and smelling flowers. Especially roses. She always loved the way every bush seemed to have a different fragrance. She never asked me to describe what I had seen. All she wanted was to make sure at least one of us had been there to enjoy the new season."

Brian lifted his gaze to the stars, and found himself seated in the midst of a storm of descending love. It was the easiest thing in the world to say, "She would be so happy to see me sitting here, talking with you, discussing a woman I've come to care for very deeply. Making friends and building a new home and a future with hope and purpose."

"My dear Brian—" Trevor faltered. "Your words leave me feeling very foolish indeed."

"They weren't meant to. I'd appreciate any advice you can offer."

Trevor collected himself and replied, "Very off the top. If you intend to become involved with Cecilia, do so honestly. Not just with her, with yourself. Ask yourself every step of the way, why am I doing this? Is it because of who she is, or what I am still carrying inside?" Trevor paused a moment, then continued, "Try to remember that your needs and your desires might remain affected by the tragedy which sent you spinning off on a tangent you never expected. It's one of life's bitterest turns to force someone to face such issues. But it has happened, and you must deal with it. Setting a proper course now, as you lift yourself up and get on with your life, is the only hope of reaching the right destination further down the line."

Brian studied the night, and found within the warm wind and the rustling trees and the starlight a presence that was both new and old as time itself. "I don't know why I've been given the chance to start over. I don't know why I've had this prospect of loving someone as fine as Cecilia. But I do know that I'll give it my very best. That I can promise you."

"I can't ask for anything more," Trevor answered.

An unexpected voice spoke softly from behind them. "I can't either." Cecilia walked over and seated herself beside Brian.

He could only ask, "How long have you been there?"

"Long enough." She took his face in both her hands—and kissed him warm and long.

It was Trevor's embarrassed cough that drew them apart. "Well, that is, perhaps I should be getting back."

"We all should," Cecilia said, her gaze speaking another language entirely. "I came out to tell you that Arthur's found something."

39

"I confess it was an utter accident," Arthur said. "I was tapping bricks in the old scullery fireplace, and found myself stuck fast."

"I told you to leave it for someone younger," Gladys reprimanded.

"Yes, well, it's a good thing I didn't. That's when I found it. Look here." Arthur lowered himself down to his hands and knees, and with Trevor and Brian and Cecilia all crowding around him, he scrambled to the back of the narrow chimney. His voice echoed tightly as he said, "Back in the days before electric cookers, the servants would slip iron rods through pot handles, and then slide the rods through these rings you see here, hanging the pots over the fire."

"I can't see a thing," Cecilia complained.

"Then you'll just have to take my word for it. I gripped this top ring here, didn't even see it until I was crammed in so. It is black as the bricks and looks to be imbedded slightly into the wall; yes, I can see now there's an indentation carved here, to keep it from being detected from outside. Quite remarkable, really."

"Do get on with it, dear," Gladys cried impatiently.

"Shine the torch over here, Trevor. That's better. Here we go, then."

Brian pressed his cheek to the cold stone floor so as to watch from underneath as Arthur gripped the ring and twisted hard. There was a faint rumble as a six-brick square rolled away from the side. Arthur eased himself backward and gave everyone a chance to admire his handiwork. "What do you think of that?"

"I am rendered positively speechless," Trevor said.

"Quite a feat for a vicar," Arthur remarked.

Brian eased in far enough to observe, "There's a set of narrow stairs." He pulled his head out to ask Arthur, "Want to go first?"

"Couldn't possibly, old chap," the old man replied cheerfully. "The honors must lie with you."

"Okay, here goes." In order to make the narrow entrance Brian had to twist and sit on the brick fireplace, then slide in one arm at a time. Once inside, however, the passage broadened and he was able to stand.

Cecilia demanded, "What do you see?"

He shone the light upward and whistled softly.

"Brian Blackstone, if you don't answer me right now, I'm going to crawl in there and inflict some serious damage!"

Arthur's chuckle echoed from down below. "I say, that sounds rather possessive."

"Hush, dear, it's none of your affair."

Brian called back, "It looks like a spiral stone ladder. I'm going up." He gripped the flashlight with his teeth, and used his hands and feet to scramble up.

"I can't stand this," Cecilia declared. "Somebody hand me a flashlight."

"I'm right behind you," Trevor announced.

Brian did a slow revolution as he climbed, the breath puffing hard through his nostrils. Up and up he went until he was certain he had risen nearly to the level of the middle floor. He was halted by a stout wooden door set into the ceiling overhead. Brian plucked the flashlight from his mouth, pressed his back into the side wall, levered one leg up against the opposite stones, and shoved hard.

The wooden grate fell back with a resounding clatter.

"I say," Arthur called from down below. "Are you all right?"

"Fine." Brian coughed and sneezed from the dust as he clambered through the opening.

"It's raining grit!" Cecilia complained.

"Don't stop," Trevor hacked. "I'm stuck halfway in and catching it all right in my face."

Brian seated himself on the lip of the opening, shone the flashlight around, and said, "I don't *believe* this."

"What?" When he did not respond, Cecilia called, "Speak to me!"

He leaned down and shouted, "Everybody get up here, fast!"

40

$\mathcal{B}$rian slid away from the opening in the floor, leaving Cecilia to help first Trevor and then Molly through the portal. He stayed where he was so as to watch their expressions. It was a vastly satisfying experience, hearing their gasps echo around the stone-lined chamber. He observed with them as they spun their cones of light about the room, flashing upon the ancient shields stacked around the walls, pausing upon the tall broadswords in their jeweled scabbards, the crosspieces supporting suits of chain mail and helmets with the same royal crests as the shields.

It was Trevor who pointed at the chamber's far end and said, "What's in the chest?"

"I don't know, I was waiting for Arthur and Gladys to come up."

"Gladys isn't coming," Molly reported. "She doesn't like dark enclosed spaces. She took one look at the opening and said she'd gone all quiffy."

"Go on and open it," Cecilia begged.

"Okay." The ceiling was not tall enough for him to stand upright, so Brian slid across the flagstones on his hands and knees. The chest was an ancient strongbox. Rusted iron bands crisscrossed the top, and some ancient seal had been stamped in colored wax across the opening. In the chamber's corner lay two other strongboxes, open and empty and laying on their sides. The seal on this box had long since been broken as well, and the lid slid back easily. The interior was far smaller than the exterior, for the wood was a good three inches thick. Gently Brian lifted up the box's uppermost contents.

Cecilia demanded, "What is it?"

"A letter from Heather." But that alone was not what caused his hands to tremble.

"What else?"

Brian found himself rocked back on his heels. "Come see for yourself."

"Why can't you just . . ." Cecilia's voice trailed off as she shone her light inside.

"What is it?" Trevor and Molly crawled across, and gasped yet again.

Brian watched as Cecilia dipped an unsteady hand into the box, lifted up a pile of gold and silver pieces, and let them slide through her fingers. The coins jingled heavily as they fell back into the chest.

Trevor lifted one coin close to his face, said to his wife, "Hold the light steady, will you?"

"I'm trying."

He squinted and said, "The inscription is in Latin and the coin looks hand-stamped. The crest appears to be the same as on the shields." Trevor looked at Brian. "Do you have any idea what you have here?"

"A fortune," Cecilia breathed for him.

"More than that." Trevor glanced from the coin to the shields and back. "My guess is you've found the royal armory. Back in the thirteenth century the prince occupying the castle supported the wrong claimant for the throne of England. A siege was laid about Knightsbridge, and when defeated the castle was demolished to ensure that no one would ever use it to stage another insurrection. The earliest manor was built long before the castle was destroyed. They must have designed this chamber during the siege, and hidden everything here before surrendering."

"The second manor was built around the remnants of the first, and the third around that," Molly added. "I remember that from my school days."

Trevor took the light from his wife and flashed it toward the empty strongboxes in the corner. "The family must have kept this hoard secret, dipping into it when times got hard."

Cecilia demanded, "What does the letter say?"

Brian looked down in surprise. He had forgotten what he held. With none-too-steady hands he slit the envelope and pulled out the single page. Time and the dry air had turned it to the brittle quality of old parchment. The scrawl slipped up and down, many letters only partly formed. Brian squinted hard as Cecilia held the light up close, and read:

"My dear Brian, now all my secrets lie revealed. Alex had always planned to bring these lovely items out into the open and make one room of our overlarge house into a village museum. But illness took him before the plans could be realized, and after his passage I let his dream fade with so much else. I congratulate you for having forged ahead to the end of our little quest. My fervent prayer is that your internal quest has been equally successful.

"The doctors tell me I do not have much time left, and my poor crumbly body is saying the same. I find it remarkable I have managed to make the journey to deposit this letter. I decided to write it here, at the old home's secret heart, for it was here that Alex and I used to come and share our most private dreams. As I sit here upon the floor with a treasure box as my writing table, I find him so very close. Perhaps this is the way our end is supposed to be, when the worldly veils slip away, and we begin to glimpse those who have gone ahead.

"But all my anticipations of the other side are not pleasant. Soon I shall find myself approaching the sacred altar. There are so many stains upon my garment, I am ashamed to say. Few of them I can do anything about, for I have left it too long. All I can do is rely upon the forgiving grace of my gentle Savior, as must we all. But even as He takes my hand and lifts me up, I will be crying tears of sorrow for having wasted so much, and having served Him so poorly."

Brian paused for a long breath, and heard Molly snuffling quietly. He glanced over, and received a quick little nod from Cecilia's overflowing eyes. He looked back to the letter and continued, "How I shall miss not seeing the coming summer. Do try and cherish this day for me, my dear Brian. The gentle press of English seasons is so subtle that one is prone to ignore the fact that time passes. Try and hold on to this moment, my new-found friend. Walk by the river for me, will you please? Listen to the swans fly and imprint upon your heart their wings' rainbow of sound. Buy the biggest, ripest strawberries the Knightsbridge market has to offer, and dine upon them with dollops of Devon cream. Taste the wind. Find a cloud and name it for me, will you? Hear the song of your heart and sing it out loud. And before you part with the day at its close, speak with the Lord your God. Thank Him for the gift of life, however imperfect, however mysterious, however tragic at times. Thank Him for the gift of another day upon this earth, another season of life. And however hard it may be for you, ask Him to complete your healing.

"I am certainly not one who can lead you forward by example, but I do so hope you will take heed of my words, and accept the blessing I know God wants to give you. As my dear friend the vicar liked to tell me, we Christians are simply beggars who happen to know where other beggars might find bread."

Brian paused until Trevor managed to regain control. Only when the chamber was silent once more did he continue: "God's perfect love waits to reveal to you a future He has already planned and waits to set in place, if you let Him. God is a gentle God, you see, and will never enter where He is not made welcome. Don't let go of God, my dear. Not even for an instant.

"So now I must depart, and I leave with you all wonders of the days yet to come. Live well, my dear Brian. With love, Heather."

Brian spent a while sitting there in the gloom, holding Cecilia's hand. As he looked about the chamber, it seemed as though he was surrounded by both a past and a future that was newly his. It took him a very long moment to realize that the others were waiting for his signal to speak, and longer still to recognize that they were one person short. "Where is Arthur?"

"I suppose the climb might have been too much for him," Trevor said.

"Or perhaps he didn't want to leave Gladys all alone down there," Cecilia said. She started back toward the portal. "I'll go tell them what we've found."

"That won't be necessary." Another head popped into view, and an unexpected voice said, "Stay right where you are."

Cecilia backed away so fast that she slipped on the dusty flag-stones and sprawled, the light clattering from her hand and rolling about to reveal a grinning Joe Eaves.

41

"My old granddad was a servant here at Castle Keep." The light glinted off the gun Joe kept trained on them as he slid the strongbox back across the floor. "When I was a kid we'd sneak into the grounds before the house woke up to fish off the river wall. The old man used to tell tales of money popping up right when things got hardest, always enough for the family, never enough to share with the hired hands. Course not. Why should they bother with the likes of us? Sickness, worries, things we wanted and never got." He arrived at the lip of the portal, and snarled back at them, "This settling of accounts is long overdue."

Brian realized then what the man had in mind. "Don't. Please. Think about the women."

Joe cast a dark glance to where Cecilia sat watching him. "Don't you worry, your lordship. I am."

"Tie us up," Cecilia pleaded softly. "That'll give you plenty of time to get away."

"Too much risk." Joe felt below him for the first step, and began easing out of sight. "I'll push in the old dear I've got tied downstairs, seal the door up tight, and have all the time in the world."

Trevor said, "I can't believe Hardy Seade would be party to such horrors."

Joe Eaves laughed out loud. "The old fool is too busy kicking the walls to know what I'm about. I never told him anything that mattered. Why should I? All he wanted was his own place on the pedestal, and hold the likes of me down." Keeping a tight grip on his gun, he fitted the box under one arm. As he slipped out of sight, he cast them a feral grin. "Thick as these old walls are, they won't find you for years and years."

As soon as the head disappeared, Brian slid as quietly as he could across the floor. Gradually he slipped his head over the edge, only to be met by a flashlight from below and the snarled, "Show your ugly face again, your lordship, and I'll shoot it off."

Brian pulled back and heard the clanking and shuffling from down below replaced suddenly by a terrified Gladys complaining, "No, please, not in there."

"Shut your gob." There was a squeal of genuine pain, followed by the sound of the door rumbling closed. Brian heard a clanking clatter from somewhere outside, then nothing.

He sat there for a long moment, feeling the stone walls begin to close in about them. The fear in Cecilia's face stabbed him hard. Then there was a gasping little sob from down below, and another muffled groan. Brian slid back over the edge. "Gladys, come on up, you'll be more comfortable."

"I'm frightened," she sniffled. "That horrid man."

"Stay there. I'll come down and help you up."

But when Brian was halfway down the winding steps, he was halted by more clanking clatter from outside. Gladys whimpered in alarm and began scrambling up toward him. Then the door slid back, and Arthur called up, "It's all right, everyone. You can come down now."

42

$\mathcal{B}$y the time Brian clambered down, Arthur was using the cord from the steam-iron to bind Joe Eaves's hands behind his back. The man lay sprawled unconscious on the kitchen floor, his legs wrapped tight with Gladys's laundry line. The revolver was jammed into Arthur's belt.

Gladys hurried in, a lamp in her hands. "Here you are, dear."

"Good show." He commanded Brian, "Help me draw his hands and legs together."

As Brian tugged the legs up and the arms down, Joe groaned softly. Arthur used the lamp's cord to bind Joe's ankles and wrists together. When he was finished, he stuffed a kitchen towel in the man's mouth, nodded a cheerful greeting to where Cecilia and Molly emerged from the fireplace, then said to Brian, "I would say Joe is trussed like the turkey he is."

Trevor rose from the fireplace, straightened slowly, and demanded, "How did you stop him?"

"Quite simple, really. You'd be surprised how much leverage you can get with a skillet." He gave a fierce two-handed swing. "Made quite a nice bong."

"No," Cecilia asserted. "How did you keep from being captured?"

"Oh, that." Arthur glanced sheepishly at his wife. "I hid."

"One moment he was here beside me, the next he had vanished," Gladys agreed.

Trevor demanded, "But where?"

The old man actually blushed. "There's a secret compartment behind the old cupboard with a hatchway leading outside." He pointed to where the corner cabinet was pulled slightly away from the wall. "Discovered it the year we moved in. Used it several times when I wanted to escape notice. Quite handy, really."

"All these years and you never told me?" Gladys looked horrified. "You shameless old goat!"

"On the contrary," Trevor corrected. "Arthur's secret just saved our lives."

To Brian, Arthur added, "Had a good look about the place soon as all these riddles started surfacing. Not a thing in there except dust."

Molly walked over and patted Gladys's arm. "Thank your husband for saving us, that's a dear."

Gladys worked her mouth a few times, then managed a weak, "Thank you."

"Don't mention it, my dear." Arthur cast Brian a pleased look, then turned to where the strongbox's contents lay scattered beside the bound man. "I say, it's like the past has come alive tonight."

Brian watched as Cecilia knelt and began scooping the coins back into the strongbox. "Past and future both."

43

The central church of Knightsbridge was filled to overflowing. Trevor led the entire service from the upper dais, for it was the only place from which all could see him. He wore his traditional white Sabbath robe, but draped about his shoulders was a brilliant collar of scarlet with an interlocking design of golden fishes falling to his ankles. He looked out over the throng, his eyes resting longest upon the row where Brian sat alongside Cecilia and Gladys and Arthur. Further along sat a sallow-faced woman Cecilia had introduced as Angeline Townsend, and beside her a small child who had clung limpet-like to Cecilia outside the church. Both the woman and her husband had embraced Cecilia with the force of deep emotional debts. Brian had watched with the sense of more dramas to learn of, more lives to entwine with his own.

Brian's gaze returned to those closer at hand—Arthur, Gladys, Trevor, Molly, Cecilia. He could never tell them what they had come to mean to him. He had arrived in England a broken man. Their friendship and the lessons they had helped him learn granted him a future he had never expected for himself. All the words to describe his tomorrows had meaning again—hope and thanksgiving and joy and planning and purpose. Cecilia chose that moment to reach over and take his hand, and Brian added one more word to his list. Yes, to love as well.

"We gather here this day to give thanks and to rededicate our village bells to the service of our Lord," Trevor began. "You may ask, how can bells serve such a divine purpose? The answer, my friends and neighbors, is not in the bells themselves, but in us. No place or possession is holy unless we make it so. But if we so choose, we can make *every* action a holy deed. Every moment can become a moment lived in God's light. Everything we own, everything we touch, can be found to contain the divine presence. But only if we so choose."

Brian had spent the last few days talking and planning. The Bible he had decided to keep. Christie's had agreed to help with the restoration and framing of the illuminated pages. Brian had decided to bring Alex's dream to life—to transform the stables and underground chapel into a village museum. And it would be named the Heather Harding Museum. That was the most fitting tribute he could think to give her, besides his desire to continue the quest she had set before him. Brian turned his attention outward and focused upon Trevor's words.

"Jesus is always available to us, as an encourager and protector and helper and teacher and healer. We must open ourselves to the divine presence, not once a week or even once a day, but constantly. The bells do not say, 'You must take yourself out of the world.' No! The bells say, 'Bring Jesus into your day. Into your hour. Into your life.'"

In the distance came the sound of a single bell being rung, over and over. Brian felt Cecilia's slender hand squeeze his own, as from the opposite side of the village another set of bells began to peal. Then a third set joined in.

Trevor waited for the congregation's murmuring to quiet, then continued, "The message of our village bells is this: 'Live in the continuous blessing of the living God.' How? By learning the discipline of regular prayer."

A fourth set of bells began to ring, closer now. Then a fifth. Brian sensed a pressure growing in his heart as the air became crowded with a new presence, a resounding power that invited his being to ring in time with the bells.

"The bells are a way to remind each and every one of us that the kingdom of God is hourly, *constantly* near. It calls us to a perpetual holy walk along the straight and narrow way. It reminds us in our daily life that God is the God of *now*." Trevor paused as a sixth set of bells began to chime, the air filled with the song of centuries. "Heed their call, and seek the Lord. Time is fleeting, life is passing. Seek Him *now*."

The seventh and final set of bells began pealing from directly overhead. Brian felt the air filled with such a power that the past, present, and future seemed melded together, compressed into a single united force. All the world was filled with the sound of bells, and something more. The power of their music rose to where he could almost hear voices singing praises of a tomorrow he now shared, chanting in a divine and heavenly tongue.

"Let us pray." The vicar raised his arms toward heaven and said in a voice that rang above the bells, "May these bells sound as the spiritual heartbeat of our beloved village. May all who hear their music as they go about their daily walk hear also Your voice, Lord. May You speak to them, and may they hear Your call. May also those who are sick or aged or steeped in sorrow, all those who are unable to draw nigh in body, may they hear these bells and know that we who are gathered here pray for their peace, their healing, their restoration to the community of the saints. We pray for them, we pray for ourselves. May we walk in Your light for evermore."

Other Titles by T. Davis Bunn

One Shenandoah Winter

It's late autumn in the mountain town of Hillsboro, and assistant mayor Connie Wilkes has her hands full. She's concerned about her beloved eighty-three-year-old uncle, Poppa Joe, and his ornery insistence that he can still be as independent as a man half his age. She's also worried about a young friend's hasty plans for marriage. And now the new doctor, Nathan Reynolds, may not even stay to help the town that so desperately needs him.

But before the first winter snowfall, a chain of events is set in motion that will transform Connie, the doctor, and the town forever. By Christmas Day, the greatest sorrow and the greatest miracle will bring reminders of the glorious possibilities of Emmanuel, God with us.

One Shenandoah Winter is a moving story of sacrifice, courage, and redemption.

0-7852-7217-8 • Hardcover • 276 pages

Tidings of Comfort and Joy

It started with an old photograph, one of Marissa's grandmother—she was younger and more beautiful than Marissa had ever seen. But the officer who was embracing her with such passion didn't look like her grandfather!

As the questions begin, an extraordinary story unfolds—a story of love and loss and caring, of separation and reunion. A story of small acts of heroism in a distant and war-weary English village half a century ago.

As Marissa's grandmother shares this story with her, they discover that the most precious gift of Christmas is the gift of the present, and the season of giving is not limited to once a year.

0-7852-7203-8 • Hardcover • 240 pages

The Warning

Buddy Korda is a mild-mannered banker who is the unlikeliest of prophets. He begins having nightmares and then, unmistakably, receives a message: *It is coming. Forty-one days*. The awful deadline leaves Buddy frightened and confused. Telling what he knows could threaten his job, his family's security, even his life. Buddy's prediction that America faces an economic collapse goes against every expert's forecast. But as much as Buddy wants to talk himself out of it—even to walk away from it—he cannot avoid God's call for his life. The futures of people he doesn't even know—even America's future—is at stake. What will happen if no one believes him?

0-7852-7516-9 • Trade Paperback • 324 pages

The Ultimatum

Economic gloom has settled across America. Eighteen months after Buddy Korda warned the nation of economic disaster, he is seized by a new vision: he must call the nation to repentance. God's call leads Buddy to Washington, D. C., where his friends, including Linda Kee, a well-known reporter who is familiar with the Washington power structure—coordinate the effort to bring America face-to-face with her heritage and destiny. This historic movement threatens to transform the political process, and the Washington power brokers will do anything to keep it—and Buddy—from succeeding.

0-7852-7086-8 • Trade Paperback • 324 pages

About the Author

*B*efore becoming an award-winning author, T. Davis Bunn earned a master's degree in international finance and worked as a business executive in Europe, Africa, and the Middle East. His books include the best-sellers *Another Homecoming* and *The Meeting Place* (both coauthored with Janette Oke), *The Quilt, The Presence*, and *To the Ends of the Earth*. His most recent titles with Thomas Nelson Publishers are *The Warning* and *The Ultimatum*. Davis and his wife, Isabella, live in Oxfordshire, England.

Author's Note: On July 8, 1999, a Book of Hours dating from the early 1500s was sold at Christie's Auction House in London. Part of the Rothschild collection, the book had been confiscated by the Nazis during World War II and was only recently recovered. The hand-sized prayer book included sixty-seven full-page illustrations by noted medieval artists, and nothing quite like it had ever been offered in the open market. The final sales price was well over fourteen million dollars, a record for an illuminated manuscript.